BUTCHERS
and Other Stories of Crime

by the same author

Wobble to Death
The Detective Wore Silk Drawers
Abracadaver
Mad Hatter's Holiday
Invitation to a Dynamite Party
A Case of Spirits
Swing, Swing Together
Waxwork
The False Inspector Dew
Keystone

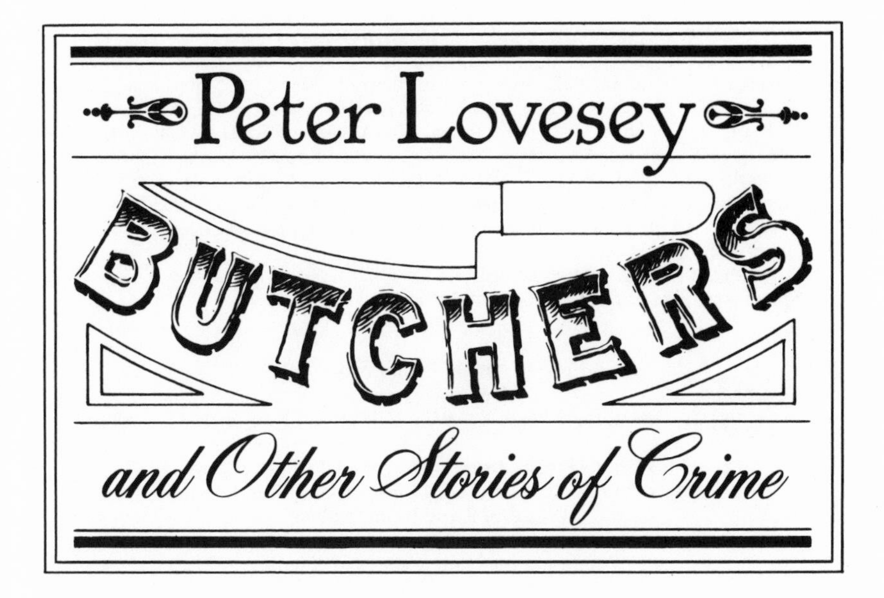

THE MYSTERIOUS PRESS

New York • London

'Arabella's Answer' was first published in *Ellery Queen's Mystery Magazine,* 1984; 'The Bathroom' in *Winter's Crimes 5,* Macmillan, 1973; 'Belly Dance' in *Winter's Crimes 15,* Macmillan 1983; 'Butchers' in *Winter's Crimes 14,* Macmillan, 1982; 'Did You Tell Daddy?' in *Ellery Queen's Mystery Magazine,* 1984; 'Fall-Out' in *Company,* 1983; 'How Mr. Smith Traced His Ancestors' in *The Mystery Guild Anthology,* Book Club Associates, 1980; 'The Locked Room' in *Winter's Crimes 10,* Macmillan, 1978; 'The Secret Lover' in *Winter's Crimes 17,* Macmillan, 1985; 'The Virgin And The Bull' in *John Creasey's Crime Collection,* Gollancz, 1983; 'Vandals' in *Woman's Own,* 1984; 'Woman And Home' (as 'Taking Possession') in *Ellery Queen's Mystery Magazine,* 1982.
'The Corder Figure', 'Private Gorman's Luck', 'The Staring Man' and 'Trace Of Spice' were first published in this collection.

The Mysterious Press, 129 West 56th Street, New York, N.Y. 10019

This Mysterious Press edition is published by arrangement with MacMillan London Limited, 4 Little Essex Street, London WC2R 3LF and Basingstoke.

Printed in the United States of America
First Printing: December 1987
10 9 8 7 6 5 4 3 2 1

Library of Congress Cataloging-in-Publication Data

Lovesey, Peter.
Butchers and other stories of crime.

1. Crime and criminals — Fiction. I. Title.
PR6062.086B8 1987 823'.914 87-7718
ISBN 0-89296-195-3

Contents

Butchers

He had passed the weekend in the cold store of Pugh the butcher's. It was now Monday morning. The door was still shut. He was unconcerned. Quite early on Saturday evening he had given up beating his fists on the door and screaming for help. He had soon tired of jumping and arm-swinging to keep his circulation going. He had become increasingly drowsy as his brain had succumbed to the deprivation of oxygen. He had lain on the tiled floor below the glistening carcases and by Sunday morning he had frozen to death.

On the other side of the door Joe Wilkins filled two mugs with instant coffee. It was still only 8 a.m. and the shop didn't open until 8.30. He was Mr Pugh's shop manager, forty-four, a master butcher, dark, good-looking with an old-fashioned Clark Gable moustache and quick, laughing eyes that had a way of involving everyone in the shop each time he passed a joke with a customer.

The second mug was for Frank, the apprentice butcher. Frank was eighteen and useful for heavy work. He earned extra money on Saturday nights as a bouncer in Stacey's , the disco across the street. When the deliveries came from the slaughterer's, Frank would take the sides of beef on his back as if they were pieces of polystyrene. The girls from Woolworth's next door often came into the shop in their lunch-hour and asked Frank for rides on his motorbike. Frank got embarrassed when Joe Wilkins teased him about it.

Frank hung up his leather jacket and put on a clean apron. Joe was already wearing his straw boater. He watched the young man struggle awkwardly with the apron strings, tying a bow so loose that it was sure to fall apart as soon as he stretched up to lift a carcase off its hook.

'Another heavy weekend, lad?'

'Not really,' answered Frank, taking his coffee and slopping some on the chopping block. 'Same as usual.'

'That's good to hear. Looks as if we've got a busy morning ahead of us.'

Frank gave a frown.

Joe snapped his fingers. 'Come on, lad, what's different this morning, or haven't you noticed yet?'

Frank looked around the shop. 'Meat's not out yet.'

'Right! And why not?'

'Percy isn't in.'

'Right again. By Jove, I was wrong about you. You ought to be on the telly with a mind as sharp as that. Why spend the rest of your life hacking at pieces of meat when you could earn millions sitting in an armchair answering questions? And now for five hundred and a holiday for two in the Bahamas, Mr Dobson, what do you think has happened to Percy?'

'Dunno,' answered Frank.

'You don't know? Come on, lad. You're not trying.'

'He could have fallen off his bike again.'

'That's more like it,' said Joe as he took his knives and cleavers from the drawer behind the counter and started sharpening them. 'Get the window ready, will you?'

Frank put down his coffee and looked for the enamel trays that usually stood in the shop window.

Joe said, 'You're probably right about Percy. He's too old to be in charge of a bike. Seven miles is a long way on a morning like this, with ice all the way up Bread and Cheese Hill and the motorists driving like lunatics. He was knocked in the ditch last week, poor old devil.'

'Where does he put the trays?' asked Frank.

'Trays?'

'For the meat – in the window.'

'Aren't they there, then?' Joe put down his knife and went to look. 'Well, I never noticed that before. I suppose he puts them away somewhere. By the time I arrive, they're always here. Have a look behind the deep-freeze cabinet. Got 'em? Good. Blowed if I understand why he bothers to do that.'

'Dust, I expect,' said Frank.

'Quite right. Wipe them over with a cloth, lad. I used to wonder what he did with himself before we arrived in the morning. He's in by six, you know, regular. How about that? He must be up at five. Could you do that six mornings a week? And it gets no easier as you get older. Percy must be pushing seventy by now.'

'What *does* he do before we get in?' asked Frank.

'Well, it's always spotless, isn't it?'

'I thought that was because he stays on of a night to clean up after we close.'

'So he does – but there's always more dust by the morning. Percy wipes all the surfaces clean. He puts out the trays, and the cuts from the cold store, and hangs up the poultry, and opens a tin of liver and checks everything against the price list and puts out the tags and the plastic parsley, and the new-laid eggs and the packets of stuffing and bread sauce. I hope you're listening, lad, because I want all those jobs done before we open.'

Frank gave another frown. 'You want me to do all that?'

'Who else, lad?' said Joe in a reasonable voice. 'It's obvious that Percy isn't going to make it this morning, and I've got the orders to get out.'

'He hasn't had a day off since I started last year,' said Frank, still unable to believe his bad luck.

'He hasn't had a day off in the twenty years I've been working here. Six in the morning till seven at night, six days a week. And what for? Boy's work. He does the work you ought to be doing, lad. No one else but Percy would stand for it. Fetching and carrying and sweeping up. Do you know, he's never once complained to me or Mr Pugh or anyone else. You've seen him bent nearly double carrying in the carcases. A man of his age shouldn't be doing work like that. It's exploitation, that's what it is.'

'Why does he do it, then? He's old enough to draw his pension.'

Joe shook his head. 'He wouldn't be happy with his feet up. He's spent the best years of his life working in this shop.

He was here before Mr Pugh took it over. It was Slater's in those days. Yes, Percy can tell you some tales about the old days. It means a lot to him, working in this shop.'

Frank gave a shrug and went to the cold store to get out the small joints left over from Saturday. The cold store consisted of two chambers, one for the chilled meat, the other for the frozen. He opened the door of the chiller and started taking out legs of lamb. He needed to hurry to fill the trays in the window by opening time.

Joe was still sharpening knives. He continued telling Frank about the injustices heaped on Percy. 'He gets no recognition for all the work he puts in. Blind loyalty, I call it, but there are some that would call it plain stupidity. Do you think Mr Pugh appreciates what Percy does? Of course he doesn't.'

'He's never here, is he?' contributed Frank, who was becoming quite skilful at fuelling Joe's maledictions against their employer.

'That's a fact. To be fair to Mr Pugh, he has to look in at the market and collect the meat from the slaughterhouse, but that shouldn't take all day. It wouldn't hurt him to show his face here more often.'

Frank gave a sly grin. 'It might hurt someone else.'

'What do you mean by that?' asked Joe, taking offence.

'Well, you and me. We don't want the boss breathing down our necks, do we?'

Joe said in a curt tone, 'Speak for yourself, boy. I'm not ashamed of my work.' He put down the knife he was holding and went to the window to rearrange the tray of lamb chops that Frank had just put there. 'Haven't you any idea how to put meat on a tray to make it look attractive?'

'I was trying to be quick.'

'You can't hurry a job like this. That's why Percy starts so early. He's an artist in his way. His windows are a picture. I wonder what's happened to him.'

'He could be dead.'

Joe turned to look at Frank with clear disfavour. 'That's a very unpleasant suggestion.'

'It's a possibility. He's always falling off that old bike. Well, he could have been taken to hospital, anyway.'

'Someone would have phoned by now.'

'All right, perhaps he died in the night,' persisted Frank. 'He could be lying in his bed. He lives alone, doesn't he?'

'You're talking nonsense, lad.'

'Can you think of anything better?'

'Any more lip from you, young man, and I'll see that you get your cards. Get the chickens out. I'll attend to this.'

'Do you mean the frozen birds, Mr Wilkins?'

'The farm birds. I'll tell you if we need any frozen in a minute or two.'

'Do you think we ought to phone the hospital, Mr Wilkins, just in case something has happened to Percy?'

'What good would that do?'

Frank took seven capons from the chiller and hung them on the rail above the window. 'That's all there is,' he told Joe. 'Shall I get out some frozen ones?'

Joe shook his head. 'It's Monday, isn't it? There isn't much call for poultry on a Monday.'

'We'll need them for tomorrow. They need to thaw. We won't be getting any farm birds this week with Mr Pugh on holiday.'

Joe hesitated in his rearrangement of the window display. 'You've got a point there, lad.'

Frank waited.

'Yes,' said Joe. 'We shall want some frozen birds.'

'Have you got the key?'

'The key?'

'There's a padlock on the freezer door.'

Joe crossed the shop to take a look. It was a heavy padlock. It secured the hasp on the freezer door over an iron staple. He said, 'Silly old beggar. What does he want to lock it for?'

'There's a lot of meat in there,' said Frank, in Percy's defence. 'Have you got the key?'

Joe shook his head. 'I reckon he takes it home with him.'

Frank swore. 'What are we going to do? We've got to get in there. It's not just the chickens. It's the New Zealand. We're right down on lamb.'

'We'd better look for the key, just in case he leaves it somewhere,' said Joe, opening one of the drawers under the counter.

Their short search did not turn up the key.

'I think I could force it with that old file of yours,' suggested Frank.

'No, lad, you might damage the door. You don't want to get your marching orders from Mr Pugh. I've got one of those small hacksaws in my toolbag in the car. We'll use that to cut through the padlock.'

A short time later he returned with the saw. He held the padlock firm while Frank started sawing through the staple.

'All this trouble because of Percy,' said Frank. 'I'd like to strangle the old git.'

'It might not be his fault after all,' said Joe. 'Mr Pugh might have given him orders to use a padlock. He's dead scared of the boss. He does exactly what he's told, and I don't blame him. I heard Mr Pugh laying into him on Saturday night after you left to deliver those orders. It was vicious, it really was.'

Frank continued sawing. 'What was it about?'

'Well, you were there when Mr Pugh walked in out of nowhere, saying he wanted to see that things were straight before he went off for his week in Majorca. That was before you left with the orders.'

'Yes, he'd just picked up his tickets from the travel agent.'

'Right. You'd think he'd be on top of the world, wouldn't you, just about to push off for a week in the sun? Not Mr Pugh. He happened to catch old Percy putting away the cuts we hadn't sold.'

'There's nothing wrong with that, is there?'

'No, but Percy left the door of the chiller open while he was doing it. We all do it, but Percy got caught. You should have heard Mr Pugh go for him, ranting and raving about the cost of running a cold chamber with employees who are so idle that they let the cold air out when they can't be bothered to open and close the door a few times. He really laid it on thick. He was quoting things about cubic feet of air and thermal units as if old Percy had done it deliberately.'

'Almost there,' said Frank. 'Mind it doesn't catch your hand.'

The hacksaw blade cut cleanly through the staple.

Joe said, 'Good.' But he was determined to finish his story. 'He told Percy he was too old for the job and he ought to retire soon. Percy started pleading with him. I tell you,

Frank, I was so embarrassed that I didn't want to hear any more. I left them to it and went home.'

'I'll get out those frozen birds,' said Frank as he slipped the padlock from the hasp.

'You'd have a job to find a meaner man than Mr Pugh,' Joe continued as Frank swung back the door of the freezer chamber. 'Going on like that at an old man who's worked here all his life – and all for the sake of a few pence more on his electricity bill, when we all know he makes enough profit to have holidays in Spain. What's the matter, lad?'

Frank had uttered a strange cry as he entered the chamber.

Joe looked in and saw him standing over the huddled, hoar-white figure of a dead man. He went closer and crouched to look at the face. It was glistening with a patina of frost.

It was the face of Mr Pugh.

Joe placed his hand on Frank's shoulder and said, 'Come away, lad. There's nothing we can do.'

From somewhere Joe produced a hipflask and poured some scotch for Frank as they sat in the shop and stared at the door of the freezer.

'We'll have to call the police,' said Frank.

'I'll do it presently.'

'He must have been trapped in there all the weekend.'

'He wouldn't have known much about it,' said Joe. 'He must have died inside a few hours.'

'How could it have happened?'

Joe stared into space and said nothing.

'There's a handle on the inside of that door,' said Frank, speaking his thoughts as they rushed through the implications. 'Anyone caught in there can open the door and walk out, usually. But he couldn't get out because the padlock was on the outside. Someone must have put it there. It must have been Percy. Why, Mr Wilkins, why would Percy do a thing like that?'

Joe gave a shrug and still kept silent.

Frank supplied his own answer: 'He must have panicked when he thought he would lose his job. He'd been in fear of losing it for years. He found some way of persuading Mr Pugh to go into the freeze chamber, and then he locked him inside. I know what he did. He told Mr Pugh the handle on the inside was too stiff to move, and he liked to leave the door open because he was scared of being trapped. Mr Pugh said he was making excuses and stepped inside to show how easy it was to get out.' Frank began to smile. 'Mr Wilkins, I think I'm going to laugh.'

The tension relaxed a little.

'I'll tell you something funnier than that,' said Joe. 'Why do you think Percy hasn't come in this morning?'

'Well, it's obvious. He knew we'd open that door and find the body.'

'Yes, but where do you think he is?'

Frank frowned and shook his head. 'At home?'

Joe grinned and said, 'Majorca.'

'No!' Frank rocked with laughter. 'The crafty old beggar!'

'When Mr Pugh came in on Saturday, he had a large brown envelope with him containing his travel tickets.'

'I remember. I saw it. He put it on the counter by the cash register.'

'Well, it isn't there now, is it?'

Frank said, 'You can't help admiring him. He's probably sitting on the hotel terrace at this minute ordering his breakfast and thinking of you and me finding Mr Pugh in the freezer.'

'I'd better phone the police,' said Joe, getting up.

'You know, if it wasn't for that padlock on the door, no one would suspect what happened,' said Frank. 'Mr Pugh might have just felt ill and fainted in there. They'd call it misadventure, or something.'

'And Percy would get away with it,' said Joe reflectively. 'It isn't as if he's a vicious murderer. He's no danger to anyone else.'

'I could get rid of it,' offered Frank. 'I could put it in the pannier on my bike and get rid of it lunchtime.'

'We'd have to stick to the same story,' said Joe. 'We just opened the door and found him lying there.'

'It's the truth,' said Frank. 'We don't need to say a word about the padlock. Shall we do it? Poor old Percy – he hasn't had many breaks.'

'All right,' confirmed Joe. 'We'll do it.'

After they had shaken hands, he picked up the phone and called the police. Frank took the padlock to his motorbike in the yard at the back of the shop, and secreted it under the toolbag in the pannier.

A squad car drew up outside the shop within five minutes of Joe's call. A bearded sergeant and a constable came in and Joe opened the freeze chamber and showed them Mr Pugh's body. Frank described how he had found the body. He omitted to mention the padlock. Joe confirmed Frank's statement.

'So it looks as if the body's been lying in there since you closed on Saturday,' said the sergeant after they had withdrawn to the warmer air of the shop. 'You say that Mr Pugh looked in late in the afternoon. What did he want?'

'He was just making sure that everything was in order before he went on holiday,' said Joe.

'He was off to Majorca for a week,' added Frank.

'Lucky man,' put in the constable.

The sergeant gave him a withering look. 'Was Mr Pugh in good health?' he asked Joe.

'I thought he looked rather off-colour,' answered Joe. 'He drove himself hard, you know.'

'He needed that holiday,' said Frank, quick to see the point of what Joe was suggesting.

'Well, he didn't get it,' said the sergeant. 'He must have collapsed. Heart, I expect. The doctor will tell us. There's an ambulance on the way. I suggest you keep the shop closed for a couple of hours. I shall want statements from both of you. Was there anyone else working here on Saturday?'

'Only Percy – Mr Maddox,' answered Joe. 'He isn't in this morning. I believe he was going to ask Mr Pugh for a few days off.'

'I see. We'll want a statement from him. Have you got his address?'

'He told me he was hoping to go away,' said Joe.

'We'll catch up with him later, then. Which of you was the last to leave on Saturday?'

'That was Percy,' said Joe.

'He stays behind to clear up,' explained Frank.

'He puts things away, you mean?' said the sergeant.

'That's right,' said Joe. 'He's getting on a bit, you know. Worked here for years. A bit slow now, but he likes to be useful. He puts everything away at the end of the day.'

'In the freezer?'

Joe shook his head. 'We don't re-freeze meat. It has to be put in the chiller at the end of the day.'

'So he wouldn't have opened the freezer door?'

'It's very unlikely,' said Joe. 'If he had, he'd have found Mr Pugh, wouldn't he?'

They took a statement from Frank. He said nothing to incriminate Percy. He simply explained how he had seen Mr Pugh come into the shop late on Saturday afternoon, shortly before he (Frank) had left to deliver the orders. As for this morning, he had opened the freezer door and found Mr Pugh dead on the floor. The constable read the statement back and Frank signed it. 'Would you like some coffee and a fresh doughnut?' he asked the policemen. 'We always have a doughnut in the morning. It's my job to collect them from Jonquil's. I go on my bike, and they're still warm when I get back.'

'I like the sound of that,' said the sergeant, putting his hand in his pocket. 'How much are they?'

Frank felt an exhilarating sense of release as he wheeled his motorcycle into the street and started the engine. He rode up the hill towards the baker's, stopping a few yards short, by the place where the front of the delicatessen was being renovated. Outside was a builder's skip containing old wood and masonry. Frank took the padlock from his pannier and dropped it unobtrusively into the skip. He collected the bag of doughnuts from the baker's and drove back to the shop.

An ambulance had drawn up outside. As Frank approached, one of the attendants was closing the rear door. The man walked round the side of the vehicle and got in. It moved away. The few bystanders who had collected outside the shop moved on.

When Frank went in, Joe had already made the coffee. He was talking to the police about football.

'We should have gone by now,' the sergeant told Frank. 'We've got both your statements and the body's been collected, but we didn't want to miss those doughnuts.'

Frank handed them around.

'Still warm,' said the sergeant. 'I hope you observed the speed limit, lad.'

Frank smiled.

The police finished their coffee and doughnuts and left the shop.

Frank heaved a huge breath of relief.

Joe took out his handkerchief and mopped his forehead. 'Did you get rid of it?'

Frank nodded.

'Well done,' said Joe. 'Well done, Frank.'

'I reckon old Percy owes us both a beer after that,' said Frank.

'It was worth more than that,' said Joe.

'We couldn't have turned him in,' said Frank.

They opened the shop. Customers who had seen the shop closed earlier now returned in force. They all wanted to know what the police had been doing there and whether it was a body that the ambulancemen had collected. Joe and Frank explained that they were unable to comment. The enquiries persisted and the queue got longer.

'If you ask me,' one woman notorious for voicing her opinions said, 'it was that old boy who sweeps the floor. He was far too old to be working in a shop.'

'If you mean Percy Maddox, you're wrong,' said the woman next in line. 'There's nothing wrong with Percy. He's coming up the street on his bike.'

Joe dropped the cleaver he was using and went to the window. He was joined by Frank, who gave a long, low whistle of amazement.

'Crazy old man!' said Joe angrily. 'What does he think he's up to? He ought to be in Spain.'

They watched through the window as Percy came to a halt outside the shop, dismounted, removed his cycle clips and wheeled his bicycle up the side passage. A moment later he appeared in the shop, a slight, bald-headed, worried-looking man in a faded grey suit. He picked his apron off the hook and started getting into it. 'Morning, ladies,' he said to the queue, then turned to Joe and said, 'Morning, Joe. Shall I tidy up the window? It's a bit of a mess.'

Joe said, 'What are you doing, coming in here?'

'Sorry I'm late,' said Percy. 'The police kept me waiting.'

'You've been to the police?' said Joe in a shrill voice. 'What did you tell them?'

Frank said, 'Listen, I've just thought of something. I'd better go and fetch it.' He started untying his apron.

But he was slower than Joe, who was already out of his. He said, 'You stay. I'll go.'

While Frank was saying, 'But you don't know where I put it,' Joe was round the corner and out to the street.

He didn't get far. Apparently from nowhere, two policemen grabbed him. A squad car drew up and he was bundled into the back. It drove away, its blue light flashing.

'Who's next?' said Percy, who had taken Joe's place at the counter.

An hour or so later, when there was no queue left and Frank and Percy had the shop to themselves, Frank said, 'What's going to happen to Joe?'

'Plenty of questions, I should think,' answered Percy. 'You know about Mr Pugh being found dead, don't you?'

'I was the one who found him.'

'Well, Joe must have murdered him.'

'Joe? We thought it was you.'

Percy blinked. 'Me, son?'

'When you didn't come in this morning, we thought you must have bunked off to Spain with that ticket Mr Pugh left on the counter.'

'But why should I want to kill Mr Pugh after all these years?'

'Well, because of the bad time he gives you, all those long hours without a word of thanks. Exploitation, Joe called it.'

'Did he, by George?' said Percy with a smile.

'He said there was a bit of a scene on Saturday because you left the freezer door open. He said he felt so embarrassed that he cleared off home while Mr Pugh was still laying into you.'

Percy shook his head. 'Son, that isn't true. I left before Joe on Friday. Mr Pugh had told me it might be better if I wasn't around while he did some stocktaking with Joe. We had our suspicions about Joe, you see. The books weren't right. There were big discrepancies. Mr Pugh and I decided to check things carefully for a week and confront Joe with the evidence on Saturday after we closed.'

Frank's eyes widened. 'Mr Pugh and *you*?'

'Yes, you weren't to know this, and nor was Joe, but Mr Pugh made me a partner last year, after I'd done fifty years in the shop. Nice of him, wasn't it? I told him I wouldn't ever make a manager, and I certainly didn't want to upset Joe, so we agreed to keep the partnership a secret, just between Mr Pugh and me, and I carried on the same as ever, with the work I know best. But as things have turned out, with me the surviving partner, I can't keep it a secret any longer, can I? It's my shop now. I'm the boss.'

Frank was shaking his head, trying to understand. 'So did you put the police on to Joe?'

Percy nodded. 'But I didn't mean to. I didn't know what had happened. On Sunday morning Joe drove over to see me. He told me Mr Pugh had changed his mind about going to Spain because the auditors were coming to look at the books. He had asked Joe to offer the ticket to me. I believed him. I thought he wanted me out of the way to spare me any unpleasantness.'

'When it was really Joe who wanted you out of the way,' said Frank. He recollected the events of the morning, the way Joe had tricked him into covering up the crime out of sympathy for Percy, when in reality Percy was innocent. The trick had almost succeeded too. The police had gone away convinced that Mr Pugh had died by misadventure. They had not suspected murder, and they certainly had not suspected Joe of committing it. But now he was under arrest. 'Well, if you weren't suspicious of Joe,' Frank said to Percy, 'why aren't you in Spain? What made you go to the police?'

Percy picked up Joe's straw boater. 'You know how it is with me, son. I haven't had a holiday in years, let alone a holiday abroad. I haven't got a passport. I dropped in at the police station to ask where I can get one, and...' He handed the boater to Frank. 'I need a new manager now, don't I?'

Vandals

Miss Parmenter disliked the young man on sight. He shocked her. She took it as a personal offence that he stood at her door in a black leather jacket, faded blue denim trousers and what she had been brought up to think of as tennis shoes.

Of an evening, she had got into the habit of standing at her window and staring down at the courtyard. The hotel brochure described it as the piazza. Piazza! *Pigsty* was nearer the truth ever since the thugs and hooligans had started meeting there in the evenings. They had ruined it. They sat on their motorcycles swilling beer and picking at food from the takeaway shop, and littering the ground with the cans and cardboard boxes it came in. Most of the food ended up on the floor. Often they threw it at each other. Sometimes they threw bottles, and the place was strewn with broken glass. They had vandalised the walls with words sprayed three or four feet high – the names, she was told, of pop groups they admired. And the worst of it was that they had no right to be there. They weren't hotel guests. The manager should have seen them off months ago, but he was weak. He claimed he had spoken to them several times.

Now here at her door was this young man dressed no differently from the thugs.

Miss Parmenter wrestled mentally with her fear. She knew she led a cloistered existence at the Ocean View. He was probably a decent young man who happened to favour leather and denim. Perhaps they all did nowadays.

She drew back from the secret eye and drew a long, uneven breath, then rubbed distractedly at her fingernails, pressing back the skin until it hurt. She could easily get rid of him by pretending she was out.

Yet she had waited twenty years for this opportunity. She would not let it pass.

She checked her hair. A wayward strand needed repinning under the coil.

He rang again.

It *had* to be him. There was no reason for anyone else to call.

She slotted the end of the safety chain into its notch and opened the door the couple of inches it allowed, half-hoping she would miraculously find the young man dressed in a three-piece suit and striped tie.

There was no miracle, but at least the jacket looked cleaner than some she had seen.

He grinned. 'I'm Paul Yarrow. Not late, am I?'

He had remarkably even teeth. They were so perfect that they could have been artificial. Perhaps he was not so young as his style of dress suggested. His eyes were hidden behind a pair of large sunglasses.

'Remember?' he said. 'I phoned last week.'

'Yes.'

She thought she had caught a whiff of liquor on his breath. It might have been something else, that after-shave they advertised on television. She tightened her grip on the door. 'How do I know who you are?'

He gave a shrug and a smile. 'I just said. I'm the guy that phoned.'

'Don't you have a card or something?'

'Sorry?'

'Some kind of identification?'

'You'll have to take my word for it.'

'I would have thought a firm as highly regarded as yours...'

'I'm not in the firm. I'm kind of, er, freelance, if you see what I mean. They called me up and asked me to do this one. Shall I come in, or would you fancy a drink somewhere?'

She didn't care at all for his manner, but she told herself

it sounded like an educated accent. Really she wanted to be convinced. She wanted passionately to go through with this.

She took a deep breath and unfixed the chain. 'You had better come in, Mr Yarrow.'

'Cheers.'

The tea things were already on the rosewood occasional table in the drawing room. She had only to fetch the teapot from the kitchen where the kettle had been simmering for the last twenty minutes, but she decided against it. She dared not leave him alone in the room.

'Won't you sit down?'

Ignoring the invitation, he crossed the carpet to the corner cupboard and picked up a large stoneware vase. He balanced it in his palm and with his free hand caressed the surface, tracing the ripples left by the potter's fingers.

'Fantastic. Fabulous glaze.'

'It is rather lovely,' Miss Parmenter agreed.

'Must date from after her trip to Japan in 1933.'

Her skin prickled. 'You know who made it?'

'Your sister – who else?'

He knew. The relief was as palpable as rain in tropical heat. For all his unprepossessing appearance, he had demonstrated his right to be there. He knew about pottery, about Maggie's pottery. He was a connoisseur. 'I couldn't say which glaze it is,' she told him in a rush of words. 'She had hundreds, well, dozens, anyway. She wrote them all down like recipes in a cookery book. She actually called them recipes. This could be anything, anything at all.'

'Celadon,' said Mr Yarrow. 'It's one of the celadons. The grey-green.'

'Really? I believe you could be right, but I couldn't for the life of me tell you what went into it.'

'Feldspar, wood ash and a small quantity of iron oxide,' said Mr Yarrow.

'You're very well informed.'

'That's why I'm here.' He replaced the vase. 'Shall we get down to business?'

Miss Parmenter said, 'I'll get some tea. You will have a cup of tea, Mr Yarrow?'

'Sure.'

She felt she *had* to trust him now, even if she still found it impossible to get those thugs and vandals out of her mind. She was in such a hurry that she deliberately omitted to heat the teapot first, a rule that she had broken only once or twice in her life. When she carried it – naked without its cosy – back into the drawing room, Mr Yarrow had picked up Maggie's pot again.

'Terrific.'

'It is a fine example of her work,' said Miss Parmenter, as she stopped to pour the tea. She had forgotten the strainer. She would break another rule and manage without one.

'No, I was talking about you,' said Mr Yarrow. 'Here you are, a little old lady tucked away in a small hotel on the south coast. Once had a famous sister, but she died twenty years ago. Who would have thought —'

'Just a minute,' broke in Miss Parmenter. 'I may be old, Mr Yarrow, but little I most certainly am not. Nor am I "tucked away", as you put it. There is an hourly train service to London if I want it.'

He shook his head and smiled. 'We haven't got off to a very good start, have we?'

'If you would be good enough to replace the pot on the shelf, I can hand you a cup of tea.'

'Right.'

'Sugar?'

'No. Do you mind if I try again? Your sister had an international reputation as a potter. She travelled the world. She worked with the greatest potters of the twentieth century, people like Hamada and Bernard Leach.'

'I met them.'

'I'm sure you did, but it must have been hell to have been the sister of Margaret Parmenter.'

'I don't know what you mean.'

'Well, did you ever travel abroad like her?'

'No.'

'Were you ever called a genius?'

'Mr Yarrow, I don't know where this is leading, but I find it intrusive and embarrassing.'

'I'm trying to pay you a compliment, Miss Parmenter. You have to be a pretty exceptional lady to go to all the trouble you have to keep your sister's name before the public, considering you had no talent of your own. That's what I call selflessness.'

'Oh, nonsense,' murmured Miss Parmenter, looking coyly into her cup.

'Not at all. Come clean with me. Didn't you ever feel a twinge of envy?'

She looked up and regarded him steadily. 'You must understand, Mr Yarrow, that I was brought up to love and respect my sister and all my family. Father believed in certain principles that I am afraid are neglected by the modern generation of parents.'

'Old-fashioned values?'

'I've heard them called that. I've heard it said that we were repressed, presumably because we didn't go about in gangs, terrifying people. If we needed to express ourselves, we learned to do it creatively, like my sister.'

'How about you?' asked Mr Yarrow. 'Did you do anything creative?'

'I would rather not talk about myself.'

'You weren't motivated?'

'I didn't have the opportunity. Mother died when I was twenty, so I had to manage the home and care for Father.'

'Ah, the parent trap,' said Mr Yarrow. 'The unmarried daughter caring for the aged parent.'

Miss Parmenter set down her cup and saucer. She was so irritated that she feared she might snap the handle from the cup. 'Mr Yarrow, I don't know whether that remark was intended to be sympathetic. If so, it was misplaced. I was pleased and privileged to be able to look after my father for over thirty years. The fact that I chose to remain unmarried is immaterial. I have nothing to hide from you or anyone else, but I will not have my life dissected by a total stranger who knows nothing about it. Nothing.'

'Easy,' said Mr Yarrow as if he were speaking to a dangerous animal. 'You did invite me here. Remember?'

'I invited the Artemis Gallery to send a representative with a view to mounting an exhibition.'

'But you didn't bargain for a guy like me who takes a personal interest in the job?'

'I don't mind telling you that I expected someone more... well, more businesslike.'

'Pinstripes and bowler?'

'Well...'

'Give me strength,' muttered Mr Yarrow. 'Okay, let's do it your way. What have you got to show me?'

Miss Parmenter folded her arms and sat back in her chair. 'In a moment. First, how much do you know about my sister's career?'

'Enough. The Royal College. The two years with Hamada in Japan. Those elegant, tall pots in the palest wood-ash glazes that she produced right through the forties and fifties.'

'How many have you seen?'

'Not many,' he admitted. 'Most of them went into private collections.'

'At least you're honest.'

'Thank you for that. The few I've seen are knock-outs.' He added for her benefit, 'Exquisite.'

'I like honesty,' Miss Parmenter observed. 'If my generation had a fault, it was putting too much stress on being tactful, sometimes at the expense of the truth. Young people are not so sensitive about what they say. They can be hurtful, but at least they are honest. I would like you to be honest with me.'

'It's okay. I was a boy scout.'

She stood, picked up the tray and carried it towards the door. 'There's no need to be facetious.'

He followed her to the door and reached for the handle. 'Miss Parmenter, I was trying to make a point. You don't have to treat me like a kid.'

She laughed. She could hardly believe that she was actually laughing, but she was. The funny thing was that he was right. She was treating him like a child. She wasn't in the least afraid of him. And this was the man she had almost refused to admit because of the intimidating clothes he wore.

'What's so funny?' he asked.

'Nothing you would understand.'

'Shall I take the tray?'

'No. I can manage, thank you. But come with me.' She was distinctly enjoying this. Her moment was approaching, and she intended to savour it. She carried the tea things through to the kitchen and set them down. She felt supremely confident.

She stood in her kitchen and emptied the teapot and said without looking at him, 'Do you know what I've been doing since Father died?'

'Tracking down your sister's pots?'

'Yes. Maggie was very meticulous. She kept a record of each one, who bought it, what they paid and when. Some have changed hands several times since then, and a few have suffered accidents, unfortunately, but I think I can account for every one.'

'Useful.'

'Some people simply refuse to sell, of course.'

'To *sell*? You buy the pots back?'

'I offer a very fair price. Since Father died I have not been short of money. Altogether, I have reclaimed over seventy pots.'

'Why? What did you do it for?'

'For this.'

'This?'

'The exhibition.'

Mr Yarrow was rubbing the back of his neck. 'I don't understand. You don't have to repossess all the pots to put them on show. People are usually willing to loan them.'

She smiled again. 'You obviously think I'm soft in the head, or whatever the current expression is.'

'I just think it's a hell of an expensive way to put on an exhibition. Okay, it's a terrific tribute to your sister, but where does it leave you? On the bread-line, if I know anything about the value of those pots. Even if we go ahead with the show, I can't guarantee that you'll get your money back.'

'The money doesn't interest me.'

'They charge a commission on anything they sell.'

Miss Parmenter scarcely heard him. She said,'I think you should see the collection now.'

'Try and stop me,' said Mr Yarrow.

'You promise to give your honest opinion?'

'You can rely on me.'

'Come this way, then.' She led him out of the kitchen and through the passage to a door at the end. She stepped aside 'You may open it and go in.'

Mr Yarrow stepped into the room.

Miss Parmenter waited outside, smiling to herself. 'Take as long as you like,' she called out. 'After all, there's a lifetime of work in there.'

A lifetime . . . and more. An old tune was going through her head. Something Father had often whistled when he was in a good mood, one of those mornings when a letter arrived. *'It's from our Maggie, and bless me if she hasn't sold another pot. Isn't she the cat's whiskers?'*

A pity Father couldn't have lived to see what his other, disregarded daughter had finally achieved. Or Maggie herself, the brilliant, celebrated Maggie. Wouldn't *she* have been astonished!

A step! Mr Yarrow was coming out!

He had taken off his sunglasses. He had blue eyes, and they were open extraordinarily wide, as they should have been after what they had just seen.

She was so anxious that she almost reached out to touch him. 'Well?'

He fiddled with the collar of his shirt. 'I'm . . . lost for words.'

Miss Parmenter gave a nervous laugh. 'I expect you are, but tell me what you think.'

With a shrug, he said, 'I'm just amazed, that's all.'

'I knew you would be. But you like it, don't you?'

He turned his eyes aside. 'It's an incredible thing to have done. Years of work, I'm sure.'

'I want to know,' she told him. 'You promised to be frank with me.'

'Right.' He rubbed his arms as if he suddenly felt a draught of cold air. 'Shall we go through to your sitting room?'

'If you wish – but you *will* be honest?'

Seated in the armchair, he said, 'Are they all your sister's pots?'

'Yes. I told you.'

'And the shells – did you collect them yourself?'

'Every morning, from the beach, very early, before anyone

else was about.'

'There must be millions.'

'I expect so. I had to use the tiny shells, you see. Big ones wouldn't have done at all. And they all had to be sorted into shapes and colours before I could use them.'

'I'm sure,' said Mr Yarrow. 'How did you fix them to the surface of the pots?'

'A tile cement. Very strong. There's no fear of them falling off, if that is what you're thinking.'

'Where did you get the idea?'

She chuckled into her handkerchief. 'Actually, from one of the souvenir shops on the way to the beach. They have all sorts of things decorated with shells. Table lamps, ashtrays, little boxes. Crudely done, of course. You couldn't call it art.'

'So you took it upon yourself to buy back every pot your sister ever made and cover them all with seashells.'

'*Decorate* them. My designs are very intricate, as I'm sure you appreciate. I have some ideas for the exhibition catalogue, if you are interested. For the cover, I think a close-up photograph of one of the pots, and, in white lettering, *Margaret and Cecily Parmenter.*'

Mr Yarrow got up and crossed to the corner cupboard. 'You missed one.' He picked up the vase he had handled before and rotated it slowly, looking at the glaze. 'Why did you leave this one?'

'This?' She took it from him. 'Because it's the only one that belonged to me. She gave it to me.'

'So it was allowed to escape.'

Miss Parmenter hesitated. 'Escape?'

His voice changed. There was something in it that made Miss Parmenter go cold. 'You wanted the truth,' he told her. 'You've ruined those pots. You've destroyed the glaze, the line, the tactile quality, everything. They are no longer works of art.'

She stared at him, unable to find words.

He replaced his sunglasses. 'I think I'd better leave. All I can say is that you must have hated that sister.' He started towards the door.

Miss Parmenter still had the vase in her hands. She lifted it high and crashed it on to the back of Mr Yarrow's skull.

He fell without a sound. Blood flowed across the rosewood table, colouring the splinters of stoneware scattered over its surface.

She went to the cupboard in the kitchen where she kept her sleeping tablets. She swallowed two handfuls and washed them down with water.

Then she went into the room where the pots were ranged on shelves. She opened the window and started dropping them slowly into the courtyard among the empty beercans.

The Corder Figure

Mrs D'Abernon frowned at the ornamental figure on the shelf above her. She leaned towards it to read the name inscribed in copperplate on the base.

'Who was William Corder?'

'A notorious murderer.'

'How horrid!' She sheered away as if the figure were alive and about to make a grab at her throat. She was in the back room of Francis Buttery's second-hand bookshop, where cheap sherry was dispensed to regular buyers of the more expensive books. As a collector of first editions of romantic novels of the twenties and thirties, she was always welcome. 'Fancy anyone wanting to make a porcelain effigy of a murderer!'

'White earthenware,' Buttery told her as if that were the only point worth taking up. 'Staffordshire. I took it over with the shop after the previous owner passed on. He specialised in criminology.' He picked it up, a glazed standing figure about ten inches in height.

'The workmanship looks crude to me,' ventured Mrs D'Abernon, determined not to like it. 'I mean, it doesn't compare with a Dresden shepherdess, does it? Look at the way the face is painted; those daubs of colour on the cheeks. You can see why they needed to write the name on the base. I ask you, Mr Buttery, it could be anyone from the Prince of Wales to a peasant, now, couldn't it?'

'Staffordshire portrait figures are not valued as good likenesses,' Buttery said in its defence, pitching his voice at a level audible to browsers in the main part of the shop. He believed that a bookshop should be a haven of culture, and when he wasn't broadcasting it himself, he played Bach on the stereo. 'The proportions are wrong and the finishing is too stylised to admit much individuality. They are primitive pieces, but they have a certain naive charm, I must insist.'

'Insist as much as you like, darling,' said Mrs D'Abernon, indomitable in her aesthetic judgements. 'You won't convince me that it is anything but grotesque.' She smiled fleetingly. 'Well, I might give you vulgar if you press me, as I'm sure you'd like to.'

Buttery sighed and offered more sherry. These sprightly married women in their thirties and forties who liked to throw in the occasional suggestive remark were a type he recognised, but hadn't learned how to handle. He was thirty-four, a bachelor, serious-minded, good-looking, gaunt, dark, with a few silver signs of maturity at the temples. He was knowledgeable about women – indeed, he had two shelf-lengths devoted to the subject, high up and close to the back room, where he could keep an eye on anyone who inspected them – but he had somehow failed to achieve what the manuals described as an intimate relationship. He was not discouraged, however; for him, the future always beckoned invitingly. 'The point about Staffordshire figures,' he persisted with Mrs D'Abernon, 'is that they give us an insight into the amusements of our Victorian ancestors.'

'Amusements such as murder?' said Mrs D'Abernon with a peal of laughter. She was still a pretty woman with blonde hair in loose curls that bobbed when she moved her head.

'Yes, indeed!' Buttery assured her. 'The blood-curdling story of a man like Corder was pure theatre, the stuff of melodrama. The arrest, the trial and even the execution. Murderers were hanged in public, and thousands came to watch, not just the rabble, but literary people like Dickens and Thackeray.'

'How macabre!'

Buttery gave the shrug of a man who understands human behaviour. 'That was the custom. Anyway, the Staffordshire potters made a tidy profit out of it. I suppose respectable Victorian gentlemen felt rather high-hat and manly with a line of convicted murderers on the mantelpiece. Of course, there were other subjects, like royalty and the theatre. Sport, as well. You collected whatever took your fancy.'

'And what did Mr William Corder do to earn his place on the mantelpiece?'

'He was a scoundrel in every way. No woman was safe with him, by all accounts,' said Buttery, trying not to sound envious. 'It happened in 1827, way out in the country in some remote village in Suffolk. He was twenty-one when he got a young lady by the name of Maria Marten into trouble.'

Mrs D'Abernon clicked her tongue as she took a sidelong glance at the figure.

'The child didn't survive,' Buttery went on, 'but Corder was persuaded to marry Maria. It was a clandestine arrangement. Maria dressed in the clothes of a man and crossed the fields with Corder to a barn with a red roof, where her luggage was stored and a gig was supposed to be waiting to take them to Ipswich. She was not seen alive again. Corder reappeared two days after, and bluffed it out for months that Maria was living in Ipswich. Then he left the district and wrote to say that they were on the Isle of Wight.'

'And was he believed?' asked Mrs D'Abernon.

'By everyone except one tenacious woman,' said Buttery. That was the feature of the case that made it exceptional. Mrs Marten, Maria's mother, had two vivid dreams that her daughter had been murdered and buried in the red barn.'

'Ah! The intrusion of the supernatural,' said Mrs D'Abernon in some excitement. 'And did they find the poor girl there?'

'No one believed Mrs Marten at first, not even her husband, but, yes, eventually they found Maria buried under the floor. It was known as the Red Barn Murder, and the whole nation was gripped by the story. Corder was arrested and duly went to the gallows.' He paused for effect, then added, 'I happen to have two good studies of the case in fine condition, if you are interested.'

Mrs D'Abernon gave him a pained look. 'Thank you, but I don't care for that sort of reading. Tell me, what is it worth?'

'The figure of Corder? I've no idea.'

'It's an antique, isn't it? You ought to get it valued.'

'It's probably worth a few pounds, but I don't know that I'd care to sell it,' said Buttery, piqued that she had dismissed the books so off-handedly.

'You might, if you knew how much you could get for it,' Mrs D'Abernon remarked with a penetrating look. 'I'll make some enquiries. I have a very dear friend in the trade.'

He would have said, 'Don't trouble,' but he knew there was no stopping her. She was a forceful personality.

And next afternoon, she was back. 'You're going to be grateful to me, Mr Buttery,' she confidently informed him as he poured the sherry. 'I asked my friend and it appears that Staffordshire figures are collectors' items.'

'I knew that,' Buttery mildly pointed out.

'But you didn't know that the murderers are among the most sought after, did you? Heaven knows why, but people try to collect them all, regardless of their horrid crimes. Some of them are relatively easy to obtain if you have a hundred pounds or so to spare, but I'm pleased to inform you that your William Corder is extremely rare. Very few copies are known to exist.'

'Are you sure of this, Mrs D'Abernon?'

'Mr Buttery, my friend is in the antique trade. She showed me books and catalogues. There are two great collections of Staffordshire figures in this country, one at the Victoria and Albert Museum and the other owned by the National Trust, at Stapleford Park. Neither of them has a Corder.'

Buttery felt his face getting warm. 'So my figure could be valuable.' He pitched his voice lower. 'Did your friend put a price on it?'

'She said you ought to get it valued by one of the big auctioneers in London and she would be surprised if their estimate was lower than a thousand pounds.'

'Good gracious!'

Mrs D'Abernon beamed. 'I thought that would take your breath away.'

'A thousand!' said Buttery. 'I had no idea.'

'These days, a thousand doesn't go far, but it's better than nothing, isn't it?' she said as if Buttery were one of her neighbours on Kingston Hill with acres of grounds and a heated swimming pool. 'You might get more, of course. If you put it up for auction, and you had the V and A bidding against the National Trust...'

'Good Lord!' said Buttery. 'I'm most obliged to you for this information, Mrs D'Abernon.'

'Don't feel under any obligation whatsoever, Mr Buttery,' she said, flashing a benevolent smile. 'After all the hospitality you've shown me in my visits to the shop, I wouldn't even suggest a lunch at the Italian restaurant to celebrate our discovery.'

'I say that *is* an idea!' Buttery enthused, then, lowering his voice again, 'That is, if your husband wouldn't object.'

Mrs D'Abernon leaned towards Buttery and said confidentially, 'I wouldn't tell him, darling.'

Buttery squirmed in his chair, made uneasy by her closeness. 'Suppose someone saw us? I'm pretty well known in the High Street.'

'You're probably right,' said Mrs D'Abernon, going into reverse. 'I must have had too much sherry to be talking like this. Let's forget it.'

'On the contrary, I shall make a point of remembering it,' Buttery assured her, sensing just in time that the coveted opportunity of a liaison was in danger of slipping by. 'If I find myself richer by a thousand pounds, I'll find some way of thanking you, Mrs D'Abernon, believe me.'

On Wednesday, he asked his part-time assistant, James, to manage the shop for the day. He got up earlier than usual, packed the Corder figure in a shoe box lined with tissue, and caught one of the commuter trains to London. In his corduroy jacket and bow-tie he felt mercifully remote from the dark-suited businessmen ranged opposite him, most of them doggedly studying the city news. He pictured Mrs D'Abernon's husband reading the same paper in the back of a chauffeur-driven limousine, his mind stuffed with stock market prices, uninterested in the dull, domestic routine he imagined his wife was following. Long might he remain uninterested!

The expert almost cooed with delight when Buttery unwrapped his figure. It was the first William Corder he had ever seen, and a particularly well-preserved piece. He explained to Buttery that Staffordshire figures were cast in simple plaster moulds, some of which were good for up to two hundred figures, while others deteriorated after as few as twenty castings. He doubted whether there were more than three or four Corders remaining in existence, and the only ones he knew about were in America.

Buttery's mouth was dry with excitement. 'What sort of price would you put on it?' he asked.

'I could sell it today for eight hundred,' the expert told him. 'I think in an auction it might fetch considerably more.'

'A thousand?'

'If it went in one of our sales of English pottery, I would suggest that figure as a reserve, sir.'

'So it might go for more?'

'That is my estimation.'

'When is the next sale?'

The expert explained the timetable for cataloguing and pre-sale publicity. Buttery wasn't happy at the prospect of waiting several months for a sale, and he enquired whether there was any way of expediting the procedure. With some reluctance, the expert made a phone call and arranged for the Corder figure to be added as a late item to the sale scheduled the following month, five weeks ahead.

Two days later, Mrs D'Abernon called at the shop and listened to Buttery's account of his day in London. She had sprayed herself lavishly with a distinctive floral perfume that subdued even the smell of the books. She appeared more alluring each time he saw her. Was it his imagination that she dressed to please him?

'I'm thrilled for you,' she said.

'And I'm profoundly grateful to you, Mrs D'Abernon,' said Buttery, ready to make the suggestion he had been rehearsing ever since he got back from London. 'In fact, I was wondering if you would care to join me for lunch next Wednesday as a mark of my thanks.'

Mrs D'Abernon raised her finely plucked eyebrows. 'I thought we had dismissed the possibility.'

'I thought we might meet in Epsom, where neither of us is so well known.'

She gave him a glimpse of her beautiful teeth. 'How intriguing!'

'You'll come?'

She put down her sherry glass. 'But I think it would be assuming too much at this stage, don't you?'

Buttery reddened. 'How, exactly?'

'One shouldn't take anything for granted, Mr Buttery. Let's wait until after the sale. When did you say it is?'

'On May the fifteenth, a Friday.'

'The fifteenth? Oh, what a pity! I shall be leaving for France the following day. I go to France every spring, before everyone else is on holiday. It's so much quieter.'

'How long will you be away?' Buttery asked, unable to conceal his disappointment.

'About a month. My husband is a duffer as a cook. He can survive for four weeks on rubbery eggs and burnt bacon, but that's his limit.'

Buttery's eyes widened. The future that had beckoned ever since he had started to shave was now practically tugging him by the sleeve. 'You go to France without your husband?'

'Yes, we always have separate holidays. He's a golfer, and you know what they're like. He takes his three weeks in July and plays every day. He doesn't care for travel at all. In fact, I sometimes wonder what we *do* have in common. Do you like foreign travel, Mr Buttery?'

'Immensely,' said Buttery huskily, 'but I've never had much opportunity... until this year.'

She traced the rim of the sherry glass with one beautifully manicured finger. 'Your thousand pounds?'

'Well, yes.' He hesitated, taking a glance through the shop to check that no one could overhear. 'I was thinking of a trip to France myself, but I don't know the country at all. I'm not sure where to head for.'

'It depends what you have in mind,' said Mrs D'Abernon, taking a sip of the sherry and giving Buttery a speculative look. 'Personally, I adore historical places, so I shall start with a few days in Orléans and then make my way slowly along the Loire Valley.'

'You can recommend that?'

'Absolutely.'

'Then perhaps I'll do the same. I say,' he added, as if the

idea had just entered his head, 'wouldn't it be fun to meet somewhere in France and have that celebration meal?'

She registered surprise like a star of the silent screen. 'Yes, but you won't be going at the same time as I . . . will you?'

Buttery allowed the ghost of a smile to materialise fleetingly on his lips. 'It could be arranged.'

'But what about the shop?'

'Young James is perfectly capable of looking after things for me.' He topped up her glass, sensing that it was up to the man to take the initiative in matters as delicate as this. 'Let's make a rendezvous on the steps of Orléans Cathedral at noon on May the eighteenth.'

'My word, Mr Buttery! . . . Why May the eighteenth?'

'So that we can drink a toast to William Corder. It's the anniversary of the Red Barn Murder. I've been reading up on the case.'

Mrs D'Abernon laughed. 'You and your murderer!' There was a worrying pause while she considered her response. 'All right, May the eighteenth it is – provided, of course, that the figure is sold.'

'I'll be there whatever the outcome of the sale,' Buttery rashly promised her.

Encouragingly, she leaned forward and kissed him lightly on the lips. 'So shall I.'

When she had gone, he went to his Physiology and Anatomy shelf and selected a number of helpful volumes to study in the back room. He didn't want his inexperience to show on May 18th.

The weeks leading up to the auction seemed insufferably long to Buttery, particularly as Mrs D'Abernon appeared in the shop only on two occasions, when by sheer bad luck he happened to be entertaining other lady customers in the back room. He wished there had been time to explain that it was all in the nature of public relations, but on each occasion Mrs D'Abernon curtly declined his invitation to join the sherry party, excusing herself by saying she had so many things to arrange before she went to France. For days, he agonised over whether to call at her house – a big detached place overlooking the golf course – and eventually decided against it. Apologies and explanations on the doorstep didn't accord with the cosmopolitan image he intended to present in Orléans.

So he made his own travel arrangements, such as they were: the purchase of an advance ticket for the cross-Channel ferry, some travellers' cheques and a map of the French railway system. Over there, he would travel by train. He gathered that Mrs D'Abernon rented a car for her sightseeing, and that would have to do for both of them after Orléans, because he had never learned to drive. He didn't book accommodation in advance, preferring to keep his arrangements flexible.

He also invested in some new clothes for the first time in years: several striped shirts and cravats, a navy blazer and two pairs of white, well-cut trousers. He bought a modern suitcase and packed it ready for departure on the morning after the auction.

On May 15th, he attended the auction. He had already been sent a catalogue, and the Corder figure was one of the final lots on the list, but he was there from the beginning, studying the form, spotting the six or seven dealers who between them seemed to account for three-quarters of the bids. They made him apprehensive after what he had once read about rings that conspired to keep the prices low, and he was even more disturbed to find that a number of items had to be withdrawn after failing to reach their reserve prices.

As the auction proceeded, Buttery felt increasingly nervous. This wasn't just the Corder figure that was under the hammer; it was his rendezvous with Mrs D'Abernon, his initiation into fleshly pleasures. He had waited all his adult life for the opportunity, and it couldn't be managed on a low budget. She was a rich, sophisticated woman, who would expect to be treated to the best food and wines available.

'And so we come to Lot 287, a very fine Staffordshire figure of the murderer, William Corder...'

A pulse throbbed in Buttery's head and he thought for a moment he would have to leave the sale room. He took deeper breaths and closed his eyes.

The bidding got under way, moving rapidly from £500 to £750. Buttery opened his eyes and saw that two of the dealers were making bids on the nod at an encouraging rate.

'Eight hundred,' said the auctioneer.

There was a pause. The bidding had lost its momentum.

'At eight hundred pounds,' said the auctioneer. 'Any more?'

Buttery leaned forward anxiously. One of the dealers indicated that he had finished. This could be disastrous. Eight hundred pounds was below the reserve. Perhaps they had overvalued the figure.

'Eight-fifty on my left,' said the auctioneer, and Buttery sat back and breathed more evenly. Another dealer had entered the bidding. Could he be buying for the V and A?

It moved on, but more slowly, as if both dealers baulked at a four-figure bid. Then it came.

'One thousand pounds.'

Buttery had a vision of Mrs D'Abernon naked as a nymph, sipping champagne in a hotel bedroom.

The bidding continued to twelve hundred and fifty pounds.

The auctioneer looked around the room. 'At twelve hundred and fifty pounds. Any more?' He raised the gavel and brought it down. 'Hudson and Black.'

And that was it. After the auctioneers' commission had been deducted, Buttery's cheque amounted to eleven hundred and twenty-five pounds.

Three days later, in his blazer and white trousers, he waited at the rendezvous. Mrs D'Abernon arrived twenty minutes late, radiant in a primrose yellow dress and wide-brimmed straw hat, and pressed her lips to Buttery's, there on the cathedral steps. He handed her the box containing an orchid that he had bought in Orléans that morning. It was clearly a good investment.

'So romantic! And two little safety-pins!' she squeaked in her excitement. 'Darling, how thoughtful. Why don't you help me pin it on?'

'I reserved a table at the Hôtel de Ville,' he told her as he fumbled with the safety-pin.

'How extravagant!'

'It's my way of saying thank you. The Corder figure sold for over a thousand pounds.'

'Wonderful!'

They had a long lunch on the hotel terrace. He ordered

champagne and the food was superb. 'You couldn't have pleased me more,' said Mrs D'Abernon. 'To be treated like this is an almost unknown pleasure for me, Mr Buttery.'

He smiled.

'I mean it,' she insisted. 'I don't mean to complain about my life. I am not unloved. But this is another thing. This is romance.'

'With undertones of wickedness,' commented Buttery.

She frowned. 'What do you mean?'

'We're here by courtesy of William Corder.'

Her smile returned. 'Your murderer. I was meaning to ask you: why did he kill poor Maria?'

'Oh, I think he felt he was trapped into marriage,' Buttery explained. 'He was a philanderer by nature. Not a nice man at all.'

'I admire restraint in a man,' said Mrs D'Abernon.

'But, of course,' Buttery responded, with what he judged to be the ironic smile of a man who knows what really pleases a woman.

It was after three when, light-headed and laughing, they stepped through the hotel foyer and into the sunny street.

'Let's look at some shops,' Mrs D'Abernon suggested.

One of the first they came to was a jeweller's. 'Aren't they geniuses at displaying things?' she said. 'I mean, there's so little to see in a way, but everything looks exquisite. That gold chain, for instance. So elegant to look at, but you can be sure if I tried it on, it wouldn't look half so lovely.'

'I'm sure it would,' said Buttery.

'No, you're mistaken.'

'Let's go in and see, then. Try it on, and I'll give you my opinion.'

They went in and, after some rapid mental arithmetic, Buttery parted with three thousand francs to convince her that he really had meant what he said.

'You shouldn't have done it, you wicked man!' she told him, pressing the chain possessively against her throat. 'It was only a meal you promised me. I can't think why you did it.'

Buttery decided to leave her in suspense. Meanwhile, he suggested a walk by the river. They made their way slowly down the Rue Royale to the Quai Cypierre. In a quiet position with a view of the river, they found a *salon de thé,* and sipped lemon tea until the shadows lengthened.

'It's been a blissful day,' said Mrs D'Abernon.

'It hasn't finished yet,' said Buttery.

'It has for me, darling.'

He smiled. 'You're joking. I'm taking you out to dinner tonight.'

'I couldn't possibly manage dinner after the lunch we had.'

'Call it supper, then. We'll eat late, like the French.'

She shook her head. 'I'm going to get an early night.'

He produced his knowing smile. 'That's not a bad idea. I'll get the bill.'

Outside, he suggested taking a taxi and asked where she was staying.

She answered vaguely, 'Somewhere in the centre of town. Put me off at the cathedral, and I can walk it from there. How about you? Where have you put up?'

'Nowhere yet,' he told her as he waved down a cab. 'My luggage is at the railway station.'

'Hadn't you better get booked in somewhere?'

He gave a quick, nervous laugh. She wasn't making this easy for him. 'I was hoping it wouldn't be necessary.' The moment he had spoken, he sensed that his opportunity had gone. He should have sounded more masculine and assertive. A woman like Mrs D'Abernon didn't want a feeble appeal to her generosity. She wanted a man who knew what he wanted and took the initiative.

The taxi had drawn up and the door was open. Mrs D'Abernon climbed in. She looked surprised when Buttery didn't take the seat beside her.

He announced, 'I'm taking you to lunch again tomorrow.'

'That would be very agreeable, but –'

'I'll be on the cathedral steps at noon. Sweet dreams.' He closed the door and strode away, feeling that he had retrieved his pride and cleared the way for a better show the next day. After all, he had waited all his life, so one more night in solitary was not of much account.

So it was a more assertive Buttery who arrived five minutes late for the rendezvous next day, found her already waiting and kissed her firmly on the mouth. 'We're going to a slightly more exotic place today,' he told her, taking a decisive grip on her arm.

It was an Algerian restaurant on the fringe of the red light district. Halfway through their meal, a belly dancer came through a bead curtain and gyrated to taped music. Buttery clapped to the rhythm. At the end, he tossed the girl a five-franc piece and ordered another bottle of wine.

Towards 3 p.m. Mrs D'Abernon began to look restless.

'Had enough?' asked Buttery.

'Yes. It was wonderfully exciting and I enjoyed every minute of it, but I have to be going. I really must get back to my hotel and wash my hair. It must be reeking of cigar smoke and I made an appointment for a massage and manicure at five.'

'I'll give you a massage,' Buttery informed her with a no-nonsense statement of intention that pleased him as he said it. It more than made up for the previous day's ineptness.

'That won't be necessary, thank you,' responded Mrs D'Abernon, matching him in firmness. 'She's a qualified masseuse and beautician. I shall probably have a facial as well.'

He gaped at her. 'How long will that take?'

'I'm in no hurry. That's the joy of a holiday, isn't it?'

Buttery might have said that it was not the joy he had in mind, but he was too disconcerted to answer.

'We could meet again tomorrow for lunch, if you like,' offered Mrs D'Abernon.

He said, letting his resentment show, 'Do you really want to?'

She smiled benignly. 'Darling, I can think of nothing I would rather do.'

That, Buttery increasingly understood, was his problem. Mrs D'Abernon liked being treated to lunch, but there was nothing she would rather do. Each day that week she made some excuse to leave him as soon as possible afterwards: a hair appointment, a toothache, uncomfortable shoes. She declined all invitations to dinner and all suggestions of night-clubbing or theatre-visiting.

Buttery considered his position. He was going through his traveller's cheques at an alarming rate. He was staying at a modest hotel near the station, but he would have to pay the bill some time, and it was mounting up, because he spent each evening drinking alone in the bar. The lunches were costing him more than he had budgeted and there was nearly always a taxi-fare to settle.

In the circumstances, most men planning what Buttery had come to France to achieve would have got discouraged, cut their losses, and given up, but Buttery was unlike most other men. He still nursed the hope that his luck would change. He spent many lonely hours trying to work out a more successful strategy. Finally, desperation and his dwindling funds drove him to formulate an all-or-nothing plan.

It was a Friday, and they had lunch at the best fish restaurant in Orléans, lobster scooped wriggling from a tank in the centre of the dining room and cooked to perfection, accompanied by a vintage champagne. Then lemon sorbet and black coffee. Before Mrs D'Abernon had a chance to make her latest unconvincing excuse, Buttery said, 'I'd better get you back to your hotel.'

She blinked in surprise.

'I'm moving on tomorrow,' Buttery explained. 'Must get my travel arrangements sorted out before the end of the afternoon.' He beckoned to the waiter.

'Where do you plan to visit next?' asked Mrs D'Abernon.

'Haven't really decided,' he said as he settled the bill. 'Nothing to keep me in Orléans.'

'I was thinking of driving to Tours,' Mrs D'Abernon quickly mentioned. 'The food is said to be outstanding there. I could offer you a lift in my car if you wish.'

'The food isn't so important to me,' said Buttery.

'It's also very convenient for the châteaux of the Loire.'

'I'll think it over,' he told her, as they left the restaurant. He hailed a taxi and one drew up immediately. He opened the door and she got in. 'Hôtel Charlemagne,' he told the driver as he closed the door on Mrs D'Abernon. He noticed her head turn at the name of the hotel. It hadn't been difficult to trace. There weren't many that offered a massage and beauty service.

She wound down the window. 'But how will I know...?' Her words were lost as the taxi pulled away.

Buttery gave a satisfied smile as he watched it go.

He went to the florist's and came out with a large bouquet of red roses. Then he returned to his hotel and took a shower.

About seven, he phoned the Hôtel Charlemagne and asked to speak to Mrs D'Abernon.

Her voice came through. 'Yes?'

In a passable imitation of a Frenchman, Buttery said, 'You are English? There is some mistake. Which room is this, please?'

'Six-five-seven.'

He replaced the phone, went downstairs to the bar and ordered his first vodka and tonic.

Two hours later, carrying the roses, he crossed the foyer of the Charlemagne and took the lift to the sixth floor. The corridor was deserted. He found 657 and knocked, pressing the bouquet against the spy-hole.

There was a delay, during which he could hear sounds inside. The door opened a fraction. Buttery pushed it firmly and went in.

Mrs D'Abernon gave a squeak of alarm. She was dressed in one of the white bathrobes that the best hotels provide for their guests. She had her hair wrapped in a towel and her face was liberally coated in a white cream.

'These are for you,' said Buttery in a slightly slurred yet, he confidently believed, sexy voice.

She took the roses and looked at them as if a summons had been served on her. 'Mr Buttery! I was getting ready for bed.'

'Good,' said Buttery, closing the door. He crossed to the fridge and took out a half-bottle of champagne. 'Let's have a nightcap.'

'No! I think you'd better leave my room at once.'

Buttery moved closer to her, smiling. 'I don't object to a little cream on your face. It's all right with me.' He snatched the towel from her head. The colour of her hair surprised him. It was brown, and grey in places, like his own. She must have been wearing a blonde wig all the times he had taken her to lunch.

Mrs D'Abernon reacted badly. She flung the roses back at him and said, 'Get out of here!'

He was not discouraged. 'You don't mean that, my dear,' he told her. 'You really want me to stay.'

She shook her head emphatically.

Buttery went on, 'We've had good times together, you and I. Expensive lunches.'

'I enjoyed the lunches,' conceded Mrs D'Abernon, in a more conciliatory vein. 'Didn't I always express my appreciation?'

'You said you felt romantic.'

'I did, and I meant it!'

'Well, then.' He reached to embrace her, but she backed away. 'What's the matter with you? Or is something the matter with me?'

'No. Don't think me unappreciative, but that's enough for me, to have an escort during the day. I like to spend my evenings alone.'

'Come on, I've treated you well. I've spent a small fortune on you.'

'I'm not to be bought,' said Mrs D'Abernon, edging away from the bed.

'It's not like that at all,' Buttery insisted. 'I fancy you, and I reckon you fancy me.'

She gave an exasperated sigh. 'For pity's sake, Mr Buttery, I'm a married woman. I'm used to being fancied, as you put it. I'm sick of it, if you want to know. All evening he ignores me, then he gets into bed and thinks he can switch me on like the electric blanket. Coupling, that's all it is, and I want a break from it. I don't want more of it. I just crave a little innocent romance, someone to pay me some attention over lunch.' Then Mrs D'Abernon made her fatal mistake. She said, 'Don't spoil it now. This isn't in your nature. I picked you out because you're safe. Any woman could tell you're safe to be with.'

Safe to be with? He winced, as if she had struck him, but the effect was worse than that. She had just robbed him of his dream, his virility, his future. He would never have the confidence now to approach a woman again. He was finished before he had ever begun. He hated her for it. He hated her for going through his money, cynically eating and spending her way through the money he had got for his Corder figure.

He grabbed her by the throat.

Three days later, he returned to England. The French papers were full of what they described as the Charlemagne killing. The police wished to interview a man, believed to be English, who had been seen with the victim in several Orléans restaurants. He was described as middle-aged, going grey, about 5 ft 8 ins and wearing a blue blazer and white trousers.

In Buttery's well-informed opinion, that description was worse than useless. He was 5 ft 9 ins in his socks, there was no grey hair that anyone would notice and thirty-four was a long way from being middle-aged. Only the blazer and trousers were correct, and he had dumped them in the Loire after buying jeans and a T-shirt. He felt amused at the problems now faced by all the middle-aged Englishmen in blue blazers staying at the Charlemagne.

He experienced a profound sense of relief at setting foot on British soil again at Dover, but it was short-lived, because the immigration officer asked him to step into an office and answer some questions. A CID officer was waiting there.

'Just routine, sir. Would you mind telling me where you stayed in France?

'Various places,' answered Buttery. 'I was moving along the Loire Valley. Angers, Tours, Poitiers.'

'Orléans?'

'No. I was told it's a disappointment historically. So much bombing in the war.'

'You heard about the murder there, I expect?'

'Vaguely. I can't read much in French.'

'An Englishwoman was strangled in her hotel bedroom,' the CID man explained. 'She happens to come from the same town as you.'

Buttery made an appropriate show of interest. 'Really? What was her name?'

'Mildred D'Abernon. You didn't meet her at any stage on your travels?'

He shook his head. 'D'Abernon. I've never heard of her.'

'You're quite sure?'

'Positive.'

'In that case, I won't detain you any longer, Mr Buttery. Thank you for your co-operation.'

In the train home, he tried to assess the case from the point of view of the police. In France, there was little, if anything, to connect him with the murder. He had travelled separately from Mrs D'Abernon and stayed in different hotels. They had met for lunch, but never more than once in the same restaurant and it was obvious that the descriptions provided by waiters and others could have applied to hundreds, if not thousands, of Englishmen. He had paid every bill in cash, so there was no question of his being traced through the traveller's cheques. The roses he had bought came from an old woman so short-sighted that she had tried to give the change to another customer. He had been careful to leave no fingerprints in the hotel room. The unremarkable fact that he came from the same Surrey suburb as Mrs D'Abernon and had been in France at the same time was hardly evidence of guilt.

All he had to do was stay cool and give nothing else away.

So he was irritated, but not unduly alarmed, when he was met off the train by a local policeman in plain clothes and escorted to a car.

'Just checking details, sir,' the officer explained. 'We'll give you a lift back to your place and save you the price of a taxi. You live over your bookshop, don't you?'

'Well, yes.'

'You answered some questions at Dover about the murder in Orléans. I believe you said you didn't know Mrs D'Abernon.'

'That's true.'

'Never met the lady?'

Buttery sensed a trap. 'I certainly didn't know her by name. Plenty of people come into the shop.'

'That clears it up then, sir. We found a number of books in her house that her husband understands had been bought from you. Do you keep any record of your customers?'

'Only if they pay by cheque,' said Buttery with a silent

prayer of thanks that Mrs D'Abernon had always paid in cash.

'You don't mind if I come in, then, just to have a glance at the accounts?'

The car drew up outside the shop and the officer helped Buttery with his cases.

It was after closing time, but James was still there. Buttery nodded to him and walked on briskly to the back room, followed by the policeman.

'Nice holiday, Mr Buttery?' James called. 'The mail is on your desk. I opened it, as you instructed.'

Buttery closed the door, and took the account book off its shelf. 'If I'd had any dealings with the woman, I'm sure I'd remember her name,' he said, as he held it out.

The officer didn't take it. He was looking at an open parcel on Buttery's desk. It was about the size of a shoe-box. 'Looks as if someone's sent you a present, sir.'

Buttery glanced into the box and saw the Corder figure lying in a bed of tissue paper. He picked it out, baffled. There was a letter with it from Hudson and Black, dealers in *objets d'art*. It said that the client they had represented in the recent auction had left instructions on the day of the sale that the figure of William Corder should be returned as a gift to its seller with the enclosed note.

The policeman picked out a small card from the wrappings, frowned at it, stared at Buttery and handed it across.

Buttery went white. The message was handwritten. It read:

You treated me to romance in a spirit of true generosity. Don't think badly of me for devising this way to show my gratitude. I can well afford it.

It was signed: *Mildred D'Abernon.*

Below was written: *P.S. Here's your murderer.*

Private Gorman's Luck

As private Gorman saw it, he was dead unlucky.

He had just been picked up by the redcaps for the seventh time. He couldn't stand the army. The snag was that he was no more of a success at deserting than he was at rifle drill. On four occasions he had got only a couple of miles from the barrack gates. Twice they had collected him from his home in Bermondsey. But the latest attempt was his most ambitious. He had managed three days on the run and all but got away. His assessment of the experience in the quiet of his cell in Hounslow Barracks was that only his stinking luck had let him down.

At first, fortune had favoured him. After two nights sleeping rough, his uniform had got too shabby to wear with confidence, so he had started to look for some civvies. He was passing a bomb site in Hounslow when he spotted a damaged house across the street. It was like looking into a doll's house; the blast had ripped away the entire front. The wardens had cleared the floor downstairs, but the upper floor was unsafe, so everything was left: two bedrooms with beds, chests of drawers, wardrobes, dressing tables and – of surpassing interest to Gorman – a blue double-breasted suit on a hanger suspended from the top of one of the wardrobe doors.

That evening in the blackout (as he told it later to Private Plumridge, who was on fatigues in the guardroom), Gorman had gone back to the house and waited nearby for an air raid to create a distraction. This was the summer of 1944, when the flying bombs were at their worst, so there was a fair chance of the siren going some time. When it did, and Gorman heard the steady drone of a V1 coming over from London, he made his move. The buzzbombs held no fears for Gorman. He had a firm conviction that he was safe from those things, however close they came. His enemy wasn't Hitler; it was the redcaps. He hopped over the rubble, through the path cleared by the wardens, into the dining room, out to the hall and up the stairs. As easy as ABC.

For the first time in his army career, he was glad of his metal-studded boots when he got up there and found the bedroom door locked by some security-minded bastard from the rescue service. Two good kicks and he was inside.

Then it was a matter of keeping close to the wall and edging around the room to the dark shape of the wardrobe. He stepped deftly over one of the fallen chairs, sidled past the dressing table and reached out his fingertips to feel for the suit. With his hand firmly over the padded shoulder, he lifted it from the wardrobe and held it against his chest. The sleeve length matched his arm to perfection. Elated, he started back around the edge of the room, blundered into the chair, went arse over tip, as he put it to Private Plumridge, and plunged alarmingly to the floor.

There was a short, uncomfortable hiatus, not unlike the seconds after a flying bomb cuts out, when Private Gorman waited for the crash. It started as a rending sound in the plaster, followed by a crack and a groan as the entire floor caved in. Gorman dropped yelling with a mass of wood, plaster and linoleum. His first thought was that the entire building would collapse on him.

After the fall, he heard himself spluttering, so he reckoned he was still alive. Most of his body had hit the mattress of the double bed. One of his legs hurt and he couldn't breathe for plaster in the air, but he was able to get up. Still holding the precious suit, he stumbled through the debris and hobbled off in the blackout as quickly as his injured leg would let him.

He passed the night at the feet of an angel in a churchyard, with the suit laid out on a granite tomb nearby. At first light, he gave himself a fitting. For off-the-peg, it was as good as anything from the Fifty Shilling Tailors. Better. In the pockets there was four and threepence, a packet of Senior Service and a box of Swan Vestas. After he had dumped his uniform under a heap of discarded wreaths and flowers, Gorman climbed over the churchyard wall into someone's garden and helped himself to a shirt from the washing line. Without clothing coupons, what else was he to do?

A smoke, a shave at a barber's in Hounslow High Street and a cup of tea at the bus station gave him the confidence he needed to enter the town hall and see the National Registration people about an identity card. If you said you had lost your card, it cost a shilling to apply for a replacement, and they would give you a receipt that you could show to anyone who challenged you. A passport to civilian life.

Gorman understood identity numbers. When the woman clerk asked him, he rattled off a number similar to his own before he was called up, AB to say he lived in the London Borough of Bermondsey, and a slight variation in the digits after, to prevent her from tracking him to his real address. He gave a false name. He was getting smart at last.

When the clerk asked him for the shilling, Gorman casually took a two-shilling piece from his pocket and placed it on the counter. She wrote out the receipt, stamped it, handed it to Gorman and passed him his shilling change. And that was when his luck ran out.

In his elation, he dropped the shilling. It fell off the counter and rolled for a short distance across the floor. Gorman pursued it. He put out his foot to step on it just as someone stooped to pick it up. With his regulation army boots Gorman crushed the fingers of the police constable on duty.

No apology could save him. He was unable to explain how a civilian in a smart blue suit came to be wearing metal-studded army boots. Inside the hour, he was collected by the redcaps.

'I was dead unlucky,' he complained once more to Private Plumridge.

'Deplorably unfortunate,' agreed Plumridge, who was socially a cut above Gorman. Plumridge was regularly in trouble for insubordination when addressing NCOs, who were apt to mistake an elegant turn of phrase for sarcasm. It was a shame he had failed the intelligence test for officer selection, yet to his credit he had come to terms with the rigours of life in the ranks. He had no plans to desert. 'To be candid with you, Gorman, I'm at a loss to understand why you keep doing it.'

Gorman scowled. 'I hate the army, don't I?'

Plumridge leaned on the polisher he was supposed to be using on the floor outside Gorman's cell. 'If it comes to that, I'm not passionately devoted to wearing khaki and living in wooden huts myself.'

'Why do you stick it, then?' asked Gorman, expecting a short sermon about King and Country and Mr Churchill.

A smug smile spread across Plumridge's face. 'I have an incentive. A certain somebody who happens to believe I'm the finest soldier in the British Army.'

'God Almighty, who's that?'

Plumridge lifted one of the flaps of his fatigue dress and took out a photograph, which he pushed through the grille of the cell door. 'Annabelle.'

Gorman studied the picture and passed it back. 'Not bad. Not bad at all. Your girl?'

'Wife, in point of fact,' Plumridge remarked with an attempt to be casual.

'You're married?' Gorman said in a shrill note. 'Give us another look at that.'

Plumridge held the picture up. 'She is rather fetching, I must admit. She agreed to marry me the day my call-up papers arrived. She adores the uniform, you see. Before that, I was merely one of a string of would-be suitors. Now Annabelle is keeping my home fire burning in Chiddingfold.'

'Where's that?'

'In a rather select part of Surrey that you wouldn't have heard of. Whenever I get a weekend pass, I'm off there. She's terribly proud of me. Fully expects me to get a stripe before Christmas.' He took the photograph away from the grille and gazed at it. 'So you see, I'm utterly committed to the army.'

The conversation was cut short by the appearance of Corporal Harker, the Military Policeman on duty. Harker was the most conscientious redcap in the barracks. 'What's that in your grubby fist, Soldier?'

'Only a photograph, Corporal,' answered Plumridge, tucking it away.

Harker snapped his fingers and held out his hand.

Plumridge reluctantly handed over the picture of Annabelle. 'My wife, actually.'

'My wife, actually, *Corporal*.'

'Sorry, Corporal.' Plumridge hesitated. 'May I have it back please? It's rather precious.'

Harker snorted his displeasure. 'You've got no business showing photographs of women to the prisoner. He's under close arrest and you're supposed to be polishing the floor. What else have you been handing over? Cigarettes? Chocolate? Turn out your pockets, at the double.'

Plumridge obeyed, producing a letter addressed to Annabelle, his pay book, a set of keys and his identity disc.

'This should be round your neck, not in your pocket,' Harker reprimanded him. 'CO's orders: identity discs will be worn by all personnel at all times so long as the air raids continue. That means round your fat neck, Plumridge, have you got that?'

'Yes, Corporal.'

'Put it on, then. Put this other rubbish back in your pockets and get polishing the floor. I'm going to search the prisoner now, and if I find so much as a peppermint on his person, you're on a charge, do you understand?'

Plumridge nodded unhappily.

The search of Private Gorman was a simple matter because he was wearing only shorts and a singlet, having disposed of his uniform and had been deprived of the blue civilian suit. To his credit, he was still wearing his identity disc around his neck. Corporal Harker could find nothing irregular, so he had to content himself with some disparaging remarks about deserters, and, when he emerged from the cell, a blistering attack on the quality of Plumridge's polishing. He ordered Plumridge to buff the entire floor again, and with that he went off duty.

'That man's an absolute sadist,' Plumridge confided through the grille to Gorman.

'Who's on duty now?'

'The tall ginger one with the moustache.'

'That's Corporal Davis. He's all right. He'll let you off in twenty minutes.'

This might have been the case, but inside three minutes, the air raid warning sounded and within seconds they could hear the ominous note of a flying bomb. The procedure in an air raid was to evacuate the guard room, which was a timber structure, and go into the underground shelter at the rear. Corporal Davis unlocked Gorman's cell. He was holding a pair of handcuffs.

'Let's have your wrist.'

'Sounds like a close one, Corp,' commented Gorman, untroubled and glad of the distraction.

In accordance with standing orders, Corporal Davis manacled Gorman to himself and shouted to Plumridge to go with them. The entrance to the shelter was about thirty yards away, across a stretch of grass. Before they were through the back door of the guard room. Gorman heard the engine of the V1 cut out. He looked up.

It was diving straight towards them out of a brilliant blue sky, its black and green camouflage clearly visible on the upper fuselage, its stubby, squared-off wings and tail giving it the look of an aircraft crudely manufactured for destruction, its propulsion unit spurting orange flames.

Corporal Davis yelled, 'Come on!' to Plumridge, who was last out of the door. Gorman, his injured leg forgotten, was already halfway across the grass towards the shelter, jerking Davis with him.

The flying bomb didn't actually hit the guard room. It crashed into the tarmac just in front of the main gates. The blast ripped the guard room and the armoury apart. Slats of wood hailed down.

Gorman was temporarily deafened, but unhurt. He had made it to the sandbags heaped outside the shelter and leapt over into the dug-out front as the explosion happened. His arm was still draped over the sandbags, attached to Corporal Davis. He tugged on it and felt no response. He hauled himself up and over the sandbags.

Corporal Davis had been hit by some piece of flying debris. He was either stunned or dead. Gorman didn't wait to check. Someone else's misfortune was his opportunity. He felt for the chain attached to Davis's belt, found the key of the handcuffs and released himself. He was about to desert for the eighth time.

He looked around him. Black smoke was blotting out the sky. The wreckage of the guard room had caught fire and the long grass at the rear was smouldering. It would probably be safe to go out by the main gate. The blokes on sentry duty must have been blasted to Kingdom Come.

As he stepped forward, he almost tripped over a body in fatigue dress. Private Plumridge was dead, dead beyond argument, with half his head blown off. Gorman's first impulse was to hare away and he had already gone a couple of paces when the thought occurred to him that Plumridge's fatigue dress might be of use. He knew from experience that nights in the open could be cold, even in August, and he didn't relish sleeping rough, dressed as he was.

He braced himself for another look at the body. The jacket was soiled with blood and ripped in a couple of places, but worth taking if there was time, and the trousers were perfectly usable. When it came to deserting, Gorman wasn't squeamish about robbing the living or the dead. So he unbuttoned the clothes and peeled them off, leaving Plumridge in singlet and shorts, just as he was himself.

Then he had his brainwave.

It was sparked by the sight of Plumridge's identity disc. The opportunity was there to free himself totally from the army. If he removed Plumridge's disc and replaced it with his own, everyone would assume that 505918 Gorman, Private E. was dead. They wouldn't be able to identify the body by looking at the face, because most of it was missing. And in a few minutes, the grass where Plumridge was lying would be alight, charring him all over.

While he was switching the discs, Gorman thought of an extra refinement. He ran back to Corporal Davis's body, dragged it the few yards across the turf and positioned it alongside Plumridge. Then he clipped the spare handcuff over Plumridge's wrist. The clincher, he told himself, grinning. That done, he grabbed the fatigue dress and dashed across the smouldering grass to freedom.

Soon after, the army tackled the job of putting out the fires and recovering the bodies. There were four dead and they were identified as Privates Harris and Parks, the two men on guard at the main gate, Corporal Davis of the Military Police and the prisoner, Private Gorman. Next of kin were informed.

After some hours, there was concern about the welfare of Private Plumridge, who was known to have been detailed to perform fatigues in the guard room and who appeared to be missing. A thorough examination of the debris failed to reveal a fifth body. Searches of the surrounding area were organised and a trail of footsteps was discovered leading from the charred area where two of the bodies had been found towards the main gate. It was assumed that Plumridge had wandered off, possibly in a state of concussion, and the civilian police were informed. Two days later, his identity disc was found by a man walking his dog on Hounslow Heath.

Plumridge's wife Annabelle was contacted, but she informed Corporal Harker, the Military Policeman who called on her in Chiddingfold, that she had heard nothing from him. She seemed mystified, but not unduly distressed by her husband's disappearance.

A week passed, and there was no further news of Plumridge. The funerals of the four men killed by the flying bomb were all attended by senior officers. Ten days after the tragedy, a service of remembrance was conducted by the padre.

After the service, the CO called at the temporary, prefabricated guard room and spoke to Corporal Harker. He expressed concern about the lack of information concerning Private Plumridge. He detested the very idea, but he felt obliged to consider the possibility that Plumridge had taken advantage of the bombing to go absent without leave. After questioning Harker closely about the reaction of Annabelle Plumridge to her husband's disappearance, he authorised Harker to make a second visit to Chiddingfold and see whether the lady could throw any more light on the mystery.

The same ten days had been a testing time for Private Gorman. To his credit, it was the longest period he had spent on the run. Yet without civilian clothes or even a passable uniform, he had been compelled to spend the days in hiding and the nights scavenging. He was living mainly on raw eggs and vegetables stolen from suburban gardens. It was much too soon after his supposed demise to think of going home. At the sight of him, his mother would scream and his father would tell the whole of Bermondsey and Rotherhithe that a miracle had happened.

He sat hunched in his latest hide-out, a delapidated boat shed at Twickenham, ironically trying to lift his spirits with what the army called planning. What he needed urgently was a set of clothes and some money. It was no use trusting to luck. He couldn't expect to come across another bomb site with a suit on a hanger waiting for him to collect. As for money, Plumridge hadn't left so much as a halfpenny in the pockets of the fatigue dress. Just the pay book, and what use was that to a deserter? Gorman had torn it into small pieces and thrown it out days ago, with the letter to Annabelle. Apart from the clothes, the only things of Plumridge's still in his possession were two keys on a ring, one that probably fitted the padlock of his locker, the other a Yale which had come in useful for scraping the dirt off carrots and parsnips. He had since picked up a knife, so the keys could be chucked out as well now. There was small chance of finding a lock they would open.

Or was there?

As he dangled the key ring on his finger, Gorman had another of his brainwaves. Wasn't it reasonable to suppose that the Yale was the key to Plumridge's house in Surrey, and wouldn't it be worth finding the place and seeing if it fitted? There were sure to be clothes there, and food and probably money. This was the luck he needed, and all this time he had been carrying it around with him!

Where was it that Plumridge had said he lived? The address had been on that blasted letter. Victoria House – it had struck Gorman as comical, Plums at Victoria House – but what the hell was the name of the village? Chittyfield? Chiddingfield? Not quite.

Chiddingfold! Victoria House, Chiddingfold.

It wasn't easy to find the place. Surrey was a large county, and signposts had been removed to frustrate troop movements in the event of an invasion. He headed south, away from London, reasoning that it must be out of the surburban reaches. Going through Hampton Court on the first night, he broke into three cars parked outside a pub before he found what he needed: a county map.

Chiddingfold was near Haslemere on the Sussex border, too far to reach in a night, so he walked the twenty miles to Guildford, and laid up in some outbuildings at a farm just south of the town. He found apples stored there in boxes, and ate enough to satisfy hunger and thirst in one.

The following night was a Saturday and a full moon, so he was glad he had not left too many miles to cover, because people would be out later than usual. It was after eleven when he started, and half-past two in the morning when he finally located Victoria House. Happily, it was a detached building in its own grounds. No telephone wires were visible. He had no wish to disturb Annabelle Plumridge's sleep if he could avoid it, but it was a relief to know that she couldn't call the police.

The first thing was to see whether the key fitted. He started up the drive towards the house.

In bed, Annabelle heard the crunch of gravel outside. 'Listen!'

'What's the matter?'

'Just listen, Simon. There's someone outside!'

'A fox, I expect.'

'No, it's too heavy for that. He's by the front door! Oh, God, what if it's my husband!'

Corporal Harker swung his legs to the floor and pulled on a pair of shorts. He went to the chair over which he had draped his uniform and drew his baton from its sheath. Then he glided out of the door and downstairs.

Annabelle shrank back in bed, pulling the sheet tight around her neck. She heard the sound of a key turning in the door, a shout of surprise and then a crack that made her gasp with terror, followed by two more, then silence.

The suspense was petrifying before the landing light came on, and Corporal Harker stood in the doorway holding his baton. 'I'm afraid I had to hit him,' he said, breathing heavily.

'Charlie? My husband?' whispered Annabelle.

He hesitated. 'Private Plumridge, yes. You don't have to come downstairs. I can deal with it.'

'Is he...?'

'I'm afraid so.'

'Oh, my poor Charlie!' Annabelle started to sob.

'Come off it,' Corporal Harker said in the sharp voice of authority he used in the guard room. 'You told me you couldn't bear to live with a deserter. You said you fancied me in my red cap and white gaiters.'

'I know, but...'

'He must have had a thin skull. Some people do. It's better this way. Your reputation, my career.'

'But what shall we do with him?'

'Easy. You don't have to do a thing. Better if you stay up here. I'll put him in the van and take him with me. I know a couple of bomb sites on the way back to barracks. I'll hide him under some rubble, and even if they find him, no one will ever guess who he was, or how it happened.'

'I suppose it was just bad luck,' Annabelle said to appease her feelings of shock.

'That's right,' Corporal Harker confirmed. 'He was unlucky. Dead unlucky.'

The Secret Lover

'Pam.'

'Yes?'

'Will you see him this weekend?'

Pam Meredith drew a long breath and stifled the impulse to scream. She knew exactly what was coming. 'See who?'

'Your secret lover.'

She summoned a coy smile, said 'Give over!' and everyone giggled.

For some reason, that last session of the working week regularly turned three efficient medical receptionists into overgrown schoolgirls. They were all over thirty, too. As soon as they arrived at the health centre on Saturday morning, they were into their routine. After flexing their imaginations with stories of what the doctors had been getting up to with the patients, they started on each other. Then it was never long before Pam's secret lover came up.

He was an inoffensive, harassed-looking man in his late thirties who happened to walk into the centre one afternoon to ask for help. A piece of grit had lodged under his left eyelid. Not one of the doctors or the district nurse had been in the building at the time, so Pam had dealt with it herself. From her own experiences with contact lenses, she had a fair idea how to persuade the eye to eject a foreign body, and she had succeeded very quickly, without causing the patient any serious discomfort. He had thanked her and left in a rush, as if the episode had embarrassed him. Pam had thought no more about him until a fortnight later, when she came on duty and was told that a man had been asking for her personally and would be calling back at lunchtime. This, understandably, created some lively interest in reception, particularly when he arrived at five minutes to one carrying a bunch of daffodils.

At thirty-three, Pam was the second youngest of the medical receptionists. She exercised, dieted and tinted her hair blonde and she was popular with many of the men who came in to collect their prescriptions, but she was not used to floral tributes. In her white overall she thought of herself as clinical and efficient. She had a pale, oval face with brown eyes and a small, neat mouth that she had been told projected refinement rather than sensuality. Lately, she had noticed some incipient wrinkles on her neck and taken to wearing polo sweaters.

Under the amused and frankly envious observation of her colleagues, Pam had blushingly accepted the flowers, trying to explain that such a tribute was not necessary, charming as it was. However, when the giver followed it up by asking her to allow him to buy her a drink at the Green Dragon, she had found him difficult to refuse. She had stuttered something about being on duty after lunch, so he had suggested tomato juice or bitter lemon, and one of the other girls had given her an unseen nudge and planted her handbag in her hand.

That was the start of the long-running joke about Pam's secret lover.

Really the joke was on the others. They hadn't guessed it in their wildest fantasies, but things had developed to the extent that Pam now slept with him regularly.

Do not assume too much about the relationship. In the common understanding of the word, he was not her lover. Sleeping together and making love are not of necessity the same thing. The possibility was not excluded, yet it was not taken as the automatic consequence of sharing a bed, and that accorded well with Pam's innate refinement.

So it wasn't entirely as the girls in the health centre might have imagined it. Pam had learned over that first tomato juice in the Green Dragon that Cliff had a job in the cider industry which entailed calling on various producers in the West Midlands and South-West, and visiting Hereford for an overnight stay once a fortnight. He liked travelling, yet he admitted that the nights away from home had been instrumental in the failure of his marriage. He had not been unfaithful, but, as he altruistically put it, anyone who read the accounts of rapes and muggings in the papers couldn't really blame a wife who sought companionship elsewhere when her husband spent every other week away on business.

Responding to his candour, Pam had found herself admitting that she, too, was divorced. The nights, she agreed, were the worst. Even in the old cathedral city of Hereford, which had no reputation for violence, she avoided going out alone after dark and she often lay awake listening acutely in case someone was tampering with the locks downstairs.

The first lunchtime drink had led to another when Cliff was next in the city. The fortnight after, Pam had invited him to the house for a 'spot of supper', explaining that it was no trouble, because you could do much more interesting things cooking for two than alone. Cliff had heaped praise on her chicken *cordon bleu*, and after that the evening meal had become a fortnightly fixture. On the first occasion, he had quite properly returned to his hotel at the end of the evening, but the following time he had introduced Pam to the old-fashioned game of cribbage, and they had both got so engrossed that neither of them had noticed the time until it was well after midnight. By then, Pam felt so relaxed and safe with Cliff that it had seemed the most natural thing in the world to make up the spare bed for him and invite him to stay the night. There had been no suggestion on either side of a more intimate arrangement. That was what she liked about Cliff. He wasn't one of those predatory males. He was enough of a gentleman to suppress his natural physical instincts. And one night six weeks after in a thunderstorm, when she had tapped on his bedroom door and said she was feeling frightened, he had offered in the same gentlemanly spirit to come to her room until the storm abated. As it happened, Pam still slept in the king-size double bed she had got used to when she was married, so there was room for Cliff without any embarrassment about inadvertent touching. They had fallen asleep listening for the thunder. By then it was the season of summer storms, so next time he had come to the house, they had agreed that it was a sensible precaution to sleep together even when the sky was clear. You could never be certain when a storm might blow up during the night. And when the first chill nights of autumn arrived, neither of them liked the prospect of sleeping apart between cool sheets. Besides, as Cliff considerately mentioned, using one bed was less expensive on the laundry.

Speaking of laundry, Pam took to washing out his shirts, underclothes and pyjamas. She had bought him a special pair of bottle-green French pyjamas without buttons and with an elasticated waistband. They were waiting on his pillow, washed and ironed, each time he came. He was very appreciative. He never failed to arrive with a bottle of cider that they drank with the meal. Once or twice he mentioned that he would have taken her out to a restaurant if her cooking had not been so excellent that it would have shown up the cook. He particularly relished the cooked breakfast on a large oval plate that she supplied before he went on his way in the morning.

So Pam staunchly tolerated the teasing in the health centre, encouraged by the certainty that it was all fantasy on their part; she had been careful never to let them know that she had invited Cliff home. She was in a better frame of mind as she walked home that lunchtime. It was always a relief to get through Saturday morning.

As she turned the corner of her street, she saw a small car, a red Mini, outside her house, with someone sitting inside it. She wasn't expecting a visitor. She strolled towards her gate, noticing that it was a woman who made no move to get out, and whom she didn't recognise, so she passed the car and let herself indoors.

There was a letter on the floor, a greetings card by the look of it. She had quite forgotten that her birthday was on Sunday. Living alone, with no family to speak of, she tended to ignore such occasions. However, someone had evidently decided that this one should not go by unremarked. She didn't recognise the handwriting, and the postmark was too faint to read. She opened it and smiled. A print of a single daffodil, and inside, under the printed birthday greeting, the handwritten letter C.

The reason why she hadn't recognised Cliff's writing was that this was the first time she had seen it. He wasn't one for sending letters. And the postmark wouldn't have given Pam a clue, even if she had deciphered it, because she didn't know where he lived. He was vague or dismissive when it came to personal information, so she hadn't pressed him. He was entitled to his privacy. She couldn't help wondering sometimes, and her best guess was that since the failure of his marriage he had tended to neglect himself and his home and devote himself to his job. He lived for the travelling, and, Pam was encouraged to believe, his fortnightly visit to Hereford.

Presently the doorbell chimed. Pam opened the door to the woman she had seen in the car, dark-haired, about her own age or a little older, good-looking, with one of those long, elegant faces with high cheekbones that you see in foreign films. She was wearing a dark blue suit and white blouse buttoned to the neck as if she were attending an interview for a job. Mainly, Pam was made aware of the woman's grey-green eyes that scrutinised her with an interest unusual in people who called casually at the door.

'Hello,' said Pam.

'Mrs Pamela Meredith?'

'Yes.'

The look became even more intense. 'We haven't met. You may not even know that I exist. I'm Tracey Gibbons.' She paused for a reaction.

Pam smiled faintly. 'You're right. I haven't heard your name before.'

Tracey Gibbons sighed and shook her head. 'I'm not surprised. I don't know what you're going to think of me, coming to your house like this, but it's reached the point when something has to be done. It's about your husband.'

Pam frowned. 'My husband?' She hadn't heard from David in six years.

'May I come in?'

'I suppose you'd better.'

As she showed the woman into her front room, Pam

couldn't help wondering if this was a confidence trick. The woman's eyes blatantly surveyed the room, the furniture, the ornaments, everything.

Pam said sharply, 'I think you'd better come to the point, Miss Gibbons.'

'Mrs, actually. Not that it matters. I'm waiting for my divorce to come through.' Suddenly the woman sounded nervous and defensive. 'I'm not promiscuous. I want you to understand that, Mrs Meredith, whatever you may think of me. And I'm not deceitful, either, or I wouldn't be here. I want to get things straight between us. I've driven over from Worcester this morning to talk to you.'

Pam was beginning to fathom what this was about. Mrs Gibbons was having an affair with David, and for some obscure reason she felt obliged to confess it to his ex-wife. Clearly the poor woman was in a state of nerves, so it was kindest to let her say her piece before gently showing her the door.

'You probably wonder how I got your address,' Mrs Gibbons went on. 'He doesn't know I'm here, I promise you. It's only over the last few weeks that I began to suspect he had a wife. Certain things you notice, like his freshly ironed shirts. He left his suitcase open the last time he came, and I happened to see the birthday card he addressed to you. That's how I got your address.'

Pam's skin prickled. 'Which card?'

'The daffodil. I looked inside, I'm ashamed to admit. I had to know.'

Pam closed her eyes. The woman wasn't talking about David at all. It was Cliff, *her* Cliff. Her head was spinning. She thought she was going to faint. She said, 'I think I need some brandy.'

Mrs Gibbons nodded. 'I'll join you, if I may.'

When she handed over the glass, Pam said in a subdued voice, 'You *are* talking about a man named Cliff?'

'Of course.'

'He is not my husband.'

'What?' Mrs Gibbons stared at her in disbelief.

'He visits me sometimes.'

'And you wash his shirts?'

'Usually.'

'The bastard!' said Mrs Gibbons, her eyes brimming. 'The rotten, two-timing bastard! I knew there was someone else, but I thought it was his wife he was so secretive about. I persuaded myself he was unhappily married and I came here to plead with you to let him go. I could kill him!'

'How do you think I feel?' Pam blurted out. 'I didn't even know there was anyone else in his life.'

'Does he keep a toothbrush and razor in your bathroom?'

'A face flannel as well.'

'And I suppose you bought him some expensive after-shave?'

Pam confirmed it bitterly. In her outraged state, she needed to talk, and sharing the trouble seemed likely to dull the pain. She related how she and Cliff had met and how she had invited him home.

'And one thing led to another?' speculated Mrs Gibbons. 'When I think of what I was induced to do in the belief that I was the love of his life . . .' She finished her brandy in a gulp.

Pam nodded. 'It was expensive, too.'

'Expensive?'

'Preparing three-course dinners and large cooked breakfasts.'

'I wasn't talking about cooking,' said Mrs Gibbons, giving Pam a penetrating look.

'Ah,' said Pam, with a slow dip of the head, in an attempt to convey that she understood exactly what Mrs Gibbons *was* talking about.

'Things I didn't get up to in ten years of marriage to a very athletic man,' Mrs Gibbons further confided, looking modestly away. 'But you know all about it. Casanova was a boy scout compared to Cliff. God, I feel so humiliated.'

'Would you like a spot more brandy, Mrs Gibbons?'

'Why don't you call me Tracey?' suggested Mrs Gibbons, holding out her glass. 'We're just his playthings, you and I. How many others are there, do you suppose?'

'Who knows?' said Pam, seizing on the appalling possibility and speaking her thoughts aloud. 'There are plenty of divorced women like you and me, living in relative comfort in what was once the marital home, pathetically grateful for any attention that comes our way. Let's face it: we're second-hand goods.'

After a sobering interval, Tracey Gibbons pushed her empty glass towards the brandy bottle again, and asked, 'What are we going to do about him?'

'Kick him out with his toothbrush and face flannel, I suppose,' Pam answered inadequately.

'So that he finds other deluded women to prey on?' said Tracey. 'That's not the treatment for the kind of animal we're dealing with. Personally, I feel so angry and abused that I could kill him if I knew how to get away with it. Wouldn't you?'

Pam stared at her. 'Are you serious?'

'Totally. He's ruined my hopes and every atom of self-respect I had left. What was I to him? His bit in Worcester, his Monday night amusement.'

'And I was Tuesday night in Hereford,' Pam added bleakly, suddenly given a cruel and vivid understanding of the way she had been used. Sex was Monday, supper Tuesday. In her own way, she felt as violated as Tracey. An arrangement that had seemed to be considerate and beautiful was revealed as cynically expedient. The reason why he had never touched her was that he was always sated after his night of unbridled passion in Worcester. 'Tracey, if you know of a way to kill him,' she stated with the calm that comes when a crucial decision is made, 'I know how to get away with it.'

Tracey's eyes opened very wide.

Pam made black coffee and sandwiches and explained her plan. To describe it as a plan is perhaps misleading, because it had only leapt to mind as they were talking. She wasn't given to thinking much about murder. Yet as she spoke, she sensed excitedly that it could work. It was simple, tidy and within her capability.

The two women talked until late in the afternoon. For the plan to work, they had to devise a way of killing without mess. The body should not be marked by violence. They solemnly debated various methods of despatching a man. Whether the intention was serious or not, Pam found that just talking about it was a balm for the pain that Cliff had inflicted on her. She and Tracey sensibly agreed to take no action until they had each had time to adjust to the shock, but they were adamant that they would meet again.

On the following Monday evening, Pam received a phone call from Tracey. 'Have you thought any more about what we were discussing?'

'On and off, yes,' Pam answered guardedly.

'Well, I've been doing some research,' Tracey told her with the excitement obvious in her voice. 'I'd better not be too specific over the phone, but I know where to get some stuff that will do the job. Do you understand me?'

'I think so.'

'It's simple, quick and very effective, and the best thing about it is that I can get it at work.'

Pam recalled that Tracey had said she worked for a firm that manufactured agricultural fertilisers. She supposed she was talking about some chemical substance.

Poison.

'The thing is,' Tracey was saying, 'if I get some, are you willing to do your part? You said it would be no problem.'

'That's true, but—'

'By the weekend? He's due to visit me on Monday.'

The reminder of Cliff's Monday assignations in Worcester was like a stab of pain to Pam. 'By the weekend,' she confirmed emphatically. 'Come over about the same time on Saturday. I'll do my part, I promise you, Tracey.'

The part Pam had to play in the killing of Cliff was to obtain a blank death certificate from one of the doctors at the centre. She had often noticed how careless Dr Holt-Wagstaff was with his paperwork. He was the oldest of the five practitioners and his desk was always in disorder. She waited for her opportunity for most of the week. On Friday morning she had to go into his surgery to ask him to clarify his handwriting on a prescription form. The death certificate pad was there on the desk. At twelve-fifteen, when he went out on his rounds, and Pam was on duty with one other girl, she slipped back into the surgery. No one saw her.

Saturday was a testing morning for Pam. The time dragged and the teasing about her secret lover was difficult to take without snapping back at the others. She kept wondering whether Dr Holt-Wagstaff had noticed anything. She need not have worried. He left at noon, wishing everyone a pleasant weekend. At twelve-thirty, the girls locked up and left.

When Pam got home, Tracey was waiting on her doorstep. 'I came by train,' she explained. 'Didn't want to leave my car outside again. It's surprising how much people notice.'

'Sensible,' said Pam, with approval, as she opened the door. 'Now I want to hear about the stuff you've got. Is it really going to work?'

Tracey put her hand on Pam's arm. 'Darling, it's foolproof. Do you want to see it?' She opened her handbag and took out a small brown glass bottle. 'Pure nicotine. We use it at work.'

Pam held the bottle in her palm. 'Nicotine? Is it a poison?'

'Deadly.'

'There isn't much here.'

'The fatal dose is measured in milligrams, Pam. A few drops will do the trick.'

'How can we get him to take it?'

'I've thought of that.' Tracey smiled. 'You're going to like this. In a glass of his own buckshee cider. Nicotine goes yellow on exposure to light and air, and there's a bitter taste which the sweet cider will mask.'

'How does it work?'

'It acts as a massive stimulant. The vital organs simply can't withstand it. He'll die of cardiac arrest in a very short time. Did you get the death certificate?'

Pam placed the poison bottle on the kitchen table and opened one of her cookbooks. The certificate was inside.

'You're careful, too,' Tracey said with a conspiratorial smile. She delved into her handbag again. 'I brought a prescription from my doctor to copy the signature, as you suggested. What else do we have to fill in here? *Name of deceased*. What shall we call him?'

'Anything but Cliff,' said Pam. 'How about Clive? Clive Jones.'

'All right. Clive Jones it is. *Date of death*. I'd better fill that in after the event. What shall we put as the cause of death? Cardiac failure?'

'No, that's likely to be a sudden death,' said Pam,

thinking of post-mortems. 'Broncho-pneumonia is better.'

'Suits me,' said Tracey, writing it down. 'After he's dead, I take this to the Registry of Births, Marriages and Deaths in Worcester, and tell them that Clive Jones was my brother, is that right?'

'Yes, it's very straightforward. They'll want his date of birth and one or two other details that you can invent. Then they issue you with another certificate that you show to the undertaker. He takes over after that.'

'I ask for a cremation, of course. Will it cost much?'

'Don't worry,' said Pam. 'He can afford it.'

'Too true!' said Tracey. 'His wallet is always stuffed with notes.'

'He never has to spend much,' Pam pointed out. 'The way he runs his life, he gets everything he wants for nothing.'

'The bastard,' said Tracey with a shudder.

'You really mean to do it, don't you?'

Tracey stood up and looked steadily at Pam with her grey-green eyes. 'On Monday evening when he comes to me. I'll phone you when it's done.'

Pam linked her arm in Tracey's. 'The first thing I'm going to do is burn those pyjamas.'

Tracey remarked, 'He never wore pyjamas with me.'

'Really?' Pam hesitated, her curiosity aroused. 'What exactly did he do with you? Are you able to talk about it?'

'I don't believe I could,' answered Tracey with eyes lowered.

'If I poured you a brandy? We *are* in this together now.'

'All right,' said Tracey with a sigh.

Sunday seemed like the longest day of Pam's life, but she finally got through it. On Monday she didn't go in to work. That evening, she waited nervously by the phone from six-thirty onwards.

The call came at a few minutes after seven. Pam snatched up the phone.

'Hello, darling.' *The voice was Cliff's.*

'Cliff?'

'Yes. Not like me to call you on a Monday, is it? The fact is, I happen to be in Worcester on my travels, and it occurred to me that I could get over to you in Hereford in half an hour if you're free this evening.'

'Has something happened?' asked Pam.

'No, my darling. Just a change of plans. I won't expect much of a meal.'

'That's good, because I haven't got one for you,' Pam candidly told him.

There was a moment's hesitation before he said, 'Are you all right, dear? You don't sound quite yourself.'

'Don't I?' said Pam flatly. 'Well, I've had a bit of a shock. My sister died here on Saturday. It wasn't entirely unexpected. Broncho-pneumonia. I've had to do everything myself. She's being cremated on Wednesday.'

'Your sister? Pam, darling, I'm terribly sorry. I didn't even know you had a sister.'

'Her name was Olive. Olive Jones,' said Pam, and she couldn't help smiling at her own resourcefulness. After she had poisoned Tracey with a drop of nicotine in her brandy, all it had wanted on the death certificate was a touch of the pen. 'We weren't close. I'm not too distressed. Yes, why don't you come over?'

'You're sure you want me?'

'Oh, I want you,' answered Pam. 'Yes, I definitely want you.'

When she had put down the phone, she didn't go to the fridge to see what food she had in there. She went upstairs to the bedroom and changed into a black lace négligé.

Did You Tell Daddy?

Jonathan Wilding, four years old, his tight curls bleached by the August sun, stepped busily through the village delivering letters. He called at every house. They were his mother Sally's love letters.

Jonathan had found them at the bottom of the spare-room wardrobe when he had gone to look for a tennis ball to replace the one he had lost over next door's wall. The moment he had slipped the elastic band off the shoe-box and lifted the lid, he had forgotten about the ball. Those bundles of letters neatly tied with coloured ribbon had seemed provided for him to realise the one ambition of his young life: to be a postman. Mr Halliwell, with his peaked hat, grey uniform, bicycle and above all, the brown bag stuffed with letters and parcels, was Jonathan's idol, a loud-voiced, bearded man with something to say to everyone he met, including the children. Sometimes he allowed Jonathan to walk along the street with him and guard the bicycle when he propped it against someone's gatepost.

Jonathan's status this afternoon was infinitely more important. With his nursery-school satchel slung from one shoulder and filled with letters, he made his way purposefully from door to door making his special delivery. He knew that ideally the envelopes should not have been torn open at the top, but every one had a long letter inside, often running to several pages, so no one ought to feel dissatisfied. By a happy chance, there were just enough letters to go round. He had covered both sides of the street, slipping two or three through the doors of people who were particular friends of the family, and he was home and watching television before the first knock came at the front door.

Sally Wilding was in the kitchen cooking plaice and chips for her husband Bernard, the author of the letters. Bernard was asleep upstairs. He was a sergeant in the police, with responsibility for one small town and seven villages, including their own, and this week he was on nights. He and Sally had lived in the village all their lives. It was often mentioned that they had been childhood sweethearts, but that was sentimental blurring of the truth. They had ignored each other in school and avoided each other outside until a month before Bernard had become a police cadet. That month, April 1969, had made nonsense of all the years before. Out of nowhere, an avalanche of passion had engulfed them. They had been eighteen and in love and facing separation, for Bernard had been due to report to Hendon Police College, two hundred miles away, on May 1st. That last weekend, they had got engaged and promised to send letters to each other every day.

Such letters! Sally still blushed at their frankness and prickled with secret pleasure at the unrestraint of Bernard's ardour. If she ever needed a testimony to the force of his passion, it was there in his neatly upright handwriting, more candid and more eloquent than he had been before or since. There had been a few times in their marriage – very few – when she had been glad to take out those letters and read them for reassurance. Bernard was almost certainly unaware that she had kept them.

She heard the doorbell.

'Michael, see who it is, please.'

Michael was her first-born, ten years old and pleased to be the man of the house when Bernard was not available.

'It's Mrs Nugent. She wants to speak to you.'

Sally sighed, took the frying pan off the gas, wiped her hands and went to see what the village do-gooder wanted this time. Probably collecting for something. Why was it always when the evening meal was on the go?

'I rather think that this belongs to you, my dear.'

Sally took the letter and stared at it, unable yet to make the mental leap that linked it with the embarrassed neighbour on her doorstep.

'Somebody pushed it through my door. I expect they got the numbers mixed. It was already open. I haven't looked inside, believe me.'

Sally went numb. She couldn't summon the words to respond to Mrs Nugent. If a chasm had opened between them, she would have jumped into it at once.

Her mind mobilised at last. Which letter was it, for heaven's sake? What was in it? How could it possibly...?

One of the boys!

Fast as her brain began to race, events outpaced it. Mr Marsh from across the street came up the path with two more letters in his hand.

She took them, managed to blurt out something approximating to thanks, closed the door and dashed upstairs to the spare room to have her worst fears confirmed: the shoe-box empty except for one elastic band and three lengths of ribbon.

'Michael, Jonathan! Come here this minute!'

'There's someone else at the door, Mummy.'

The reckoning would have to wait. And so would Bernard's dinner.

The front door stood open for the next twenty minutes as Sally's letters were returned to her by a succession of blushing, grinning or frowning neighbours. Some cheerfully admitted having read the letters. For Sally, the ordeal was worse than a day in the stocks. 'I expect it was one of the children,' suggested the vicar's wife. 'Little scamps. What will they think of next?'

From upstairs, Bernard called out, 'Sally, are you there? You didn't call me. Is anything the matter?'

She nodded to the vicar's wife, closed the door and called upstairs, 'Sorry, darling. People at the door. You'd better hurry.'

She scooped up the letters from the hall table, hurried back into the kitchen and thrust them into the drawer with the teacloths just before Bernard came down.

'Who was it?'

'Oh, just about everybody. I'll tell you later. I'm afraid the chips are ruined, but the fish is still all right.'

'I'll have some bread with it. One of the boys up to some mischief?'

'I honestly don't know.'

'Want to deal with it yourself?'

Sally nodded.

The doorbell rang again.

'Oh, no!'

She answered it. Miss Sharp, the doctor's receptionist, with two more letters.

Sally returned to the kitchen.

'Letters as late in the day as this?'

She whisked them into the drawer. 'Old ones. Got to keep the place tidy.' It was hateful deceiving him, but she couldn't face the eruption when he found out. He set high standards for himself, and he expected his family to follow.

He picked up his tunic. 'If there's trouble, you can bet your life it's Jonathan. Time we stopped treating him as the baby of the family. He's got to learn.'

Sally agreed. Bernard had been more strict with Michael than ever he had been with Jonathan. It showed. Michael was dependable, a quiet, self-sufficient lad with a good capacity for concentration. He liked reading, stamps and model-making. If he misbehaved, it was generally because he put a higher priority on his hobbies than cleaning his teeth or tidying his room.

Jonathan was the adventurous one, and naughty with it. He had more than his share of personal charm, which he exploited to the limit.

As soon as Bernard had left for work, Sally questioned Michael. She had always tried to treat the boys even-handedly, even though they responded differently.

'Michael, what were you doing this afternoon?'

'I was at school.'

'After that.'

'I came home.'

'Straight home?'

'Yes.'

'What did you do when you came in?'

'Looked at my stamps.'

'You didn't go to the spare room for anything?'

'No, Mummy.'

Jonathan, when Sally spoke to him, cheerfully admitted playing postman with her letters. He told her everything. Five minutes later, he was in bed with his bottom smarting.

Downstairs, Sally took out the letters. Two more were returned during the evening. She had decided to destroy them all. She could never read them again without being conscious that the words meant only for her had been looked at by others. First, she needed to be sure that they had all come back. She sorted them into sequence. She had never counted them, but she knew Bernard had written her two a week for the whole of his cadet course.

One was missing: the first in the first week of July.

She soon recalled it, by glancing at the next one. Bernard had been waiting for the mid-course tests to be assessed. Keyed up, perhaps, he had poured out his desire for her in a long letter that was a kind of prose-poem to her physical attractions, a mixture of recollection and speculation that she had found wickedly delightful at the time, but now painfully embarrassing.

Which of her neighbours had got the letter and not returned it?

She mentally reviewed everyone who had called, and then in her mind's eye went up and down the village street, checking the houses and their inmates. When she came to Primrose Cottage she stopped. Ruby Simmons. Ruby had not returned a letter.

Ruby was Sally's age. They had gone through school together, but they had never been friends. In those days, Ruby had been an outrageous flirt, the first in their year to appear in eye shadow and a smear of lipstick, and the leader in every other step towards maturity. The boys had fought battles in the playground over her and she had rewarded them with favours in the cycle shed that were whispered about with sly smiles and sniggers. Sally, who could only guess, had disliked everything about her.

Worse, Ruby had been Bernard's girl for nearly a year before he fell for Sally. This was after they had all left school. Ruby had bleached her carroty-red hair and Bernard had succumbed as if he had never seen a blonde before. She had got a job assisting Mrs Parker in the general store – after leaving school with deplorable grades – and every night at seven when it closed, Bernard would be waiting to escort her up the street to Primrose Cottage, where she lived with her Aunt Lucy.

That was all a dozen years ago. It had turned out to be the high point of Ruby's life. Events since then had not been kind to her. First, Bernard had abandoned her for Sally. Then she had started going out with the doctor's son, until she had found out that a girl in the next village was pregnant by him. Soon after, she had lost her job in the store. It had been no fault of hers; simply that trade was falling off and Mrs Parker could no longer pay the wages. Since then, Ruby had lived off social security. When her aunt died in the winter of 1973, Ruby was faced with extra payments for the rent – or moving out of Primrose Cottage. She had found it necessary to take on casual work as a domestic help, occasional mornings that she probably didn't mention when she collected her unemployment money. Her hair had reverted to its natural red. She rarely spoke to anyone, and never to Sally.

Was Ruby still so bitter about the past that she couldn't bring herself to return the letter? If she didn't want to speak, she could easily have pushed it through the door and walked away.

Sally got up and went to see if there was anything on the doormat, but there was not. She opened the door to see if the light was on in Primrose Cottage. It was, but she told herself to be reasonable. Ruby might have come home late. Probably she would return the letter in the morning. If she couldn't face bringing it herself, she might well give it to George Halliwell, the postman, and George would know where it belonged.

Bernard was home and reading the paper when Sally got up next morning. She put her hand on his shoulder and kissed him.

'What was that for?'

'Just for you.'

'There's something you want to tell me?'

'No.'

The post arrived. Sally said, 'I'll get it.' She hurried to the door and found two bills. Nothing else.

'What were you expecting?' Bernard asked.

'Nothing in particular.'

'Want anything from the store? I think I'll take a walk presently and pick up a *Radio Times*.'

Sally said quickly, 'I can get it.'

Bernard said, 'I need some fresh air.'

She hated herself for her cowardice. She ought to have told him what had happened. He was entitled to hear it from her. It was practically certain that he would hear it from *someone* in the village. Even if by some miracle he didn't, he still had a right to know that the love letters he had written for her alone had been read in every house in the village. She would have to tell him, but she couldn't face it yet.

She bit her lip as she watched him stroll serenely up the street in his uniform, confident of the respect that was his entitlement. She almost ran after him, but she did not.

She watched him pass Primrose Cottage, and a horrid possibility occurred to her. Had Ruby kept the letter to hand to Bernard himself, out of some embittered notion of revenge? But he went past and on his way. There was no sign of Ruby.

He was back in twenty minutes with the magazine. He smiled at Sally and said, 'How about a coffee?'

'Of course. Who did you meet?'

'Only old George. And Mrs Parker, of course. I want to do a spot of gardening before I have my sleep. The weeds are taking over in the front.'

The morning passed with agonising slowness. Bernard worked steadily in the garden, greeting people as they passed. From the window, Sally saw Ruby emerge from the cottage, but she turned in the other direction, probably to do some cleaning for Miss Seddon, who had the big house by the church.

Jonathan was understandably subdued that morning. He lingered in his room, keeping out of his father's way.

'Did you tell Daddy?' he asked Sally over breakfast.

'Not yet.'

'Will he have to know?'

'I expect so.' She hesitated. 'Jonathan, did you post all the letters that you found upstairs? Every single one?'

'Yes.' He gave a sniff. 'I'm sorry, Mummy.'

'You went up and down the street posting them in all the houses?'

'Yes. I thought they were just old letters.'

'They were, but you had no right to do it.'

At noon, Bernard had lunch and went to get some sleep.

Michael was back from school. 'Everyone knows about Jon and the letters.'

'I'm sure,' said Sally, 'but as far as we're concerned, it's finished. Go and tell your brother lunch is ready.'

Early in the afternoon, she crossed the street and rang the bell at Primrose Cottage.

Ruby Simmons was definitely back. Sally could hear her moving about inside. But she didn't come to the door.

Sally pressed the bell a second time. And a third. She refused to be ignored. Recovering that letter mattered more to her than some schoolgirlish feud.

She called out, 'Ruby, this is Sally Wilding. I want to speak to you. It's important.'

There was no response.

'I think you have something that belongs to me. I want it back, please.'

She walked around the cottage to the back door. Before she got there, she heard the bolt drawn across. She stared through the kitchen window. Ruby must have run upstairs.

It was a seventeenth-century cottage, and Ruby had not done much to keep it up. Sally could easily have forced a window open and got inside, but that would have been a criminal offence. She came away.

At home, she wrote a note politely asking Ruby to return the letter. She delivered it herself. She heard Ruby come and pick it off the mat. That was all that happened.

That evening, after Bernard had gone back on duty, Sally sat listening for footsteps on the path. Several times, when something in the cottage creaked, she got up to check the letterbox.

She was beginning to feel desperate. She could think of nothing else but recovering that letter. She had tried to shake off the obsession by telling herself that as she planned to destroy the letter anyway, she didn't care about it. But of course she did. She cared for Bernard's sake. And hers. And Jonathan's – that small boy who had given her a lesson in telling the truth.

In bed that night, she thought of a way to get her letter back.

Over breakfast, she said to Bernard, 'It's such a lovely morning. Why don't you take Jonathan fishing? You've often promised him, and you said yourself that we should stop treating him as the baby. It will do him good to have an outing with his father.'

She watched from the front-room window as they went, and she remained there, watching Primrose Cottage.

At about the same time as the previous morning, Ruby came out and turned in the direction of Miss Seddon's.

Sally waited until the street was clear and then crossed to Primrose Cottage and went straight around the side to the back door. It was bolted. She glanced about her. The back windows of the cottage were not overlooked. She took a steel knitting needle from her waistband and pushed it where the wood had warped between one window and the frame.

The catch lifted at the second attempt. She pulled the window open and climbed through.

There were letters on the kitchen table. Hers was not among them. She went into the living room and searched the dresser and the writing bureau. Drawers, bookshelves, window sills. Where had Ruby put it?

She went upstairs. A tidy bedroom. The bed made. She spotted the photo at once: a small, framed portrait of Bernard as he had been at seventeen, before he had cut his hair to join the police. Across it, in his handwriting, the words *To Ruby, lots of love, Bernard.* Sally wished she had not seen it.

She went to the dressing table and opened the drawers. She was feeling sick inside. This was the first really bad thing she had done in her life. It was despicable. It was a crime. Yet she had to go on with it.

She started on the chest of drawers. Passed her hand between the layers of clothes. Crossed to the bed and lifted the pillow.

'What are you doing here?'

Sally dropped the pillow and froze.

'What are you doing in my bedroom?' Ruby demanded in a measured voice.

Sally turned. Ruby had the knitting needle in her hand, holding it like a knife. She must have found it by the open window. She must have only gone as far as the store when she went out.

Sally answered with an effort to sound calm, 'Looking for my letter.'

'It isn't here.'

'What have you done with it, then?'

'I haven't got your letter.'

'Ruby, I wish I hadn't had to do this, but that letter belongs to me. I want it back.'

'And you think that gives you the right to force your way into my home and search my things? That's unlawful entry, Sally Wilding, even if you *are* married to the policeman.'

'I'm sorry. If you had opened the door to me yesterday—'

'I didn't wish to. There's no law that says I have to speak to you, but there is a law to protect my home from sneak thieves and intruders, and it's your husband's duty to enforce it. Does he know you're here?'

'No.'

There was a moment's pause.

Ruby's mouth twitched. 'Get you in a nice spot of trouble if I report this to the police, won't it?'

'Don't. Please.'

'Why shouldn't I?'

Sally glanced towards the photograph of Bernard.

Ruby said, 'You're scum. What are you?'

'Scum.'

'Get downstairs. I'll be close behind you.'

Sally obeyed. She was humiliated. She didn't know what to expect.

At the foot of the stairs, Ruby said, 'Which of your boys was it?'

'Jonathan.'

'The little one? How tall is he?'

Sally indicated. 'About this high.'

'Look at my front door,' said Ruby. 'See where the letterbox is? My Aunt Lucy had it specially made when the new door was fitted. The kids next door were always playing knock down ginger when they were small, so she had the letterbox as high as possible. Your Jonathan couldn't possibly reach it.'

Sally could see that she was right. She should have seen before. She shook her head. She was close to tears. 'I don't know what to say.'

Ruby said, 'Does he know yet?'

'Bernard? No.'

There was another pause.

Then Ruby began to laugh. 'You poor sap! For the first time in twelve years I wouldn't want to be in your shoes.' She opened the door. 'Go on, clear off and get what's coming to you.'

'Thank you.'

'Better take your knitting needle. You may need it.'

By the time that Bernard came back from the fishing, Sally had braced herself to tell him everything, but he stopped her. He said, 'If this is about those letters, save your breath. I heard it all from Jonathan this morning. That little lad is growing up. He thought it was up to him to put me in the picture. That's worth a lot to me.'

'Did he tell you about the letter that hasn't come back?'

'He told me you were still upset. I guessed there had to be a reason.'

'You're not too angry?'

'How can I be? It's Friday. I'm off nights.'

As they prepared for bed that night, Bernard held up an envelope. 'Is this what you were looking for?'

She took it from him. 'Yes! Where did you find it?'

'Not a million miles from here. I had another chat with Jonathan. Asked him if he stopped at every house.'

'But so did I. He answered that he did. He really did. It just happened that he couldn't reach the letterbox at Primrose Cottage.' Sally caught her breath. 'He must have pushed it under the door! It was under Ruby's doormat all the time!'

'No. Forget about Ruby. *Every house,* Jon said. That includes this one. He didn't leave us out.'

'Here?' Sally frowned. 'Jonathan posted one to us? I didn't find it.'

'Neither did I.'

Her eyes opened wide. *'Michael?'*

'Look at the stamp. That, my darling, was posted on July 1st, 1969, the day Prince Charles was invested as Prince of Wales. The commemorative stamp. It's gold dust to a stamp collector: a first day cover.'

'Michael had it all the time?'

'Picked it off the mat and put it in his album. Most of this time he's been at school. Didn't think we'd miss it. I found the letter in his waste bin. I don't believe he gave it more than a glance.'

She felt herself blush. 'I hope not. Bernard, you didn't punish him?'

He shook his head. 'As a matter of fact, I promised to look through mine for stamps.'

'Your what?'

'My love letters from you.'

'You kept the letters I wrote *you*?'

Bernard took her hand. 'But I had the foresight to keep mine on *top* of the wardrobe.'

The Bathroom

'Sorry, darling. I mean to have my bath and that's the end of it!' With a giggle and a swift movement of her right hand, Melanie Lloyd closed the sliding door of her bathroom. The catch fastened automatically with a reassuring click. Her husband William, frustrated on the other side, had installed the gadget himself. 'None of your old-fashioned bolts or keys for us,' he had announced, demonstrating it a week before the wedding. 'The door secures itself when you slide it across from the inside. You can move it with one finger, you see, but once closed, it's as safe as your money in the bank.'

She felt between her shoulders for the tab of her zip. William could wait for her. Sit in bed and wait whilst she had a leisurely bath. What was the purpose of a luxurious modern bathroom if not to enjoy a bath at one's leisure? William, after all, had spent *weeks* before the wedding modernising it. 'Everything but asses' milk,' he had joked. 'Mixer taps, spray attachment, separate shower, bidet, heated towel-rails and built-in cupboards. You shall bathe like a queen, my love. Like a queen.'

Queenly she had felt when she first stepped through the sliding door and saw what he had prepared for her. It was all there exactly as he had promised, in white and gold. All that he had promised, and more. Ceramic mosaic tiles. Concealed lighting. Steam-proof mirrors. And the floor – wantonly impractical! – carpeted in white, with a white fur rug beside the bath. There was also a chair, an elegant antique chair, over which he had draped a full-length lace négligé.

'Shameless Victoriana,' he had whispered. 'Quite out of keeping with contemporary design, but I'm incurably sentimental.' Then he had kissed her.

In that meeting of lips she had shed her last doubts about William, those small nagging uncertainties that would probably never have troubled her if Daddy had not kept on so. 'I'm old-fashioned, I know, Melanie, but it seems to me an extraordinarily short engagement. *You* feel that you know him, I've no doubt, but he's met your mother and me only once – and that was by accident. The fellow seemed downright evasive when I questioned him about his background. It's an awkward thing to do, asking a man things like that when he's damned near as old as you are, but, hang it, it's a father's right to know the circumstances of the man who proposes marrying his daughter, even if he is past fifty. Oh, I've nothing against his age; there are plenty of successful marriages on record between young women and older men. Nothing we could do to stop you, or would. You're over twenty-one and old enough to decide such things for yourself. The point is that he knew why I was making my enquiries. I wasn't probing his affairs from idle curiosity. I had your interests at heart, damn it. If the fellow hasn't much behind him, I'd be obliged if he'd say so, so that I can make a decent contribution. Set you both up properly. I would, you know. I've never kept you short, have I? Wouldn't see you come upon hard times for anything in the world. If only the fellow would make an honest statement...'

One didn't argue with Daddy. It was no use trying to talk to him about self-respect. Every argument was always swept aside by that familiar outpouring of middle-class propriety. God, if anything drove her into William Lloyd's arms, Daddy did!

She stepped out of the dress and hung it on one of the hooks provided on the wall of the shower compartment. Before removing her slip, she closed the Venetian blind; not that she was excessively modest, nor, for that matter, that she imagined her new neighbours in Bismarck Road were the sort who looked up at bathroom windows. The plain fact was that she was used to frosted glass. When she and William had first looked over the house – it seemed years ago, but it could only have been last April – the windows, more than anything else, had given her that feeling of unease. There were several in the house – they had been common enough in Victorian times when the place was built – small oblong frames of glass with frostwork designs and narrow stained-glass borders in deep red and blue. They would have to come out, she decided at once, if William insisted on living there. They seemed so out of keeping, vaguely ecclesiastical, splendid in a chapel or an undertaker's office, but not in *her* new home. William agreed at once to take them out – he seemed so determined to buy that one house. 'You won't recognise the place when I've done it up. I'll put a picture window in the bathroom. The old frames need to come out anyway. The wood's half-rotten outside.' So the old windows went and the picture window, a large single sheet of glass, replaced them. 'Don't worry about ventilation,' William assured her. 'There's an extractor fan built in above the cabinet there.' He had thought of everything.

Except frosted glass. She *would* have felt more comfortable behind frosted glass. But it wasn't *contemporary,* she supposed. William hadn't consulted her, anyway. He seemed to know about these things. And there *were* the Venetian blinds, pretty plastic things, so much more attractive than the old brown pelmet they replaced.

She fitted the plug and ran the water. Hot and cold came together from a lion's-head tap; you blended the water by operating a lever. Once you were in the bath you could control the intake of water with your foot, using a push-button mechanism. What would the first occupants of 9 Bismarck Road, eighty years ago, have thought of that?

Melanie reviewed the array of ornamental bottles on the shelf above the taps. Salts, oils, crystals and foam baths were prodigally provided. She selected an expensive bath oil and upended the bottle, watching the green liquid dispersed by the cascading water. Its musky fragrance was borne up on spirals of steam. How odd that William should provide all this and seem unwilling for her to use it! Each evening since Monday, when they had returned from the honeymoon, she had suggested she might take a bath and he had found some pretext for discouraging her. It didn't matter *that* much to her, of course. At the hotel in Herne Bay she had taken a daily bath, so she didn't feel desperately in need of one immediately they got back. It was altogether too trivial to make an issue of, she was quite sure. If William and she *had* to have words some time, it wasn't going to be about bath nights, at any rate. So she had played the part of the complaisant wife and fallen in with whatever distractions he provided.

Tonight, though, she had deliberately taken him by surprise. She had hidden nightie and book in the towel chest earlier in the day, so when she hesitated at the head of the stairs as they came to bed he was quite unprepared. You don't go for a late-night bath empty-handed, even when your bathroom has every convenience known to the modern home designer. She was sliding the bathroom door across before he realised what had happened. 'Sorry, darling! I mean to have my bath and that's the end of it!'

The door slid gently across on its runners and clicked, the whole movement perfectly timed, without a suspicion of haste, as neatly executed as a pass in the bull ring. That was the way to handle an obstructive husband. Never mind persuasion and pleading; intelligent action was much more dignified, and infinitely more satisfying. Besides, she *had* waited till Friday.

She tested the water with her hand, removed her slip, took her book and plastic shower-cap from the towel chest, shook her mass of flaxen hair, and then imprisoned it in the cap. She turned, saw herself unexpectedly in a mirror, and pulled a comical face. If she had remembered, she would have brought in a face pack – the one thing William had overlooked when he stocked the cosmetic shelf. She wasn't going into the bedroom to collect one now, anyway. She took off the last of her underclothes and stepped into the bath.

It was longer than the bath at home or the one in the hotel. Silly really: neither William nor she was tall, but they had installed a six foot, six inch bath – 'Two metres, you see,' the salesman had pointed out, as though that had some bearing on their requirements. Over the years it would probably use gallons more hot water, but it was a beautiful shape, made for luxuriating in, with the back at the angle of a deckchair on the lowest notch, quite unlike the utility five-footer at home, with its chipped sides and overhanging geyser that allowed you enough hot water to cover your knees and no more. William had even insisted on a sunken bath. 'It will sink to four inches below floor level, but that's the limit, I'm afraid, or we'll see the bottom of it through the kitchen ceiling.'

Accustomed to the temperature now, she pressed the button with her toe for more hot water. There was no hurry to rise from this bath. It wouldn't do Mr William Lloyd any harm to wait. Not simply from pique, of course; she felt no malice towards him at all. No, there was just a certain deliciousness – a man wouldn't understand it even if you tried to explain – in taking one's time. Besides, it was a change, a relief if she was honest, to enjoy an hour of solitude, a break from the new experience of being some-one's partner, accountable for every action in the day from cooking a dinner to clipping one's toenails.

She reached for the book – one she had found on William's bookshelf with an intriguing title, *Murder is Methodical*. Where better to read a thriller than in a warm bath behind locked doors? There hadn't been much opportunity for reading in the last three weeks. Or before, for that matter, with curtains to make and bridesmaids to dress.

She turned to the first page. Disappointing. It was not detective fiction at all. Just a dreary old manual on criminolo-gy. *William Palmer: the Rugeley Poisoner* was the first chapter. She thumbed the pages absently. *Dr Crippen: a Crime in Camden Town*. How was it that these monsters continued to exert such a fascination on people, years after their trials and executions? The pages fell open at a more whimsical title – from her present position, anyway – *George Joseph Smith: the Brides in the Bath.* Melanie smiled. That chapter ought to have a certain piquancy, particularly as one of the first place-names to catch her eye was Herne Bay. Strange how very often one comes across a reference to a place soon after visiting there. With some slight stirring of interest, she propped the book in the chromium soap-holder that bridged the sides of the bath, dipped her arms under the water, leaned back and began to read.

George Joseph Smith had stayed in Herne Bay, but not at the New Excelsior. Wise man! If the food in 1912 was anything like the apologies for cuisine they dished up these days, he and his wife were far better off at the house they took in the High Street. But it wasn't really a honeymoon the Smiths – or the Williamses, as they called themselves – spent at Herne Bay, because they had been married two years before and he had deserted her soon after, only to meet her again in 1912 on the prom at Weston-super-Mare. In May they had come to Herne Bay and on July 8th they made mutual wills. On July 9th, Smith purchased a new five-foot bath. Bessie, it seemed, decided to take a bath on the 12th, a Friday. At 8 a.m. next morning a local doctor received a note: *Can you come at once? I am afraid my wife is dead.* On July 16th, she was buried in a common grave, and Smith returned the bath to the supplier, saying he did not require it after all. He inherited £2,500.

£2,500. That must have been worth a lot in 1912. More, almost certainly, than the £5,000 policy William had taken out on her life. Really, when she considered it, the value of money declined so steadily that she doubted whether £5,000 would seem very much when they got it in 1995, or whenever it was. They might do better to spend the premiums now on decorating some of the rooms downstairs. *Super* to have a luxury bathroom, but they would have to spend a lot to bring the other rooms up to standard. 'Insurance policies are security,' William had said. 'You never know when we might need it.' Well, security seemed important to him, and she could understand why. When you'd spent your childhood in an orphanage, with not a member of your family in the least interested in you, security was not such a remarkable thing to strive for. So he should have his insurance – it was rather flattering, anyway, to be worth £5000 – and the rest of the house would get decorated in due course.

There was another reason for insurance which she did not much like to think about. For all his energy and good looks William was fifty-six. When the policy matured he would be over eighty, she fifty-two. No good trying to insure him; the premiums would be exorbitant.

For distraction she returned to the book, and read of the death of Alice Burnham in Blackpool in 1913. Miss Burnham's personal fortune had amounted to £140, but the resourceful George Smith had insured her life for a further £500. She had drowned in her bath a month after her wedding, on a Friday night in December. Strange, that Friday night again! Really, it was exquisitely spine-chilling to be sitting in one's bath on a Friday night reading such things, even if they had happened half a century ago. The Friday bath night, in fact, she learned as she read on, was an important part of Smith's infamous system. Inquest and funeral were arranged before there was time to contact the relatives, even when he wrote to them on the Saturday. Alice Burnham, like Bessie Mundy, was buried in a common grave early the following week. 'When they're dead, they're dead,' Smith had explained to his landlord.

Melanie shuddered slightly and looked up from the book. The appalling callousness of the murderer was conveyed with extraordinary vividness in that remark of his. For nearly twenty years he had exploited impressionable girls for profit, using a variety of names, marrying them, if necessary, as unconcernedly as he seduced them, and disappearing with their savings. In the early encounters, those who escaped being burdened with a child could consider themselves fortunate; his later brides were lucky if they escaped with their lives.

It was reassuring for a moment to set her eyes on her modern bathroom, its white carpet and ceramic tiles. Modern, luxurious and *civilised.* Smith and his pathetic brides inhabited a different world. What kind of bathroom had those poor creatures met their fates in? She had a vision of a cheap tin bath set on cold linoleum and filled from water jugs, illuminated by windows with coloured-glass panels. Not so different, she mused, from the shabby room William had converted – transformed rather – for her into this dream of a modern bathroom. Lying back in the water, she caught sight of the cornice William had repainted, highlighting the moulding with gold paint. So like him to preserve what he admired from the past and reconcile it with the strictly contemporary.

Friday night! She cupped some water in her hands and wetted her face. George Joseph Smith and his crimes had already receded enough for her to amuse herself with the thought that his system would probably work just as well today as it did in 1914. The postal service hadn't improved much in all those years. If, like Daddy, you insisted on living without a telephone, you couldn't get a letter in Bristol before Monday to say that your daughter had drowned in London on Friday evening.

How dreadfully morbid! More hot water with the right toe and back to the murders, quite remote now. When had Smith been tried and executed? 1915 – well, her own William had been alive then, if only a baby. Perhaps it wasn't so long. Poor William, patiently waiting for her to come to bed. It wouldn't be fair to delay much longer. How many pages to go?

She turned to the end to see, and her eye was drawn at once to a paragraph describing the medical evidence at Smith's trial. *The great pathologist, Sir Bernard Spilsbury, stated unequivocally that a person who fainted whilst taking a bath sitting in the ordinary position would fall against the sloping back of the bath. If water were then taken in through the mouth or nose it would have a marked stimulating effect and probably recover the person. There was no position, he contended, in which a person could easily become submerged in fainting. A person standing or kneeling might fall forward on the face and then might easily be drowned. Then, however, the body would be lying face downwards in the water. The jury already knew that all three women had been found lying on their backs, for Smith's claim that Miss Lofty was lying on her side was nonsense in view of the size of the bath in Bismarck Road.*

Bismarck Road. Melanie jerked up in the water and read the words again. Extraordinary. God, how horrible! It couldn't possibly be. She snatched up the book and turned back the pages, careless of her wet hands. There it was again! *Margaret made her will and bequeathed everything, nineteen pounds (but he had insured her life for £700) to her husband. Back at Bismarck Road, Highgate, a bath was installed that Friday night. Soon after 7.30 the landlady, who was ironing in her kitchen, heard splashes from upstairs and a sound which might have been wet hands being drawn down the side of the bath. Then there was a sigh. Shortly after, she was jolted by the sound of her own harmonium in the sitting-room. Mr John Lloyd, alias George Joseph Smith, was playing 'Nearer, my God to Thee'.*

Mr John Lloyd. Mr John *Lloyd*. That name. Was it possible? William said he knew nothing of his parents. He had grown up in the orphanage. A foundling, he said, with nothing but a scrap of paper bearing his name; abandoned, apparently, by his mother in the summer of 1915. The summer, she now realised, of the trial of George Joseph Smith, alias John Lloyd, the deceiver and murderer of women. It was too fantastic to contemplate. Too awful... An unhappy coincidence. She refused to believe it.

But William – what if he believed it? Rightly or wrongly believed himself the son of a murderer. Might that belief have affected his mind, become a fixation, a dreadful, morbid urge to relive George Joseph Smith's crimes? It would explain all those coincidences: the honeymoon in Herne Bay; the insurance policy; the house in Bismarck Road; the new bath. Yet he had tried to keep her from having a bath, barred the way, as if unable to face the last stage of the ritual. And tonight she had tricked him and she was there, a bride in the bath. And it was Friday.

Melanie's book fell in the water and she sank against the back of the bath and fainted. An hour later, her husband, having repeatedly called her name from outside the bathroom, broke through the sliding door and found her. That, at any rate, was the account William Lloyd gave of it at the inquest. She had fainted. Accidental death. A pity Sir Bernard Spilsbury could not have been in court to demonstrate that it was impossible. Even in a two-metre bath.

Arabella's Answer

ANSWERS TO CORRESPONDENTS

January, 1878

ARABELLA. If you are serious in aspiring to elicit a reply from a reputable journal such as ours, you should take the elementary trouble to express yourself in legible handwriting.

March, 1878

ARABELLA. Your Papa is perfectly right. A young girl of fifteen should not be seen at a dinner party at which unmarried gentlemen are guests. Your protestations at being, as you express it, 'confined' to your room do you no credit. A wiser girl would be content to occupy herself in some profitably quiet pastime, such as sewing, for the duration of the party. So long as you childishly persist in questioning decorum, you reveal your utter unreadiness for adult society.

October, 1879

ARABELLA. No gentleman sends flowers or any other presents to a young lady to whom he has not been introduced. Let him learn some manners and present his card to your parents if he entertains a notion of making your acquaintance. We doubt whether his conduct thus far will commend itself to your Papa.

Arabella's Answer

December, 1879

ARABELLA. In common civility you are bound to receive the young gentleman if he has called on your Papa and satisfied him that his intentions are honourable. The 'misgivings' that you instance in your letter are of no consequence. A gentleman should be judged by his conduct, not his outward imperfections. The protruding teeth and shortness of stature are no fault of his, any more than your tallness is of your making. We expect to hear that you have set aside these absurd objections and obeyed your parents, who clearly have a more enlightened apprehension of this young gentleman than yourself.

February 1880

ARABELLA. We suspect that your anxieties are prompted by the shyness which is natural in a young girl, but which properly must grow into the self-possession of a lady. How can you possibly say that the gentleman's blandishments are unwelcome when you have met him only once in your parents' home?

June, 1880

ARABELLA. She who finds difficulty in making conversation with her escort should not despair. There are many talkers, but few who know how to converse agreeably. The art of conversation may be learned. Mark how the most accomplished of conversationalists avoid conceit and affectation. Their speech is characterised by naturalness and sincerity which may be spiced with humour, but never oversteps the limits of propriety.

August, 1880

ARABELLA. We are surprised by your enquiry. Kissing is not a subject that we care to give advice upon, particularly to members of the sex that may receive such tokens of affection, in certain circumstances, but ought never to initiate them.

January, 1881

ARABELLA. To give no answer if the young man proposes to marry you would not only be discourteous; it would not achieve the outcome you apparently expect. When the lady is so ill-advised as to say nothing, the gentleman is entitled to publish the banns at once, for 'silence gives consent'. Have you really considered how the gentleman is placed? Making a declaration of love is one of the most trying ordeals he will experience in his life. We counsel you to give the most earnest consideration to the question, if you are so fortunate as to be asked it. Many are not, and live to regret it. Some have been known to say 'No' when they meant 'Yes'.

March, 1881

ARABELLA. Your letter reaffirms our faith in the innate wisdom of womankind. In conveying our felicities on your forthcoming marriage, we would advise you that a gown of ivory satin trimmed with lace and orange blossom is *de rigueur*.

August, 1881

ARABELLA. We see no reason why you should object to cleaning your husband's boots, as you have no servant, but we cannot comprehend your meaning when you state that he 'leaves them outside his bedroom door at night'. Are we to gather from this that you occupy a different bedroom from your husband? If so, is this at your behest, or his?

October, 1881

ARABELLA. As we have frequently reiterated in this column, the joys of marriage grow out of duty, honesty and fidelity. If, as you assure us, you have not been negligent in any of these, you must ask yourself if there is not some other impediment in your behaviour, which, when remedied, will allow a happier intimacy to ripen. Have you considered whether your choice of clothes and the way you dress your hair are pleasing to your husband?

November, 1881

ARABELLA. As a rule we deprecate the recourse to powder and rouge as an enhancement to good looks. It is possible, however, that ill-health or the anxiety sometimes experienced in the first months of marriage may deprive the skin of its colour and complexion, and in such cases art may be called in as an aid to nature.

January, 1882

ARABELLA. We condemn in the strongest possible terms the practice of using drops of belladonna in the eyes. Belladonna is the extract from that noxious plant, the deadly nightshade (*atropa belladonna*). To keep it on one's dressing table would be dangerous and foolish. A pinch of boracic powder dissolved in warm water and used with an eye-cup is a safe and beneficial tonic that may be relied upon to bring a brightness to the eyes. A little vaseline or cocoa-butter well rubbed into the eyebrows and lashes at night will promote their growth. Frequent brushing with a small brow-brush is also efficacious.

March, 1882

ARABELLA. Your difficulties are more common among newly married wives than probably you realise.

May, 1882

ARABELLA. We think it most injudicious for a wife to listen to tale-bearing neighbours. The company a husband keeps is usually dictated by the duties and obligations of his professional and business life. To expect a man to pursue his manifold interests without ever communicating with the sex who make up half of humanity is to expect the impossible. Shut your ears to gossip. If you have genuine cause for concern, it will manifest itself in other ways. Hold fast to our previous advice. Endeavour to be as pleasant and engaging as possible, to keep your husband at home. Propagate the first shoots of affection as soon as they appear.

July, 1882

ARABELLA. The experience you describe is both regrettable and deplorable, and we trust that there has been no recurrence of the incident since you wrote your letter. If the gentleman concerned was a Frenchman, as you suppose, he may be unused to our British code of decorum. He may, to be as charitable as we can to our cousins from across the Channel, have been under a misapprehension as to your married state. Yet we are bound to observe that a gentleman who attempts to ingratiate himself with a lady, whether married or not, *in a public street*, is a disgrace to his nation. If he should importune you again, look straight onwards, ignore his addresses and tell your husband as soon as you get home. We assume, of course, that the Frenchman's conduct was not encouraged by any light manner on your part.

September, 1882

ARABELLA. We sympathise with your position. It is true that in a previous issue we gave our approval to the judicious use of rouge and powder to enhance your pale complexion in the expectation that it would please your husband. Now that he appears to blame the rouge-box for the excessive behaviour of the foreign gentleman who pesters you, we think you are bound to give up using it.

January, 1883

ARABELLA. We seem to remember cautioning you last year of the dangers attendant upon the use of belladonna drops and we are surprised that you should waste our time with a further enquiry. For the benefit of other readers we repeat that belladonna is a deadly poison and ought never to be used for cosmetic purposes.

March, 1883

ARABELLA. A bereavement such as you have so tragically and so suddenly suffered will strike a chord of sympathy in every young wife who has known the dread fear of impending tragedy when her husband is unwell. You may console yourself with the knowledge that you did all that was possible to comfort your brave consort in the throes of his delirium and convulsion. To have abandoned him even for a short time to have summoned a physician was unthinkable, and, from your account of the severity of the onset, would not have made a jot of difference. The proper dress materials for deep mourning are crêpe and silk. We can recommend Messrs Jay of Regent Street, the London General Mourning Warehouse, for the most sympathetic assistance and advice on suitable costumes, mantles and millinery. Their advertisement will be found elsewhere on these pages.

July, 1883

ARABELLA. We are surprised that you should ask such a question. Velvet is utterly inadmissible for a widow in deep mourning.

September, 1883

ARABELLA. Certainly not. In the first year of mourning, a jersey would be unseemly in the extreme.

October, 1883

ARABELLA. Any person who has the temerity to address a widow of less than one year in familiar terms forfeits the right to the title of gentleman. The fact that he is French is no mitigation of the offence. Indeed, if he is the same person of whom you had cause to complain on a previous occasion, he must be a blackguard of the deepest dye. On no account should you permit him to engage you in conversation. Avoid the possibility of meeting him again by varying the route you are accustomed to taking when walking to the shops. As the proverb wisely cautions us, better go round than fall into the ditch.

March, 1884

ARABELLA. Black beads are permissible in the second year of

mourning, but gold or silver or pearls would be disrespectful. We cannot understand how any widow could consider adorning herself in jewellery so soon after the loss of the one to whom she pledged her entire life. We are shocked at your enquiry, and we can only ascribe it to an aberration consequent upon your grief. Set aside all thoughts of gratifying yourself by such vanities.

May, 1884

ARABELLA. It would be in the worst possible taste for a widow of fifteen months to 'walk out' with a gentleman, whatever he professes in the name of sympathy for you and respect for the one you mourn. Let him show his sympathy and respect by leaving you to your private grief until at least two years have passed since your bereavement. As to the 'restlessness' that you admit to feeling, this may be subdued by turning your energy to some useful occupation in the house or garden. Many a widow has found solace in the later stages of mourning by cultivating flowers.

July, 1884

ARABELLA. How can we proffer advice if you do not fully acquaint us with the circumstances in which you live? Of course you cannot employ your time in the garden if you live in a second-floor apartment without a garden, but there is no reason why you should not cultivate plants of the indoor variety. Contrary to a widely held belief, it is not necessary to have a conservatory for the successful rearing of plants in the home. Certain varieties of fern may be cultivated with gratifying success in, say, a drawing room or dining room. All that they require is a little water regularly given. We have seen some most attractive species growing under glass domes, and some prefer them to wax flowers.

September, 1884

ARABELLA. The variety known as maidenhair is in our opinion the prettiest. Perhaps you over-watered the lady fern.

November, 1884

ARABELLA. Since you seem unable to care adequately for the ferns we recommend, we suggest you try a hardier indoor plant of the palm variety, such as an aspidistra. The aspidistra will grow best in a pot of sufficient size to allow for the roots to develop. A brass plant-pot of the largest size supplied by Messrs Pugh & Martindale would be ideal. Their shop is not far from where you live. The address may be found in the advertisement on the back page of this issue.

January, 1885

ARABELLA. We are gratified to hear that you purchased a large brass pot for your aspidistra, as we suggested in our November issue, and that it is thriving. With regard to another matter that you mention, we wish it to be known that your letters until the latest did not make it clear that the French gentleman, whose attentions to you appeared so importunate, is, in fact, the owner of the art gallery over which you live. Had we been privy to this information before, we might have taken a different view of his conduct. It is only civil for a neighbour to raise his hat and pass the time of day to a lady, and his invitation to 'walk out', while still unthinkable, may now be seen in a more favourable light, with allowance for alien customs. Your own sentiments towards this gentleman must remain irreproachable.

February, 1885

ARABELLA. We did not expect that our altruistic comments in the last issue would encourage an effusion of such unseemliness. No man, however 'handsome, immaculately tailored and charmingly civil towards the fair sex', be he from France or Timbuktu, ought to be described in such unbecoming terms by one who, not two years since, buried her dear departed husband. If you have a vestige of propriety left, dismiss him from your thoughts.

March, 1885

ARABELLA. Your latest communication unhappily confirms what we have for some time suspected: that you are suffering from the delusions of a foolish, infatuated female. How can you otherwise suppose that a lady who has chanced to stand below your window in the vicinity of the art gallery on one or two occasions has 'designs' on the owner, even if he were 'the most eligible man in London'? Clear your mind of such nonsense and attend to the horticultural interests we have been at such pains to foster.

April, 1885

It is with profound regret and a deep sense of shock that we announce the death of Miss Gertrude Smyth, who edited our *Answers to Correspondents* since this journal was founded six years ago. Miss Smyth was the victim last month of a singularly unfortunate and distressing accident in Chelsea, when she was struck on the head by a brass flower-pot that fell from an upper window ledge. Miss Smyth's sagacious and authoritative advice was of the greatest service to myriads of our readers. Out of respect for her memory, we are publishing no *Answers to Correspondents* this month. The column will be resumed in our next issue.

May, 1885

ARABELLA. We can see no impediment to your being married in September in Paris.

How Mr Smith Traced His Ancestors

Most of the passengers were looking right, treating themselves to the breath-catching view of San Francisco Bay that the captain of the 747 had invited them to enjoy. Not Eva. Her eyes were locked on the lighted no-smoking symbol and the order to fasten seat belts. Until that was switched off she could not think of relaxing. She knew that the take-off was the most dangerous part of the flight, and it was a delusion to think you were safe the moment the plane was airborne. She refused to be distracted. She would wait for the proof that the take-off had been safely accomplished: the switching off of that small, lighted sign.

'Your first time?' The man on her left spoke with a West Coast accent. She had sensed that he had been waiting to speak since they took their seats, darting glances her way. Probably he was just friendly like most San Franciscans she had met on the trip, but she could not possibly start a conversation now.

Without turning, she mouthed a negative.

'I mean your first time to England,' he went on. 'Anyone can see you've flown before, the way you put your hand luggage under the seat before they even asked us, and fixed your belt. I just wondered if this is your first trip to England.'

She didn't want to seem ungracious. He was obviously trying to put her at ease. She smiled at the no-smoking sign and nodded. It was, after all, her first flight in this direction. The fact that she was English and had just been on a business trip to California was too much to explain.

'Mine, too,' he said. 'Promised myself this for years. My people came from England, you see, forty, fifty years back. All dead now, the old folk. I'm the only one of my family left, and I ain't so fit myself.' He planted his hand on his chest. 'Heart condition.'

Eva gave a slight start as an electronic signal sounded and the light went off on the panel she was watching. A stewardess's voice announced that it was now permissible to smoke in the seats reserved for smoking, to the back of the cabin. Seat belts could also be unfastened. Eva closed her eyes a moment and felt the tension ease.

'The doc says I could go any time,' her companion continued. 'I could have six months or six years. You know how old I am? Forty-two. When you hear something like that at my age it kinda changes your priorities. I figured I should do what I always promised myself – go to England and see if I had any people left over there. So here I am, and I feel like a kid again. Terrific.'

She smiled, mainly from the sense of release from her anxiety at the take-off, but also at the discovery that the man she was seated beside was as generous and open in expression as he was in conversation. In no way was he a predatory male. She warmed to him – his shining blue eyes in a round, tanned face topped with a patch of hair like cropped corn, his small hands holding tight to the armrests, his check Levi shirt bulging over the seat belt he had not troubled to unclasp. 'You on a vacation too?' he asked.

She felt able to respond now. 'Actually I live in England.'

'You're English? How about that!' He made it sound like one of the more momentous discoveries of his life, oblivious that there must have been at least a hundred Britons on the flight. 'You've been on vacation in California, and now you're travelling home?'

There was a ten-hour flight ahead of them, and Eva's innately shy personality flinched at the prospect of an extended conversation, but the man's candour deserved an honest reply. 'Not exactly a vacation. I work in the electronics industry. My company wants to make a big push in the production of microcomputers. They sent me to see the latest developments in your country.'

'Around Santa Clara?'

'That's right,' said Eva, surprised that he should know. 'Are you by any chance in electronics?'

He laughed. 'No, I'm just one of the locals. The place is known as Silicon Valley, did you know that? I'm in farming, and I take an interest in the way the land is used. Excuse me for saying this: you're pretty young to be representing your company on a trip like this.'

'Not so young really. I'm twenty-eight.' But she understood his reaction. She herself had been amazed when the Director of Research had called her into his office and asked her to make the trip. Some of her colleagues were equally astonished. The most incredulous was her flat-mate, Janet, suave, sophisticated Janet, who was on the editorial side at the *Sunday Telegraph,* and had been on assignments to Dublin, Paris and Geneva, and was always telling Eva how deadly dull it was to be confined to an electronics lab.

'Wish I were twenty-eight,' said her fellow traveller. 'That was the year I was married. Patty was a wonderful wife to me. We had some great times.'

He paused in a way that begged Eva's next question. 'Something went wrong?'

'She went missing three years back. Just disappeared. No note. Nothing. I came home one night and she was gone.'

'That's terrible.'

'It broke me up. There was no accounting for it. We were very happily married.'

'Did you tell the police?'

'Yes, but they have hundreds of missing persons on their files. They got nowhere. I have to presume she is dead. Patty was happy with me. We had a beautiful home and more money than we could spend. I own two vineyards, big ones. We had grapes in California before silicon chips, you know.'

She smiled, and as it seemed that he didn't want to speak any more about his wife, she said, 'People try to grow grapes in England, but you wouldn't think too much of them. When I left London the temperature was in the low fifties, and that's our so-called summer.'

'I'm not too interested in the weather. I just want to find the place where all the records of births, marriages and deaths are stored, so I can find if I have any family left.'

Eva understood now. This was not just the trip to England to acquire a few generations of ancestors and a family coat of arms. Here was a desperately lonely man. He had lost his wife and abandoned hope of finding her. But he was still searching for someone he could call his own.

'Would that be Somerset House?'

His question broke through her thoughts.

'Yes. That is to say, I think the records are kept now in a building in Kingsway, just a few minutes' walk from there. If you asked at Somerset House, they'd tell you.'

'And is it easy to look someone up?'

'It should be, if you have names and dates.'

'I figured I would start with my grandfather. He was born in a village called Edgecombe in Dorset in 1868, and he had three older brothers. Their names were Matthew, Mark and Luke, and I'm offering no prize for guessing what Grandfather was called. My pa was given the same name and so was I. Each of us was an only child. I'd like to find out if any of Grandfather's brothers got married and had families. If they did, it's possible that I have some second cousins alive somewhere. Do you think I could get this information?'

'Well, it's all there somewhere,' said Eva.

'Does it take long?'

'That's up to you. You have to find the names in the index first. That can take some time, depending how common the name is. Unfortunately they're not computerised. You just have to work through the lists.'

'You're serious?'

'Absolutely. There are hundreds of enormous books full of names.'

For the first time in the flight, his brow creased into a frown.

'Is something wrong?' asked Eva.

'Just that my name happens to be Smith.'

Janet thought it was hilarious when Eva told her. 'All those Smiths! How long has he got, for God's sake?'

'In England? Three weeks, I think.'

'He could spend the whole time working through the index

and still get nowhere. Darling, have you ever been there? The scale of the thing beggars description. I bet he gives up on the first day.'

'Oh, I don't think he will. This was very important to him.'

'Whatever for? Does he hope to get a title out of it? Lord Smith of San Francisco?'

'I told you. He's alone in the world. His wife disappeared. And he has a weak heart. He expects to die soon.'

'Probably when he tries to lift one of those index volumes off the shelf,' said Janet. 'He must be out of his mind.' She could never fathom why other people didn't conform to her ideas of the way life should be conducted.

'He's no fool,' said Eva. 'He owns two vineyards, and in California that's big business.'

'A rich man?' There was a note of respect in Janet's voice.

'Very.'

'That begins to make sense. He wants his fortune to stay in the family – if he has one.'

'He didn't say that, exactly.'

'Darling, it's obvious. He's over here to find his people and see if he likes them enough to make them his beneficiaries.' Her lower lip pouted in a way that was meant to be amusing, but might have been involuntary. 'Two vineyards in California! Someone stands to inherit all that, and doesn't know a thing about it!'

'If he finds them,' said Eva. 'From what you say, the chance is quite remote.'

'Just about impossible, the way he's going about it. You say he's starting with the grandfather and his three brothers, and hoping to draw up a family tree. It sounds beautiful in theory, but it's a lost cause. I happen to know a little about this sort of thing. When I was at Oxford I got involved in organising an exhibition to commemorate Thomas Hughes – *Tom Brown's Schooldays*, right? I volunteered to try and find his descendants, just to see if they had any unpublished correspondence or photographs in the family. It seemed a marvellous idea at the time, but it was hopeless. I did the General Register Office bit, just like your American, and I discovered you simply cannot trace people that way. You can work backwards if you know the names and ages of the present generation, but it's practically impossible to do it in reverse. That was with a name like Hughes. Imagine the problems with Smiths.'

Eva could see that Janet was right. She pictured John Smith III at his impossible task, and she was touched with pity. 'There must be some other way he could do this.'

Janet grinned. 'Like working through the phone book, ringing up all the Smiths?'

'I feel really bad about this. I encouraged him.'

'Darling, you couldn't have done anything else. If this was the guy's only reason for making the trip, you couldn't tell him to abandon it before the plane touched down at Heathrow. Who knows – he might have incredible luck and actually chance on the right name.'

'That *would* be incredible.'

Janet took a sip of the Californian wine Eva had brought back as duty-free. 'Actually, there is another way.'

'What's that?'

'Through parish records. He told you his grandfather was born somewhere in Dorset.'

'Edgecombe.'

'And the four brothers were named after the gospel writers, so it's a good bet they were Church of England. Did all the brothers live in Edgecombe?'

'I think so.'

'Then it's easy! Start with the baptisms. When was his grandfather born?'

'1868.'

'Right. Look up the Edgecombe baptisms for 1868. There can't be so many John Smiths in a small Dorset village. You'll get the father's name in the register – he signs it, you see – and then you can start looking through other years for the brothers' entries. That's only the beginning. There are the marriage registers and the banns. If the Edgecombe register doesn't have them, they could be in an adjoining parish.'

'Hold on, Janet. You're talking as if I'm going off to Dorset myself.'

Janet's eyes shone. 'Eva, you don't need to go there. The Society of Genealogists in Kensington has copies of thousands of parish registers. Anyone can go there and pay a fee for a few hours in the library. I've got the address somewhere.' She got up and went to her bookshelf.

'Don't bother,' said Eva. 'It's John Smith who needs the information, not me, and I wouldn't know how to find him now. He didn't tell me where he's staying. Even if I knew, I'd feel embarrassed getting in contact again. It was just a conversation on a plane.'

'Eva, I despair of you. When it comes to the point, you're so deplorably shy. I can tell you exactly where to find him: in the General Register Office in Kingsway, working through the Smiths. He'll be there for the next three weeks if someone doesn't help him out.'

'Meaning me?'

'No, I can see it's not your scene. Let's handle this another way. Tomorrow I'll take a long lunch break and pop along to the Society of Genealogists to see if they have a copy of the parish registers for Edgecombe. If they haven't, or there's no mention of the Smith family, we'll forget the whole thing.'

'But if you *do* find something?'

'Then we'll consider what to do next.' Casually, Janet added, 'You know, I wouldn't mind telling him myself.'

'But you don't know him.'

'You could tell me what he looks like.'

'How would you introduce yourself?'

'Eva, you're so stuffy! It's easy in a place like that, where everyone is shoulder to shoulder at the indexes.'

'You make it sound like a cocktail bar.'

'Better.'

Eva couldn't help smiling.

'Besides,' said Janet. 'I do have something in common with him. My mother's maiden name was Smith.'

The search rooms of the General Register Office were filled with the steady sound of index volumes being lifted from the shelves, deposited on the reading tables and then returned. There was an intense air of industry as the searchers worked up and down the columns of names, stopping only to note some discovery that usually was marked by a moment of reflection, followed by redoubled activity.

Janet had no trouble recognising John Smith. He was

where she expected to find him: at the indexes of births for 1868. He was the reader with one volume open in front of him that he had not exchanged in ten minutes. Probably not all morning. His stumpy right hand, wearing three gold rings, checked the rows of Victorian copperplate at a rate appropriate to a marathon effort. But when he turned a page he shook his head and sighed.

Eva had described him accurately enough without really conveying the total impression he made on Janet. Yes, he was short and slightly overweight and his hair was cut to within a half-inch of his scalp, yet he had a teddy-bear quality that would definitely help Janet to be warm towards him. Her worry had been that he would be too pitiable.

She waited for the person next to him to return a volume, then moved to his side, put down the notebook she had brought, and asked him, 'Would you be so kind as to keep my place while I look for a missing volume? I think someone must have put it back in the wrong place.'

He looked up, quite startled to be addressed. 'Why, sure.'

Janet thanked him and walked round to the next row of shelves.

In a few minutes she was back. 'I can't find it. I must have spent twenty minutes looking for it, and my lunch-hour will be over soon.'

He kept his finger against the place of birth he had reached and said, 'Maybe I could help. Which one are you looking for, miss?'

'Could you? It's P to S for the second quarter of 1868.'

'Really? I happen to have it right here.'

'Oh, I didn't realise . . .' Janet managed to blush a little.

'Please.' He slid the book in front of her. 'Go ahead; I have all day for this. Your time is more valuable than mine.'

'Well, thank you.' She turned a couple of pages. 'Oh dear, this is going to be much more difficult than I imagined. Why did my mother have to be born with a name as common as Smith?'

'Your name is Smith?' He beamed at the discovery, then nodded. 'I guess it's not such a coincidence.'

'My mother's name, actually. I'm Janet Murdoch.'

'John Smith.' He held out his hand. 'I'm a stranger here

myself, but if I can help in any way . . .'

Janet said, 'I'm interested in tracing my ancestors, but looking at this, I think I'd better give up. My great-grandfather's name was Matthew Smith, and there are pages and pages of them. I'm not even sure of the year he was born. It was either 1868 or 1869.'

'Do you know the place he was born?'

'Somewhere in Dorset. Wait, I've got it written here.' She opened the notebook to the page where she had made her notes at the Society of Genealogists. 'Edgecombe.'

'May I see that?' John Smith held it and his hand shook. 'Janet, I'm going to tell you something that you'll find hard to believe.'

He took her to lunch at Rules. It tested her nerve as he questioned her about Matthew Smith of Edgecombe, but she was well prepared. She said she knew there had been four brothers, only she was deliberately vague about their names. Two, she said, had married, and she was the solitary survivor of Matthew's line.

John Smith ate very little lunch. Most of the time, he sat staring at Janet and grinning. He was very like a teddy bear. She found it pleasing at first, because it seemed to show he was a little light-headed at the surprise she had served him. As the meal went on, it made her feel slightly uneasy, as if he had something in mind that she had not foreseen.

'I have an idea,' he said, just before they got up to leave, 'only I hope you won't get me wrong, Janet. What I would like is to go out to Dorset at the weekend and find Edgecombe, and have you come with me. Maybe we could locate the church and see if they still have a record of our people. Would you come with me?'

It suited her perfectly. The parish records would confirm everything she had copied at the Society of Genealogists. Any doubts John Smith might have of her integrity would be removed. And if her information on the Smiths of Edgecombe was shown to be correct, no suspicion need arise that she was not related to them at all. John Smith would accept her as his sole surviving relative. He would return to California in three weeks with his quest accomplished. Sooner or later Janet would inherit two vineyards and a fortune.

'It's a wonderful idea! I'll be delighted to come.'

Nearly a fortnight passed before Eva started to be anxious about Janet's absence. Once or twice before, she had gone away on assignments for the newspaper without saying that she was going: secretly Eva suspected she did it to make her work seem more glamorous – the sudden flight to an undisclosed destination on a mission so delicate that it could not be whispered to a friend. But this time the *Sunday Telegraph* called to ask why Janet had not been seen at the office for over a week.

When they called again a day or two later, and Eva still had no news, she decided she had no choice but to make a search of Janet's room for some clues as to her whereabouts. At least she would see which clothes Janet had taken – whether she had packed for a fortnight's absence. With luck she might find a note of the flight number.

The room was in its usual disorder, as if Janet had just gone for a shower and would sweep in at any moment in her white Dior bathrobe. By the phone, Eva found the calendar Janet used to jot down appointments. There was no entry for the last fortnight. On the dressing table was her passport. The suitcase she always took on trips of a week or more was still on top of the wardrobe.

Janet was not the sort of person you worried over, but this *was* becoming a mystery. Eva systematically searched the room, and found no clue. She phoned the *Sunday Telegraph* and told them she was sorry she could not help. As she put down the phone, her attention was taken by the letters beside it. She had put them there herself, the dozen or so items of mail that had arrived for Janet.

Opening someone else's private correspondence was a step up from searching their room, and she hesitated. What right had she to do such a thing? She could tell by the envelopes that two were from the Inland Revenue, and she put them back by the phone. Then she noticed one addressed by hand. It was postmarked Edgecombe, Dorset.

Her meeting with the friendly Californian named John Smith had been pushed to the edge of her memory by more immediate matters, and it took a few moments' thought to recall the significance of Edgecombe. Even then, she was baffled. Janet had told her that Edgecombe was a dead end. She had checked it at the Society of Genealogists. It had no parish register because there was no church there. They had agreed to drop their plan to help John Smith trace his ancestors.

But why should Janet receive a letter from Edgecombe?

Eva decided to open it.

The address on the headed notepaper was The Vicarage, Edgecombe, Dorset.

Dear Miss Murdoch,

I must apologise for the delay in replying to your letter. I fear that this may arrive after you have left for Dorset. However, it is only to confirm that I shall be pleased to show you the entries in our register pertaining to your family, although I doubt if we have anything you have not seen at the Society of Genealogists.

Yours sincerely,
Denis Harcourt, Vicar

A dead end? No church in Edgecombe?
Eva decided to go there herself.

The Vicar of Edgecombe had no difficulty in remembering Janet's visit. 'Yes, Miss Murdoch called on a Saturday afternoon. At the time, I was conducting a baptism, but they waited until it was over and I took them to the vicarage for a cup of tea.'

'She had someone with her?'

'Her cousin.'

'Cousin?'

'Well, I gather he was not a first cousin, but they were related in some way. He was from America, and his name was John Smith. He was very appreciative of everything I showed him. You see, his father and his grandfather were born here, so I was able to look up their baptisms and their marriages in the register. It goes back to the sixteenth century. We're very proud of our register.'

'I'm sure you must be. Tell me, did Janet – Miss Murdoch – claim to be related to the Smiths of Edgecombe?'

'Certainly. Her great-grandfather, Matthew Smith, is buried in the churchyard. He was the brother of the American gentleman's grandfather, if I have it right.'

Eva felt the anger like a kick in the stomach. Not only had Janet Murdoch deceived her. She had committed an appalling fraud on a sweet-natured man. And Eva herself had passed on the information that enabled her to do it. She would never forgive her for this.

'That's the only Smith grave we have in the churchyard,' the Vicar continued. 'When I first got Miss Murdoch's letter, I had hopes of locating the stones of the two John Smiths, the father and grandfather of our American visitor, but it was not to be. They were buried elsewhere.'

Something in the Vicar's tone made Eva ask, 'Do you know where they were buried?'

'Yes, indeed. I got it from Mr Harper, the Sexton. He's been here much longer than I.'

There was a pause.

'Is it confidential?' Eva asked.

'Not really.' The Vicar eased a finger round his collar, as if it were uncomfortable. 'It was information that I decided in the circumstances not to volunteer to Miss Murdoch and Mr Smith. You are not one of the family yourself?'

'Absolutely not.'

'Then I might as well tell you. It appears that the first John Smith developed some form of insanity. He was given to fits of violence and became quite dangerous. He was committed to a private asylum in London and died there a year or two later. His only son, the second John Smith, also ended his life in distressing circumstances. He was convicted of murdering two local girls by strangulation, and there was believed to have been a third, but the charge was never brought. He was found guilty but insane, and sent to Broadmoor. To compound the tragedy, he had a wife and baby son. They went to America after the trial.' The Vicar gave a shrug. 'Who knows whether the child was ever told the truth about his father, or his grandfather, for that matter? Perhaps you can understand why I was silent on the matter when Mr Smith and Miss Murdoch were here. I may be old-fashioned, but I think the pyschiatrists make too much of heredity, don't you? If you took it seriously, you'd think no woman was safe with Mr Smith.'

From the vicarage, Eva went straight to the house of the Edgecombe police constable and told her story.

The officer listened patiently. When Eva had finished, he said, 'Right, miss. I'll certainly look into it. Just for the record: this American – what did he say his name was?'

Fall-Out

'I need an axe.'

Everyone in the garden shop turned to look at the man who needed an axe. He was not dressed like the other customers in blue and beige gabardine jackets and creased trousers. He was in a string vest and faded jeans. His long, blond hair was drawn back and fixed behind his neck with a leather bootlace. He had a silver earring. And around his neck a string of wooden beads.

Mr Padmore, the shop owner, believed in giving all his customers the same courteous service. He had not served the man before, but he had sometimes seen him passing up the street. 'An axe, sir?' I think you'll find a good selection here. The size you have depends on the job you need it for.'

'How much is that one?'

'The big one? Beautiful to handle, and razor sharp. Twenty-one fifty.'

The man picked it up and felt the weight. He put his two hands on the shaft and raised it. For one petrifying moment, Mr Padmore thought he was about to bring it crashing down on a display of ornamental plaster animals. Instead he let the length of the shaft slip through his hands and examined the head.

'I'll take it.'

He placed the axe on the counter and took a wad of crumpled banknotes from his back pocket.

Mr Padmore grinned companionably. 'Shall I wrap it? You

might get arrested carrying it through the street.'

'No need. I live just around the corner.'

'Really?' said Mr Padmore as he checked the money. 'I ought to know you, then.'

'You wouldn't. I haven't been in here before.' He gave Mr Padmore a steady look with his pale blue eyes. 'I'm not interested in gardening. I hate it.'

Mr Padmore was so anxious not to provoke a scene in his shop that he practically agreed that he, too, hated gardening. 'It's a heavy commitment. No end of work. No joy in it unless you're dedicated.' He added knowingly, 'Nothing like a good, old-fashioned log fire to get you through the winter.'

The man who needed an axe stared back at him.

Mr Padmore explained, 'I thought you wanted it for chopping firewood.'

'No.' The man picked the axe off the counter and walked out of the shop.

When the door closed, Mr Padmore said, to break the tension, 'What else could he want it for, except to chop his neighbours into little pieces?' He turned to his next customer, who was wearing tweeds, and wanted hyacinth bulbs.

On the far side of the display of garden furniture in the centre of the shop, one of Mr Padmore's regular customers was in a state of shock. Gilbert Crawshaw happened to be the next-door neighbour of the man who had bought the axe. He had twitched with horror at Mr Padmore's last remark.

Crawshaw was tall, which was an asset, with a narrow build, which was not. He had grey hair and black-framed bifocals. He was fifty-one, and he worked in the treasurer's department at County Hall, where his status was senior clerical officer. But if his career had not been notably successful, he had the consolation of a marriage which was in every way satisfactory to him. Joan understood him, cared for his house, cooked well and was ten years younger than he, which was good for his self-esteem.

Theirs was a council house in Jubilee Road, a pleasant street in a good locality, close to the shops and surrounded by a private housing development that the estate agents described as exclusive and sought after. Crawshaw had qualified for a council house because of his job at County

Hall, and he had made sure that the house he got was in Jubilee Road. He liked to think that he had helped to set the standard that made it harmonise with the gracious streets of private housing.

His fastidiously tidy garden typified his life. There was a square lawn surrounded with herbaceous border plants that he bought each spring at Mr Padmore's and planted in the same regularly spaced arrangement. No weeds grew there. No slugs skulked under leaves. The garden was sprayed and fed with recommended products from the shop.

It had been a shock for Crawshaw eight months earlier when the new people had moved in next door. The old couple they replaced had lived there over thirty years – quiet, decent people who minded their own business and didn't keep animals. Towards the end they had tended to let the garden go and turn up the volume on the television, but you had to make allowances for old age.

These new ones – their name was Stock, or *his* was, at any rate – were disquieting in quite another respect. They had arrived in a Transit van one Sunday morning with several friends, similarly long-haired and sandalled. Crawshaw had been trimming the privet in the front. He had gone inside to watch from behind the net curtains in the spare bedroom. His first suspicion was that they were squatters. All the furniture they possessed had travelled in the back of that small van. It included two mattresses and several cushions, but no bed. There were also a number of indoor plants of a type he had never seen in the garden shop.

The next day, Crawshaw had called into the housing department across the corridor from his office to check whether the house had yet been allocated. That was how he had learned that the man's name was Stock. He was now the lawful occupant. He had been given the house because he was homeless and unemployed and his wife was six months pregnant.

'His wife?' Crawshaw had repeated. 'I may be mistaken, but I don't think she wears a wedding ring.'

'Wife, common law wife, we make no distinction these days,' the woman in housing had explained. 'You and I may not approve, Mr Crawshaw, but those are our instructions.'

That evening, Crawshaw told his wife Joan what he had learned.

'I know,' she told him. 'I met them this afternoon.'

Joan had a quiet style of speech that Crawshaw usually found congenial, but occasionally she shocked him. He was never certain from her mild expression whether she meant to shock.

'*Met* them?'

'I baked some cakes and took them round. You have to be neighbourly, Gilbert. They invited me in for a coffee.'

'You went in?'

'Yes,' Joan answered matter-of-factly. 'Poor dears, they haven't any chairs yet, so I sat on a cushion on the floor. They're really quite sweet.'

'You shouldn't have done it,' Crawshaw told her. 'Sometimes I despair of you, Joan. We don't know what sort of people they are.'

'We never will, if you have your way,' she pointed out.

Crawshaw's usually pale face turned purple. 'Joan, I forbid you, I absolutely forbid you to make any more overtures to Stock and his woman.'

He had never spoken to her like that in their fifteen years of married life, and it stunned her into silence.

In the months since then, Crawshaw had noticed other disturbing developments. There had been parties. He had counted as many as fifty-six guests on one occasion and some of them had stayed all night. He knew because he had counted everyone who had left. About one-thirty, the music had stopped and there were still at least a dozen in the house. He was sure that if there was no music, sinister things were going on. Joan told him to be grateful for the chance to get some sleep, but he was quite unable to relax.

One evening in the summer, Crawshaw had decided to walk home through the park instead of taking his customary route down Mason's Lane and along the High Street. It had meant using the subway to cross the railway. Halfway through the tunnel, his thoughts had been disturbed by the sound of a woman singing. Her voice had a clear tone that Crawshaw found quite pleasant until he noticed who she was and who was the person accompanying her on a guitar.

They were the people from next door.

She had the baby slung in front of her on a harness and was standing beside Stock, who was sitting on the stone floor with a wooden bowl between his feet to collect coins thrown by passers-by. Stock actually nodded to Crawshaw as he moved stiffly past them without putting his hand anywhere near his pocket.

'Can you imagine how I felt?' he asked Joan when he got home. 'Our neighbours, for heaven's sake, begging for money in a public thoroughfare.'

'It's not really begging,' Joan commented.

'That's what it amounts to.'

'Well, at least it's not dishonest.'

'It's degrading. How would you feel if I stood in the subway strumming a guitar?'

'Certainly surprised and probably elated, if you really want to know,' Joan answered, more to herself than her husband.

It didn't matter, because Crawshaw wasn't listening. He said, 'I think the social security people ought to be told. Stock has no right to public hand-outs if he has an income of his own.'

'Gilbert, let it rest,' Joan urged.

He did not. The next morning, before the office was open to the public, he saw the senior administrative officer in the social security wing. She said she was grateful for the information and they would ask Stock about it next time he came in, but these casual earnings were impossible to assess with accuracy. Crawshaw challenged this assumption. He said it was no good tamely asking Stock for information. It should be the subject of a departmental investigation. He went on to mention the parties. 'I counted fifty-six guests. Anyone with the means to entertain on that scale should not be living off the state.'

The senior administrative officer said she would do all she reasonably could to see that Mr Stock was not defrauding the department, but Crawshaw heard no more about it.

That is, until the incident in the garden shop.

'I tell you, he bought an axe,' he told Joan as soon as he got back, 'and Padmore said it was obvious what he wanted it for – to attack the neighbours.'

'He must have been joking, Gilbert.'

'What sort of joke is that? I don't find it funny.'

Joan sighed and shook her head. 'People are not very tolerant. The Stocks dress differently from most of us, so it gives rise to silly comments. It's a basic instinct, a tribal thing.'

Crawshaw sniffed. 'I don't need you to tell me that. I can recognise a couple of savages for myself.'

'Gilbert, that's unworthy of you. I took you for a tolerant man.'

'Not much use being tolerant when there's someone coming at you with an axe.'

'Now you're being melodramatic. What have we ever done to antagonise Mr Stock?'

Crawshaw turned his head and stared out of the window. He hadn't mentioned his conversation with the senior administrative officer in social security. Joan had tried to discourage him from reporting on the neighbours. It was no use talking to her about social duty. She hadn't progressed beyond the morality of the playground, when 'telling' was a crime. Yet he was beginning to wish he hadn't interfered.

No more was said on the matter until mid-afternoon, when Crawshaw was in the garden mowing his lawn. He favoured the conventional mower with a roller that left a pleasing pattern of stripes. He had sometimes looked at the rotary mowers in Padmore's shop, but they didn't give the same finish. It was while he was making his journeys up and down the lawn that he heard a sound above the whirr of the mower. He thought at first that a stone had lodged between the blades, but when he stopped, the sound persisted. It was coming from the next garden, a knock as steady as a steam-hammer.

There was a six-foot fence between the gardens, so he had to go indoors and upstairs to see what was happening.

Joan was already in the spare bedroom watching. 'You see?' she said, as he joined her at the curtain. 'I told you there was nothing to get alarmed about.'

Crawshaw stared down at the spectacle of his neighbour Stock hacking with the axe at the only tree in his garden.

He said, 'Disgusting.'

'Oh, come, Gilbert,' said Joan. 'It's a stifling afternoon and that's warm work. A man is entitled to take off his shirt in the privacy of his own garden. It's in no way offensive.'

'I can see it doesn't offend *you*,' Crawshaw commented pointedly.

Joan coloured and said, 'What do you mean?'

'If you really want to know,' Crawshaw said with condescension in his voice, 'I wasn't speaking about his naked torso when I used the word "disgusting". Obviously that sprang to your mind first. What I had in mind was the destruction of that apple tree, which I regard as an act of senseless vandalism. That tree is the last beautiful thing in their neglected garden, and there he is destroying it.'

Joan was silent, nursing her private hurt.

'If it falls against our fence,' Crawshaw went on, 'he'll be hearing from my solicitor.'

Joan said, 'At least we know why he bought the axe.' She waited for some response and, getting none, added, 'He wasn't planning to attack you.'

'I'm going down to finish the lawn,' said Crawshaw. 'No, there's no need for you to come. You carry on goggling at the ape-man.'

'That's unfair, Gilbert,' Joan said, but he was already on his way downstairs.

A short while later, Crawshaw looked up from his mowing and saw the top of the apple tree shudder and lurch. He stopped to watch which way it fell. There was no damage to his fence. The tree fell the other way.

He still said, 'Vandal,' before resuming his work. Later, he was obliged to go indoors. Stock had started a bonfire to burn the tree. Smoke was billowing across Crawshaw's garden.

'That's green wood,' he told Joan as they stood in the bedroom watching. 'It's not fit for burning. It'll smoke out the entire neighbourhood. The man has no consideration for other people.'

During that week, Stock made more bonfires, generally in the evening when Crawshaw was home from work. By sheer persistence, the wood was reduced to ashes by the weekend.

Crawshaw called at the garden shop on Saturday. He needed something to treat a patch of moss which had appeared on his lawn. Mr Padmore selected a packet from the shelves behind the counter and handed it to Crawshaw.

'That should do the trick,' he told him. 'One sachet to a gallon of water. Funny you should come in, Mr Crawshaw. We were talking about you earlier this morning.'

'In what connection?' Crawshaw asked uneasily.

'Nothing personal. That neighbour of yours came in. Long-haired chap. He *does* live next door to you, doesn't he?'

Crawshaw nodded.

'That was how your name came up,' said Mr Padmore.

'Did *he* mention it?'

Mr Padmore's mouth gave nothing away, but his eyes glittered artfully. 'Don't you two get on very well?' he asked.

'We don't have much in common,' Crawshaw guardedly answered.

'I can see that, Mr Crawshaw, I can see that.'

Crawshaw didn't altogether like Padmore's tone, but curiosity kept him from cutting the conversation short. He remarked, 'I can't think what my neighbour would want from this shop. He hasn't shown any interest in his garden in the time he's lived there.'

'He bought a spade,' said Mr Padmore. 'Last week it was an axe.' He winked at Crawshaw. 'You keep an eye on him, Mr Crawshaw.'

'Why?'

'It's obvious, isn't it? What does he want with a spade if he doesn't go in for gardening? He must be planning to bury something.'

When Crawshaw got home, he told Joan precisely what Mr Padmore had said.

'And you took it seriously?' she said. 'Gilbert, what's the matter with you?'

'There's nothing the matter with me.'

'You must have a persecution complex, or something.'

Crawshaw reached out and gripped her by the arms so tightly that she gave a cry of pain. He said, 'Listen to me, will you? If anyone is behaving oddly, it's that blighter next door. You won't find me scrounging off social security, or squatting in the subway with a begging bowl between my legs. I don't hack down healthy fruit trees and pollute the atmosphere with filthy bonfires. Just think of that before you try your pseudo-psychology on me.'

'Gilbert, you're hurting me,' said Joan.

That afternoon they watched Stock use the spade to dig out the stump of the apple tree.

'Are you satisfied?' Joan asked.

Crawshaw didn't answer, so she went downstairs and put on the television.

The next morning, she was surprised to find when she woke that her husband was not in bed. She checked the time and found that it was not yet 8 a.m. It was Crawshaw's invariable custom on Sunday mornings to remain in bed until 8.15 a.m., when the papers came. Joan drew on her housecoat, sensing that something disturbing had occurred.

She found him in the spare bedroom, staring out of the window, his back and shoulders rigid with tension.

'What is it, Gilbert?'

He said in a low voice that she scarcely heard, 'See for yourself.'

She stood at his side and looked down into the garden next door. There was no one there. There was just the hole where the stump of the apple tree had been. It had been shaped and extended into a rectangular shaft about seven feet in length and three feet wide. It was at least five feet deep.

'There must be an explanation,' said Joan.

'It's a grave,' whispered Crawshaw.

'It can't be,' said Joan. 'Let's get some breakfast.'

But Crawshaw remained where he was. Joan made some coffee and took it to him, but he didn't drink it. Nor did he speak to her.

Down below, Stock had resumed his digging.

By eleven, Joan had decided to talk to the woman next door. As a pretext, she found some soft wool left over from a jacket she had knitted for her niece's baby. She took it round and offered it for their child.

The woman was very appreciative. She invited Joan in for coffee. When it was made, she called Mr Stock in from the garden. Without Joan having to enquire, he explained what he was doing.

When Joan went back to her house, Crawshaw was still at

the window in the spare bedroom. He was still in his dressing gown. He hadn't even noticed that she had gone next door.

'It's not what you think,' she told him gently. 'I've been talking to them. They are very concerned about the prospect of a nuclear war. Mr Stock is building a fall-out shelter.'

Crawshaw said nothing then. Nearly an hour later, when Joan was putting the beef joint into the oven, she heard his voice behind her. She almost dropped the tin in surprise.

He said, 'It's idiotic, trying to build a nuclear shelter.'

'Possibly,' conceded Joan, 'but it shows a pleasing regard for the safety of his wife and child. They say it should be big enough for us as well if we care to share it with them.'

'He won't get any help from me, if that's what he's after.'

'I'm sure he doesn't expect it,' said Joan.

Later, over lunch, Crawshaw said, 'I don't suppose he got planning permission for this.'

'Does it matter?'

'Of course it matters. You can't build things like that without clearing it first with the council. There are pipes and cables and heaven knows what buried underground. There's also the danger of subsidence. He might undermine the foundations of my house.'

'Gilbert, let's talk about something else.'

'Not until I've settled this. Tomorrow morning, I want you to go to the borough surveyor's department and find out whether Stock obtained the necessary planning permission.'

'You want me to go? Why me?'

'Because they know me at the council. You needn't give your name. Everyone is entitled to look at the list.'

'Then why don't you do it yourself?'

'I didn't tell you before, but you might as well know now that I reported them to social security. For all the good it did, I might as well have saved myself the trouble, but you see that I don't want it thought that I have a grudge against the neighbours.'

'You don't want it known,' said Joan quietly.

Crawshaw put down his knife and fork and said in a low voice that she found more menacing than a shout, 'You will do as I say. If you choose to defy me, you must suffer the consequences.'

He had frightened her. There had been no violence in their marriage, but she knew him well enough to fear the force of retribution in his character. She knew better than to rouse it.

Next morning, she did as he instructed. She went to the borough surveyor's department and enquired whether there was planning permission for a nuclear fall-out shelter at 9 Jubilee Road. To her amazement and relief, the clerk confirmed that there was. He got out the detailed plan for Joan to examine. It had the council stamp on it, and the signature of the borough surveyor.

She thought that her morning's work would bring reassurance to her husband, but she should have known better. When she told him that evening, he accepted the information with a shrug and went upstairs to take another look at the excavations.

Through that summer, Crawshaw kept vigil for hours on end in the spare bedroom. Joan rarely saw him except when it was too dark to stare out of the window. Their own garden began to show signs of neglect. Daisies and dandelions flourished on the lawn. The flowerbeds dried out in the warm spell at the end of August.

Joan often spoke to the people next door. She always found them friendly. They told her that the shelter would be ready before the winter. The main chamber was complete. There was still construction work inside, to fit it out and make it habitable.

One evening in October, Crawshaw came downstairs and said, 'You've been talking to them again, haven't you?'

Joan answered, 'There's no law against it, Gilbert. They *are* our neighbours. And you must admit I don't get much conversation with you these days.'

He ignored that. 'What's happening with the shelter?'

'Well, if you don't know, I'm sure I don't.'

'He's working underground now. I can't see what he's doing.'

'How maddening for you.'

'Don't be provocative, Joan. You've been talking to them. Tell me what's going on.'

'Why don't you ask them yourself? It wouldn't hurt to

exchange a few civil words, Gilbert. They're very approachable people.'

He glared at her, and said no more. She felt for the first time in months that she had won a point.

One evening later in the week, he asked, 'Is the digging finished?'

Joan looked up and answered mildly, 'I haven't enquired.'

'Have you looked inside? Have they shown it to you?'

'Gilbert, I'm not interested in looking inside their shelter. I'm sure Mr Stock would be delighted to show it to you if you asked him.'

'I think he's still extending it,' said Crawshaw. 'He wouldn't want me to see it.'

'Oh, that's it, is it? You think he's burrowing like a mole. Under the fence and under our garden? Perhaps that's why our clematis died.'

Crawshaw's eyes widened. 'Has it?'

Joan was not sure what had prompted her to mention the clematis. She knew she was making mischief. The combination of a baking sun and the lack of any watering had killed the clematis. Gilbert had not even noticed its demise, but he would seize on it as evidence of subterranean invasion.

He took the next day off from work, something he had never done in his life, apart from a few days for illness. By 8 a.m., he was out there with his spade and wheelbarrow. Joan supposed at first that he intended catching up on the backlog of weeding, but it was soon apparent that he was otherwise engaged.

He was digging a hole.

He had started in the flowerbed where the dead clematis was, beside the fence separating their garden from the Stocks'. By lunchtime, the hole had developed into a trench. By mid-afternoon, the trench extended along the length of the fence. Plants and young trees that Crawshaw had tended for years were dug out and left to wither on the piles of topsoil and clay. He was working like a man possessed.

About 4 p.m., Joan went out to him and said, 'Gilbert, you're destroying our garden.'

Crawshaw carried on digging. He was chest-deep in the trench. 'Better than having it destroyed by someone else.'

'What are you doing this for?'

'To find where the damned shelter comes out.'

'It isn't in our garden, Gilbert.'

'It is. You'll see.'

'I saw the plans,' said Joan.

'Plans!' said Crawshaw, spitting into his trench.

Joan looked up at the house next door and noticed Mr and Mrs Stock standing at their bedroom window staring down at them. They didn't have net curtains. She ran indoors.

Crawshaw didn't come in from the garden until after eight. By then it was dark, and raining, and the wet mud was gleaming on his clothes and body. He was standing in the kitchen doorway holding out a plug attached to a length of cable. 'Plug that in, would you?'

'You're not carrying on with this?' said Joan in disbelief.

'It's dark. I need a lamp.'

'You'll get pneumonia.'

'Do as I tell you. I haven't time to stand here talking.'

She sighed, took the plug and pressed it into the socket. 'Why, Gilbert? At least tell me why.'

He laughed.

It was so unusual for him to laugh that Joan found it no comfort at all.

Crawshaw said smugly, 'I've found it. I've found the top edge of his infernal shelter projecting nearly three feet into our garden. I knew I'd find it if I went deep enough. And now I'm going to attack it with a sledge and crowbar. It might withstand a nuclear blast, but it won't stop me from exercising my rights as the lawful tenant of this land. Do you want to try and stop me?'

Joan answered quietly, 'You must do as you think fit, Gilbert.'

As soon as he had gone, she went out through the front and knocked on the Stocks' door. Mr Stock opened it. He said, 'You look as if you could do with a drink.'

He invited her in. They were very kind to her. They produced a glass of sherry. She was grateful. She explained about the digging and said, 'Gilbert says he has found something. He's convinced that it must be your shelter.'

Mr Stock shook his head. 'Impossible. It stops at least five feet our side of the fence. There's nothing underground on your side except the conduit for the main electric cable. I saw the plans. God, if he cuts through that . . .' He got up and went to the window, but before he reached it, the lights went out.

In the garden next door, the lights had gone out for ever for Gilbert Crawshaw.

And in the darkness of the Stocks' living room, Joan Crawshaw permitted herself a sigh. No one else could have noticed that it was more a sigh of relief than regret. She was free.

She, too, had taken note of those plans.

Belly Dance

This all happened through the keep-fit class. I had been going for two years and by that time I was the mainstay of the class. I attended mainly for the company. After my divorce from Mike, I lived alone in Kingston, feeling sorry for myself. On Wednesday evenings I slipped into my black leotard and joined the human race again. There is definitely something therapeutic about exercise. I can recommend it to any woman living alone.

I had better confess to you that I enjoyed the classes for another reason too. I have a better than average figure. It used to boost my confidence no end to get envious glances from the other girls. We were all 'girls' to each other, by the way – and 'students' to the teacher – although not one of us was under twenty-six. Some of the shapes that wobbled out of the changing room at half-past six on Wednesdays had to be seen to be believed, but we all got on together like a bunch of kids. Some of the heavier girls would tell me that they felt encouraged to do the exercises beside a trimmer figure. I'm not the owner of an especially pretty face, but my body is a winner. My legs are long enough to look lovely in the leotard. I have full, firm breasts, a smallish waist and Mike, my 'ex', used to say I had the perkiest bottom in the whole of Surrey. From what I later learned, he was qualifed to judge.

I was coming to the belly dancing. At seven-thirty, when the class was over, just to have a giggle, our teacher Angela would put on a record of Arabian music and we would all gyrate our hips like harem girls. It happens that I have excellent hip mobility, and the session would regularly end with everyone but me abandoning the attempt. They would form a ring around me and clap hands while I wiggled sensuously to the music. Fabulous. But I had no idea where it would lead.

One evening after I had done my party piece, Angela had a quiet word with me. She was a fine teacher, dignified, not matey, and we all respected her.

'Have you ever danced in public?'

'Like this, you mean?' I laughed. 'Not likely.'

'You're very good. You have the figure and the flexibility. With your dark hair and dreamy eyes, if you were dressed for the part, you could convince anyone you were a proper belly dancer. I'll tell you why I mentioned it. My fellow Duncan is chairman of the summer fair this year. You know the keep-fit students always give a demonstration. Well, Duncan sometimes meets me after class, and the other week he happened to be outside the window when you did your belly dance.'

'Oh, how embarrassing!' I felt myself go crimson.

'No, he adored it, really. He was so impressed that he came up with this idea of asking you to do a solo dance at the fair. We could dress you up in beads and chiffon and call you Yasmin the Belly Dancer and I guarantee you'd be the sensation of the fair. It's for charity, of course – the old folk. Would you do it?'

Naturally I made protesting sounds, but in short I allowed myself to be persuaded. I admit it: I was secretly delighted.

I had five weeks to prepare. Angela let me take the Arabian record home, and each night after work, my flat became the Kasbah. At the weekend, I made my costume. By good fortune, I had a peach-coloured bikini that I had worn one holiday with Mike in the Canaries. The pants became the basis of the costume. With a few yards of matching chiffon, I made diaphanous harem trousers fitting from the hips. I bought some satin in a similar shade and ran up the sweetest little bodice with short sleeves and a reckless plunge. Angela had given me a box of hundreds of tiny glass and gold beads, and I strung them together to make a head-dress with a fringe. The rest I used to decorate the pants and bodice. With my black hair combed out and my eyes heavily made up to gaze mysteriously above the yashmak, I was almost ready. All it wanted was a pot of that stuff that gives you an overnight tan. Dusky Bronze.

Two weeks before the fair, Angela invited me to dinner. It was a chance to let her see the costume. Duncan was also there; I got the impression that he lived there, although it wasn't mentioned. He was some kind of foreman in a wholesale business, I gathered, an animated, vocal, not bad-looking guy, splendid for the chairman of the fair committee and probably just as capable in bed, but far too similar to Mike to interest me. He had the same irritating way of totally ignoring things you said.

While they cleared the table, I went into Angela's room and changed. They adored the costume. Angela put on a record that was more Spanish than Arabian, and I went through my dance, into which I had introduced some extra and voluptuous movements, and they played besotted sheiks, cooing and shouting encouragement. We all finished helpless with amusement.

'Sensational! You're going to be the biggest attraction in the fair,' said Duncan as he took my hand in his.

'Prettiest sounds better,' said Angela. 'I *love* the colours. How did you get this marvellous tan? I've got a few gold bangles I must give you. Wear them on your wrists and ankles and they'll show up beautifully against your skin.'

'Do you know, I've had an idea?' said Duncan.

'I bet you have,' said Angela. 'What man wouldn't, watching a dance like that?'

'Seriously, Ange, it's a way of netting extra profit. After the belly dance, we announce an auction. Yasmin the Belly Dancer will perform in private at the place of the winner's choice.'

I said at once, 'I'm not sure if I like that.'

'There's nothing to worry about. As the organiser, I'll see that it's all right. It's all for charity. Once I get the bidding going, I reckon I can get it up to fifty, with some of the stockbroker types round here.'

'Fifty pounds would help the old folk quite a lot,' said Angela. 'Darling, it's just a dance. You like old people, don't you?'

As a matter of fact, I do. Older men, in my experience, have far more genuine charm than thrusting, self-assertive blokes like Mike or Duncan. 'If you promise to come with me,' I reluctantly agreed. I didn't fancy doing a private dance for some character with fantasies that he was King Farouk.

'You're on,' said Duncan. 'I'll see it gets top billing in the programme. This will guarantee we get a record-breaking profit. The old people are going to be grateful to this year's fair committee, I can tell you.'

'I can tell you how to earn some gratitude round here,' said Angela with an unadmiring smile. 'Wash the dishes while I help the lovely Yasmin out of her costume – and no, I won't switch jobs.' When the bedroom door was closed, she told me, 'I'll be glad when the damned thing is over. He talks of nothing else, even in bed. It's the first time he's been chairman of anything, and he desperately wants a huge success.'

'That's rather sweet,' I said.

'It might help matters if he put some energy into his career. I've told him marriage is out of the question while he's still earning less than I do shouting at schoolgirls all day and flabby housewives in the evening. Sorry – nothing personal.'

'You're right about marriage if that's the way you feel, Angela. You want to be sure before you take it on.'

'I love him really, but it's no good making it too easy for them, is it? Let's find those bangles for you.'

The programme for the summer fair was dropped through my letterbox two weeks before the date. Duncan had kept his promise: I was top of the bill. The wording was a bit excessive, I thought, but I suppose that's how you sell things.

3 p.m. Recently Escaped from the Harem of a Sultan
YASMIN THE BELLY DANCER
You have heard of Eastern Promise; here is the
PERFORMANCE
Admission 20p. To be followed by a sensational
GRAND AUCTION OF THE LOVELY YASMIN
Who agrees to dance in private at a date and place to be nominated by the highest bidder. Yasmin could be yours!

It certainly aroused some interest. The same afternoon, I had a call from Duncan. The local paper wanted to photograph me in my costume. Duncan was elated. It was marvellous publicity for the fair. I agreed provided that my name did not appear.

I took my costume to the keep fit and they took my picture there. The girls were very excited about it. I felt terribly self-conscious. Angela made them all work forty minutes over to rehearse the music and movement programme for the fair. Because of the time it took me to get ready, I was not in the team this year.

Well, the fair was all that Duncan could have wished. A brilliant day, every programme sold and no problems with the sideshows. I'll be brief about my dancing, because it is secondary to the story. Let's say only that the large marquee was so packed with people that my space for dancing had to be reduced to a ten-foot square. They clapped and cheered and called out things I would be mortified to put in print. But not unflattering things. I gave them both sides of the 45 called *An Arabian Night*. I swayed and swivelled and jigged my stomach until it ached. There was tumultuous applause.

Then a table was brought in. They stood me on it, still panting with the effort. Duncan stood on a chair to conduct the auction.

It was a revelation to me. The bidding started at ten pounds and rapidly got up to fifty. Then Duncan murmured to me to wriggle my hips again. That put the figure up to seventy. A rivalry developed between my local butcher and some lads in leather who seemed to have formed a syndicate. I didn't altogether like the idea of that, but at eighty pounds they reached their limit. The butcher bid eighty-five. Then Duncan held up a piece of paper.

'Ladies and gentlemen, a secret bidder has entered the auction. I have a bid of one hundred pounds. Do I hear one hundred and five?'

The butcher bleakly shook his head.

I was sold for a hundred pounds.

'Who is it?' I asked Duncan as soon as I got near him.

'It isn't clear, but here's the money in an envelope. The minute I find out I'll let you know.'

I heard nothing for four days. I couldn't sleep for thinking of it. I was in quite a state: frightened, yes, a little, but excited, too. Someone had paid a hundred pounds to have me dance for him. I considered all the affluent gentlemen of the district, from the scrap merchant to the Mayor. Who had I left out?

On Wednesday morning came a call from Duncan. The mysterious bidder had named a time and place. Saturday afternoon at an address in Esher. I asked Duncan who it was. He still didn't know. The message had been left for him. However, he would collect me in his car on Saturday and make sure everything was proper. He suggested that I put on the costume first and wore my raincoat over it.

That evening at the keep fit I asked Angela if she knew any more, but she was in the dark as well. She said the whole thing bored her now. I had a suspicion she was slightly peeved at Duncan sacrificing a Saturday afternoon he should have spent with her. She also made what I thought was a rather bitchy joke in the presence of the others, suggesting my new shoes were a present from the butcher.

Saturday was hot again. People were mowing lawns and cleaning cars along my suburban street. I looked at my glittering, semi-naked image in the mirror and thought how bizarre this episode was. A car horn sounded. I draped the raincoat round my shoulders, picked up my disc and hurried out to Duncan's unexotic old Cortina.

'All set, my precious?'

I gave him a terse, 'Yes.' He would never have called me his precious when Angela was about, and I wasn't certain that I liked it. Perhaps it was my state of nerves.

As we drove out of Kingston along the Portsmouth Road, his conversation made me increasingly uneasy.

'Super write-up in the local, wasn't it? I didn't think the picture did you justice. They should have had a full-length shot, in my opinion. Criminal not to show a gorgeous pair of legs like yours. Are you getting warm? You could slip the coat off now.'

I kept it on. 'Has this man been in touch again?' I asked him. 'Do you know any more about him?'

'Nothing of importance. I think he must be some kind of

rich recluse. It's a smart address.'

We had gone through the town of Esher, and past the race course. We took the road to Oxshott for about a mile, and then turned left, along a shadowy, wooded lane.

'A little off the beaten track,' said Duncan. 'Barely a mile to go now.'

I kept the raincoat tightly across my legs. I had a strong suspicion that Duncan had not been frank with me. He seemed to know exactly where he was taking me. Suppose there was no secret bidder other than himself? Suppose he had set me up for something? Like some frightened school-girl, I considered what to do if he stopped the car.

'Nervous?' he enquired. 'I keep a flask of brandy in the glove compartment. Have a nip if you want.'

'No thanks.'

'I could easily stop a minute.'

'I'd rather get there and get it over.'

A short way on, we came to an entrance with wrought iron gates about ten feet high.

'This is it. Better get your yashmak on, my darling, while I open up.'

I had a girlish impulse to get out and run, but I wouldn't have got far in the satin mules I had put on for the journey, and the gravel would have cut my feet to shreds. I dutifully fixed on the yashmak.

'I'll leave the gates open in case we want to exit quickly,' said Duncan with a laugh. He drove us through more trees to a mansion constructed in Bath stone almost covered in some kind of creeper. I was shivering.

'Better leave the coat behind,' suggested Duncan as I got out.

I also took off the mules.

There was a bell, but Duncan didn't use it. He tried the handle. The door opened. He knew it would. At that moment I was certain he had tricked me. There was nobody inside.

I said, 'We can't walk in like this.'

'Why not? He knows we're coming.' He pressed his hand against my back and firmly guided me inside. I felt it linger and I must have tensed, for he withdrew it.

The interior was dazzling, decorated like a Moorish palace: a carved wooden screen, illuminated windows, carpets of deepest red and gold, bejewelled scimitars and daggers ranged along one wall and tapestries along another.

But nobody came out to us.

'Duncan, what is this about?'

He winked. 'Come upstairs. You'll see.'

'No.'

'All right. Wait here. Give me the record.'

I passed it to him, still wondering whether to turn and run, but how, and where to, dressed like this? I comforted myself with the thought that if this *was* an elaborate plot to get me into bed, it was shaping up as more of a seduction than a rape. I still didn't fancy Duncan.

From upstairs came the strains of *An Arabian Night*.

'It's all right,' called Duncan's voice. 'He's here and waiting for you.' He was looking over the banisters.

'Upstairs?'

'Come on up.'

'No. You come down.'

'Very well.' He joined me in the hall. 'I don't believe you trust me. I'll tell you what. You go up and do your dance. I'll stay downstairs. There's a swimming pool round the back – you can see it from the window. I'll be there. Call down if you want me.'

For the first time since I had entered the house, I considered the possibility that the secret bidder might actually be there. 'Why does it have to be upstairs?'

'That's where the hi-fi is. He's bedridden, poor fellow. Go and give him his treat. He's really looking forward to it.'

I suppose it was the familiarity of the music that finally drew me up those stairs. I was quivering inside. Out of the corner of an eye I watched Duncan cross the hall and go outside. He was not the seducer I had taken him for.

Halfway up the stairs was a niche containing an open box. Laid across it was a necklace of lapis lazuli. I was sure it was from ancient Egypt. I moved on.

The music was coming from behind the first door on the landing. It was ajar. I considered whether to knock. It seemed inappropriate. I sidled to the door, paused, took a breath and moved inside, gyrating gently to the music.

It was a large, panelled room, dominated by a single bed with the headboard outlined in the tulip shape so beloved of Eastern craftsmen. There was a small figure sitting in its centre like a bee, an old man in a gold quilted smoking jacket, white-haired, bright-eyed and smiling. He was waving his hands, keeping the music's beat.

I warmed to him. I danced.

I had hardly started when the rhythm broke. I hesitated. Then I saw the reason. The deck for the hi-fi was beside the old man's bed. He had lifted the playing arm and set the stylus back towards the beginning of the disc.

I gave him a roguish look. He beckoned with his hand and patted the bed beside him. I glanced out of the window. Duncan was lying by the pool below. He had stripped to a pair of trunks.

I perched myself on the edge of the bed.

'What's he doing?' asked the old man in a surprisingly silky voice.

'Sunbathing.'

He smiled. 'I'm not supposed to talk to you. The money was only for the dance.'

'I don't mind.'

'I like your dancing. I used to watch the Cairo belly dancers years ago, before the war. I was in the Embassy. Had most of my career out there. I often watched the belly dancing.'

'Better than mine, I'm sure. I'm an impostor.'

'A very acceptable one, my dear. Lovely to watch. Just a little at a time, though. Blood pressure. Lost my tablets a week ago. Can't find the pesky things however hard I look.'

'Can't you get some more?'

'I've got some coming. As a matter of fact, my housekeeper – she looks after me – is picking up the prescription this afternoon. Duncan promised, but I rather think he must have forgotton it.'

'I see.'

'Duncan's a brick, bringing you here like this. I'm his Uncle Norman, as I expect he told you.'

'No.'

'Didn't he? He's absent-minded sometimes. Still, he's the

only family I have. He takes a lot of interest. He'll inherit all this when I go, of course. How's the needle going?'

I stretched across to move it back. Uncle Norman watched me and went visibly more pink.

He said, 'What a state I'm in. Wish I could find those wretched tablets.'

'Shall I look for them?'

'No use, my dear. Duncan searched the room from top to bottom the afternoon they disappeared. I'll be all right as long as I don't get too excited. Doctor's orders. Tablets keep the pressure down, you see. Duncan says I can take the dancing in my stride, but I know my ticker better than he does.'

I heard all this with mounting horror. I could have killed Uncle Norman with the belly dance. He knew it and I was damned sure Duncan knew it.

I got up.

'Where are you going, my dear? Don't go yet.'

'I'd like to find the bathroom.'

'Oh. Along the passage. Last door facing you. Come back, won't you?'

I ran downstairs. Through the open door I glimpsed a second car beside our own. The housekeeper's, I presumed. It didn't matter. I was incensed. I was going to have this out with Duncan. I could see it all: the old man forever reminiscing about his Cairo belly dancers; Duncan spying on me at the keep fit; the fair; the auction; the missing tablets. It was tantamount to murder. And Duncan would inherit this enormous house and all its treasures and marry Angela. For all her reservations about men, she'd have him at the altar like a shot.

He was still lying on his stomach.

'Duncan.'

He turned and sat up. 'Something wrong?' He didn't look too concerned.

I said, 'Is that what you expected?'

He stood up.

I said, 'You bastard. You tried to kill him.'

Duncan said, 'What happened? Is he having an attack? We're in this together. You'd better tell me.'

'He's your uncle. You're his heir. You didn't tell me.'

'So what? I didn't tell Angela either. It's my business.'

'You fixed the auction.'

Duncan grabbed my wrist. 'I've had enough of this. You and I are going upstairs to see what's happened.'

'No!'

He started pulling me along.

'Leave me alone!'

'If he's alive, you can damned well do your belly dance until you drop or he does. Move yourself!' He slapped me hard across the face.

We had reached the house. I screamed. He dragged me across the hall, twisting my arm behind me. Stair by stair he forced me upwards, his bare legs thrusting against mine.

'Let me go!' I screamed. 'Duncan, for God's sake, let me go!'

At the top of the stairs, I grabbed the rail and tried to kick him.

Suddenly he released me and gave an appalling shriek. What I saw then amazed me. His chest was spurting blood. There was a dagger in it, one of those ornamental daggers from the hall with vicious curved blades.

Angela had stabbed him. She was facing him and screaming in his face, 'I knew it, knew it, knew it!'

Duncan lurched forward. She pushed him back. Angela's vocation had made her very strong. Duncan fell backwards down the stairs. He did not move again. The post-mortem showed a broken neck.

Angela reached out and held me. We clung to each other, overcome by what had happened. She said between her sobs, 'I always knew he fancied you. I followed you in the car. I knew what he was planning, knew it, knew it.' She was hysterical again.

Of course, she didn't know it. She killed the man who loved her, would have got rich and married her. She got two years in Holloway to ruminate on that. She's still there.

And Uncle Norman? He survived the shock. He's doing well. He takes his tablets and gets a lot of pleasure twice a week watching his wife belly dancing for him to *An Arabian Night*.

Trace Of Spice

The detective story writer, Lavinia Quan, blessed with a physique that was difficult to sidestep, had succeeded in stopping Justin Fletcher, who reviewed crime fiction for one of the Sunday papers. 'Just the man I want a few words with,' she told him ominously. 'I wish to inform you that I have not altered my style of book in twenty years and I will not be bludgeoned into doing it by a newspaper critic.'

'Bravely spoken,' Fletcher tactfully remarked. 'Why change a formula that pleases so many readers and brings you all those royalities?' Stupid old bat. Even if she turned her Inspector Fotherby into a compulsive flasher, it wouldn't salvage her books from their monumental tedium. 'I hope my review last Sunday didn't upset you.'

'Your phrase, Mr Fletcher, was *"same old recipe without a trace of spice"*.'

He coughed. Why the hell had she invited him to the party if the piece offended her? 'Yes. The metaphor came over a trifle more strongly than I intended. But as a reviewer, Miss Quan, I'm bound to be sensitive to new trends in crime-writing. Frankly your world of country house parties and decent-mannered detectives is somewhat outmoded.'

'My stories have a foundation in fact, Mr Fletcher, and so do my characters.' The sweep of Miss Quan's glance took in most of the room.

God, yes! Why hadn't he seen it? This house of hers was the country mansion of all her novels. The people standing around were the stock set of suspects who inhabited it. He had already met half a dozen of them, and it had simply not dawned on him. There was the colonel by the french windows with the vicar. Under the chandelier was the eccentric professor making conversation with the inevitable doctor whose eyebrows twitched. The world of Miss Quan's books was still in existence, preserved like a pharaoh's tomb here in rural Sussex. There was even a butler – the butler who had done it nine times out of ten! – possibly on hire from a catering firm, but here to the life in tie and tails, carrying a tray of drinks.

Fletcher recovered himself. 'Your characters, Miss Quan? Straight from life. It's your plots I find predictable.'

She frowned. 'Really? You attacked my last novel but one for being too implausible. Remember your words? I do. "*Miss Quan is welcome to select any murderer she likes from her cardboard cut-out kit of suspects. After twenty or more of her novels, I am indifferent to the latest arrangement. But I am bound to protest when she asks me to believe all fifteen of her suspects are equally guilty.*" That was unkind, Mr Fletcher. It spoiled the book for thousands who would have read it. I shall not forgive you for revealing the dénouement of that book.'

Fletcher bridled. He had taken enough of this. If she wanted the truth she could have it. 'The story was totally implausible. *Fifteen* people with grudges against one man, all combining to murder him? Pure fantasy. Any thriller-writer deals in the bizarre and absurd to some extent, but a plot must have its thread of logic. Your book didn't. That's why I hammered it.' He smiled. 'Even so, I expect your loyal readers bought it in thousands.'

'That isn't the point,' said Miss Quan icily. Then, with an effort at sociability, 'However, you'll have a drink? I didn't invite you here to have an argument.'

'No argument,' said Fletcher charitably. 'Better if these matters are aired.' He took a whisky from the butler's tray. There was a good selection of drinks, generous quantities ready poured in English cut-glass. The old girl wasn't in penury yet, for all the hostile reviews.

Miss Quan took a glass of Madeira and placed it on the mantelpiece nearby. 'Implausible, you said. Suppose I told you, Mr Fletcher, that I have devised another plot – a neater one, I believe – with the same result, that fifteen people are so united in hatred of one man that they combine to murder him?'

He laughed aloud. '*Julius Caesar*, eh? That wasn't a whodunit, as far as I recollect.'

'No,' said Miss Quan quietly. 'I'm speaking of something more modern. Right up to date, in fact.'

Fletcher was suddenly conscious that Miss Quan's voice was the only one in the room. All the other guests stood facing them, glasses in hand, listening.

She went on portentously. 'If I told you that we are here tonight to participate in a murder, would you believe me, Mr Fletcher? There are fifteen of us, if you include the butler, and he most certainly wishes to be included.'

Fletcher's laugh had a note of unease. 'What do you mean? Party games?'

'Not really. We invited you here to exact a kind of justice. You probably assumed that my guests were neighbours. Not so. The vicar there came up from his parish in Cornwall for tonight's party. You will know him better as Arnold Dellar, the author of *A Box for the Bishop*. Remember your review last October?'

The vicar himself recited it, intoning the words like the last rites: '"*Murder in the Cathedral, modern-style. Plot rattles like a collection box. Enough padding to upholster all the pews in St Paul's*".'

Nobody smiled.

'You were no less vitriolic towards the colonel over there,' Miss Quan continued. '*The Bloody Brigadier* was his first crime novel and will be his last thanks to you. Yes, we are all crime-writers who have suffered from your obnoxious brand of criticism – even the butler. Remember *Skulduggery in the Scullery?*'

Too well. Fletcher nodded, liking the situation less and less.

'I won't bore you by listing all the books you have destroyed in your column, Mr Fletcher, although they meant a good deal to their authors. I shall return to an earlier point.'

Thank God for that! Cold sweat was rolling down his sides.

'You dismissed the notion of fifteen people participating jointly in a murder as preposterous. Look around you, Mr Fletcher. Do you doubt our ability to commit a crime? Aren't we the experts? And haven't we motive enough? When you have sacrificed countless precious hours to bring to life a work that a critic snuffs out in two sentences you have the motive, believe me.'

He was ready to believe anything.

'Since you are a connoisseur, Mr Fletcher, I'll tell you how this plot unfolds. Each of us, naturally, is conversant with the properties of the deadly poisons. Instead of bringing bottles to the party tonight, my guests brought phials, of strychnine, cyanide, digitalis and others they could obtain. Everyone brought something – isn't that the rule at all the best modern parties? We added something deadly and quick-acting to each of the drinks on the butler's tray. You took a whisky, I notice, and you haven't tried it yet. I can't tell you what went into it, but we may know from your reaction. Aren't you going to try it?' Remembering something, Miss Quan snapped her fingers. 'Of course! As a connoisseur, you want to know how we plan to dispose of the, em, inevitable. With a doctor and a vicar in our group, need I say more? Drink up, Mr Fletcher.'

He looked at the yellowy liquid. The idea was outrageous. Pure fantasy. A party joke. His gaze returned to the faces watching him, decent, inoffensive people anyone would respect. Would a doctor or a vicar countenance such a thing? It had to be an elaborate practical joke. The hell with them all.

He raised his glass high. 'To crime, then, ladies and gentlemen,' he announced, his confidence returning, 'of the fictional kind!' Without another thought, he gulped it down and looked around the room.

No one else had lifted a glass.

The Virgin And The Bull

She was the only daughter of the vicar and he was the publican's son. She was called Alison, he Tom. Alison had long, flaxen hair. It had once been the envy of every girl in the village school. She had let it grow so long that she could sit on it. Now, at seventeen, she wore it shorter, in a simple ponytail. She had peachy, luminous skin to match the fine fair hair. She wore no make-up. Her dresses were simple and old-fashioned and her shoes flat-heeled and practical, yet there was not a young man in Middle Slaughter whose thoughts had not been disturbed by her.

Tom Hunt was reckoned to be the only one with any prospect of turning dream into reality. Large, rough and rebellious, he had not impressed Alison in the least when they were at school together. He had ruled the playground by sheer tyranny. She had been pleased to forget him when she had transferred to secondary school, a Church of England boarding school for daughters of the clergy. The bullying in a school for girls was of a different order from Tom Hunt's brutish behaviour. He became as unreal as the ogres in the fairy stories she had left at home on the bookshelf in her bedroom.

He had surfaced unexpectedly this summer. Alison was home from school. She had been sent into the vicarage garden to pick greengages for the jam her mother always made in the last week of August. Shyly she pretended not to notice the bare-chested young man at work repairing the stone wall in the field adjoining the garden. She started gathering the fruit on the lower branches.

Tom's work on the wall brought him to a point where the greengage tree overhung the wheat field. Alison endeavoured to move around the tree so that she would not be forced to catch his eye.

Tom was not the sort to be ignored. He picked a greengage and tossed it neatly into the basket she was using. Alison heard him say, 'Funny how the best ones are always out of reach.'

She made no response.

'I was speaking of the plums, of course,' he went on. 'I meant nothing personal. Do you remember me?' He moved along the wall to where she could not fail to see his grinning features and bare, brown torso. He had the physique of a man now, a strong, broad man, but she recognised his smile.

She said, 'Tom Hunt. You used to chase the girls with nettles and sting their legs.'

He laughed. 'I've given it up now.'

It was fascinating to see how the obnoxious features Alison remembered were still traceable in this ruggedly attractive face.

At the church fête the following Sunday he helped her sell programmes at the gate. He seemed quite popular with the villagers, even girls and boys he had once persecuted unmercifully.

That evening there was a barn dance in aid of parish funds. As soon as Alison appeared with her father, Tom Hunt crossed the floor and asked her to join him in a St Bernard's Waltz.

'That's the way I do things,' Tom told her as they linked arms. 'Straight to it, like a bull at a gate. I don't stand on ceremony.'

'And you'd better not stand on my feet,' said Alison, as their shoes touched. 'Haven't you danced a St Bernard's before?'

'Not very often. Have you? You seem to know the steps.'

'Yes.'

'Where did you learn – at school?'

She gave a nod. She did not like being reminded that she was still a schoolgirl.

'I thought so,' Tom said with a trace of condescension.

'Girls' schools do a lot of that, don't they? Singing and dancing and skipping.'

'They do other things too,' Alison pointed out.

'Cookery?'

'Farming. My school has a Jersey herd and twelve acres put out to wheat and barley. The girls do all the work. It's not just skipping and dancing. So it follows,' she said with a level look at Tom, 'that bulls don't impress me overmuch.'

Against all the indications, the friendship between them took root. They were seen together hand in hand, walking the lanes and footpaths around the village each evening after work until it got dark. Then Tom would escort her to the vicarage porch and, according to report, kiss her briefly before making his way, whistling, to the Harrow. There, over his beer, he would shrug aside the good-natured banter of the regulars, the enquiries after the vicar's health and whether Tom proposed to join the choir. Any young man who courted a village girl was a target for the locals' wit. The wooing of the vicar's daughter was better than a game of darts.

The baiting of Tom was rendered more entertaining by the knowledge that, not many months before, it would have roused him to violence. Perhaps it was the onset of maturity, or perhaps it was the fact that his father was landlord of the Harrow that kept Tom in check. He seemed to accept the chaffing in good sport, which of course was demanded by the time-honoured ritual. He even summoned an occasional smile.

On some evenings Rufus Peel added his comments to the rest. Rufus was the only one of the regulars capable of rankling Tom. He was one of Tom's generation. Most of the others were older men. Rufus had been through the village school with Alison and Tom. He had been the star pupil, the boy who played Joseph in the nativity play to Alison's Mary, when Tom had not even aspired to the part of third shepherd. At secondary school, Rufus had won the biology prize. He had joined the school combined cadet force and risen to the rank of junior officer. The headmaster had chosen him for school captain. Unaccountably his public examination results had fallen below average, but the head's strong recommendation had secured him an interview for agricultural college, and he had been accepted unconditionally.

Rufus was the first Middle Slaughter boy ever to win a place at college. He was regarded with awe. He started talking to the older men as if they were his contemporaries, and they accepted it. His middle-aged manner and short, portly stature undoubtedly helped, as did his generosity in buying rounds in the Harrow. He was getting a generous grant towards his living expenses.

When Rufus joined in the wisecracks at Tom's expense, there was often a cutting edge to his comments that seemed calculated to test the victim's passivity to the limit. 'Tom's no fool,' he told the others. 'He's after a cheap wedding. There'll be no church fees, you see. It's all on the Lord, if you're smart enough to marry a vicar's daughter.'

Tom would usually look as if he had not heard a word. He knew what lay behind the barbed remarks. Rufus had wanted Alison for years. He had pestered her for friendship ever since they were in junior school. He had passed notes to her and tried to arrange meetings. He had thought at first that she would be flattered by his interest. Each success in his life – the biology prize, the school captaincy, the commission in the CCF – had cued another bid for Alison's approval.

Alison had lately described to Tom how difficult her life had become through Rufus's persistence. She had treated him politely, but coolly. In reality she disliked everything about him.

Rufus had refused to give up. One Saturday in May, Alison had been playing tennis at boarding school, when she had noticed a persistent giggling from the benches by the sidelines. Along one side of the courts was a beech hedge, intended to isolate the daughters of the clergy from the pernicious world at large. The smaller girls had spotted a young man peering through a gap in the hedge. It had been Rufus. He had cycled sixty miles to let Alison know that he had won a place in agricultural college. Burning with embarrassment and with the second-formers tittering in chorus, Alison had approached the gap, lowered her head and listened to Rufus's jubilant announcement. She had stared at the ridiculous, smug face framed by the beech leaves and she had told Rufus that she was glad he would be going to agricultural college, and she hoped it was as far away as possible. They had not spoken since.

The summer passed. In September, Rufus went off to college in a dark blue suit and a striped scarf, and Alison started her last year at boarding school. Tom stayed in Middle Slaughter and helped burn the stubble on Hopkin's Farm. In the next weeks, he wrote a few letters to Alison, but he had difficulty in expressing himself in words. He knew better than to surprise her with a visit.

It was a profound relief when she came back for the Christmas vacation and was still content to meet him. They went for long walks on the frost-white footpaths around the village. They always parted at the vicarage porch with a short embrace and a few kisses. Alison was very proper. Tom had more than once invited her home, but she had resolutely declined. The reason, he suspected, was that his home was the Harrow, and her father would be shocked if Alison set foot in a public house. This seemed to be confirmed when she told Tom, 'I'll be eighteen next holiday, and then I can do as I please. Let's wait till then.'

So the next vacation, on the Friday after Easter, the day finally arrived when Tom treated Alison to her first drink in the Harrow. He secretly dreaded the amusement it would give the regulars, but as it turned out, their arrival caused no comment at all, for there was a bigger diversion. There were strangers in the Harrow.

They were a couple from London on their way, as the man explained with a wink, to spend the weekend at a cottage in Wales. He was a freelance journalist, a fluent, amusing talker who was soon entertaining the entire clientele with stories of famous people whose secrets he had somehow discovered. He had one of those prodigious moustaches once known as 'RAF', though he belonged to a later generation. He smoked cigars and seemed to have rubbed shoulders with everyone of note in London, yet it was obvious to all that the collar of his shirt was frayed and his suit was shiny at the points of wear and tear.

If either of them had money, it was she. Her sable jacket was the real thing and so were the diamond and ruby rings and earrings. She had blonde hair worn long, with silver highlights. She wore a musky perfume that penetrated the cigar fumes. She might have been thirty-nine; forty was unthinkable. The thoughts that were abroad in the Harrow that night were laced with envy of her weekend companion.

He emptied his glass. 'Not a bad beer,' he said. 'Not bad at all.'

'Have another?' offered Rufus, who was back from college with some of his grant unspent.

'That's very decent of you. The lady's is a Pimm's.'

'I don't think I'd better, Charlie,' said the woman.

'Of course you will. I'll drive the rest of the way. I'm steady as a rock if I stay on beer.' Charlie turned to Rufus. 'You take the order, old chum, and I'll collect the empties.'

Rufus may not have intended to buy drinks for everyone, but that was what happened. The regulars needed no prompting. They chanted their orders with the familiarity of monks at prayer.

While the order was being set up, the man called Charlie said confidentially to Rufus, 'Any idea who she is?'

'Who do you mean?'

'The little raver I'm with. In the fur jacket.'

Rufus shook his head. 'Should I know her?'

Charlie nodded. 'You've seen her picture plenty of times. Come on, you recognise her.'

Rufus gave the woman another look. 'I'm sorry. I'm damned sure I don't.'

Charlie looked as if he had taken offence. 'She's famous, man.'

'I'm a student at college,' said Rufus in his defence. 'I don't watch the telly.'

'You read the papers, don't you?'

'She's not a politician?'

'Does she look like one?'

'I give up. Who is she?'

'Which paper do you read?'

'The *Chronicle*.'

'I thought so. You really ought to know her.'

'Well, there's something familiar, I admit,' said Rufus so as not to appear completely ignorant.

Charlie addressed the room in general. 'Anyone got a copy

of the *Chronicle?'*

On the window seat to the right of the door, Tom and Alison were drinking white wine, grateful for the attention the strangers were getting. Nobody had passed a comment yet about Alison's presence.

Tom's father, the landlord, retrieved a copy of the *Chronicle* from under the counter and handed it to Charlie, who passed it to Rufus. The mystery of the woman's identity was now the focus of attention of every person present.

'Turn to the centre pages, lad,' instructed Charlie. 'Now turn over again. What do you find?'

'Letters to the Editor,' Rufus read aloud. *'Your Stars Today.* Well, I'll be damned!' He stared at the page and across the room at the woman. Her large brown eyes returned his gaze without self-consciousness. She was used to being pointed out as a celebrity. 'Deborah Kristal!' said Rufus. 'The fortune-teller.'

'Don't call her that, for heaven's sake,' said Charlie between his teeth. 'She's not some gypsy at the Derby with a crystal ball. She's an astrologist, and she takes it very seriously. It's highly technical. They use computers these days.' He picked up a tray of drinks and carried it across the room. 'Anyone had a birthday lately?'

The question produced a sudden silence in the room.

In the window seat, Alison whispered urgently to Tom, 'Take me home now.' They got up to leave.

Charlie turned back to Rufus. 'Never mind. What's your birth month, old boy?'

Desperate to escape the spotlight, Rufus had an inspiration. 'It's Alison's birthday today. Her eighteenth!'

'Marvellous!' said Charlie. 'Come over here, my dear, and Miss Kristal will tell you what the future holds.'

'No, thank you,' said Alison quickly.

'She's the vicar's daughter,' someone explained. 'She's shy, poor child. She's had a very sheltered life.'

'Do it for both of 'em, then,' Tom's father suggested. 'My Tom isn't bashful.'

'What a splendid idea,' said Rufus at once. 'Cast their horoscopes and tell them if they have any future together.'

'I would need more information,' said Miss Kristal. 'I do

not have my charts with me. I can make only a few broad observations.'

'Tom was born on August the twenty-eighth,' said his father.

'In that case he is not afraid of a good day's work,' said Miss Kristal. 'He is healthy and strong, loyal and courageous. He does nothing by halves. He knows what he wants out of life and he will move mountains to get it. His manner may be a shade too overbearing at times, but he hides nothing from the world. He is an honest, open-hearted man.'

'Tom, I'd like to leave,' said Alison for the second time, but Tom lingered by the door, too interested to move.

'The young lady has positive qualities, too,' went on Miss Kristal. 'She has the highest standards and she expects others to conform to them.'

'That's true,' said Tom. 'It's absolutely true!'

'She has exceptional powers of concentration,' said Miss Kristal. 'She is not easily deceived. But when she gives her word, she means it.'

'What about the future?' asked Tom's father. 'Would you advise them to get hitched?'

'Dad!' said Tom in embarrassment.

There was a pause.

'I would rather not say,' said Miss Kristal. 'Charlie, it's getting late. We still have a long way to drive.'

Rufus had been listening intently. The answer had not satisfied him. 'But you must have *some* idea whether he is suited to her.'

'In general,' said Miss Kristal, choosing her words with care, 'I would not recommend a partnership between a Virgoan and a Taurean.'

'A what?' said Tom's father.

'A Virgoan and a Taurean. Virgo and Taurus are the virgin and the bull.'

'The virgin and the bull! I like that!' said Charlie.

'It's laughable,' said Rufus with a sneer.

'What do you mean?' demanded Tom in a spasm of anger. 'What's there to laugh about?'

'It's so ridiculous,' Rufus answered insensitively. 'The

virgin and the bull. It's a joke. It's got to be a joke!'

Rufus had scarcely finished speaking before Tom was across the floor and gripping him by the shirt front. 'What are you getting at, you louse? You'd better take that back, before I break every bone in your body.'

'Tom!' ordered his father. 'Take your hands off him! I want no violence here.'

'He's going to take back every word,' said Tom, tightening his grip. 'He insulted Alison. She's a decent girl.'

Rufus hissed at Tom, 'Is that what you think, or what she told you?'

Behind Tom, Alison gave a whimper of distress and ran from the pub.

Tom brought back his fist to strike Rufus, but his arm was seized from behind and forced against his back in a savage half-nelson. 'There'll be no brawling in this house,' his father's voice snarled into his ear. 'Not from my own son, or anybody. I'm going to put you out, and you'd better cool off.'

Tom was strongly built, yet in that grip he could do nothing to prevent his father marching him to the door and thrusting him outside. It was debatable whether the father or the son suffered the greater humiliation.

The subdued atmosphere in the Harrow lasted only a short time. At Charlie's prompting, Miss Kristal obligingly cast the horoscopes of almost everyone in the bar. Rufus, who had two quick double brandies and left early, was one of the few who professed to be uninterested in knowing the future. As events turned out, this proved to have been a fatal error, because he never reached home that night.

It was the following morning before his disappearance was reported by his parents. The overnight absence from home of a young man in his late teens is not usually treated by the police as a matter of grave concern. Yet in this case it was difficult to understand what might have happened. It was established that Rufus had left the Harrow soon after 9.45 p.m. He usually took some twenty minutes to walk the mile and a quarter along the Harford Road. It was a minor road that eventually linked with the A436, and it would have taken him past a couple of cottages and Hopkin's Farm. A search of the road, ditches and adjoining fields yielded no clue to his disappearance.

The enquiries inevitably led to a reconstruction of the events the evening of the incident in the Harrow. Everyone present was questioned except Miss Kristal and her companion Charlie, who had left in their Alfa-Romeo about 10 p.m. As they would have driven along the Harford Road, it was possible that they would have passed Rufus, but no one knew where to trace them in Wales, not even Miss Kristal's newspaper office. It seemed that Miss Kristal had anticipated a longish stay in Wales, because before leaving Fleet Street she had filed *Your Stars Today* for the next four weeks.

Tom and his father were questioned closely about the incident in the public bar. Tom stated that after his father had ejected him, he ran after Alison and escorted her home. The vicarage was in the opposite direction from Rufus's route. Alison was able to corroborate what Tom had said.

A theory was advanced in the village that the journalist, Charlie, well over the limit by the time he had left the Harrow with Miss Kristal and taken the wheel of the Alfa-Romeo, had run Rufus down and killed him, then taken fright and bundled the body into the boot of the car to dispose of it in some remote lake in Wales. But at the end of the month Charlie and Miss Kristal were traced by the police, and the car was examined by forensic experts. There was no evidence to support the theory. The couple claimed that they had no recollection of having seen Rufus or anyone else on the Harford Road after they had left the Harrow.

So Rufus Peel was listed as a missing person, one of the tens of thousands on the police computer. For two years there were no developments in the case. Tom and Alison were married in the village church and the reception was held at the Harrow. Then, within a fortnight of the wedding, the remains of Rufus were discovered at the bottom of a silage tank on Hopkin's Farm.

The autopsy revealed that he had died violently. Both legs and one arm were shattered, the rib cage had been crushed, the spinal column had been severed and the skull splintered. The Home Office pathologist stated his opinion that the multiple injuries had been caused by a heavy motor vehicle, probably a tractor. It was likely that the victim had been run over not once, but repeatedly, as if deliberately.

The police picked up Tom and took him to Gloucester for questioning. After several hours he made a confession. He admitted having caused Rufus's death. He stated that on the night his father had ejected him from the Harrow he had not, as previously claimed, taken Alison home. He had made his way to the farm, sat in the seat of a tractor at the farm entrance and waited for Rufus to come along the road. His fury at what had happened in the Harrow, the slanderous insinuation Rufus had made about Alison in the public bar the first time she had ever set foot in the place, had turned him crazy for vengeance. He had driven the tractor straight at Rufus and felled him. He had driven over him and then reversed the tractor and crushed the body again. He had done it again, and then dragged the lifeless body into the yard and disposed of it under the silage.

At the assizes, Tom pleaded guilty to the murder of Rufus. In sentencing him, the judge allowed that there had been strong provocation, but ruled that the interval between the provocation and the crime did not allow sufficient grounds for a verdict of manslaughter. Tom was given a life sentence.

In Middle Slaughter there was considerable sympathy for Tom. When he was released on parole after serving eleven years, he was given back his job on Hopkin's Farm. He was given a cottage on the site and he lived there with Alison, who had waited loyally for him to serve his sentence. The villagers still called them the virgin and the bull.

One lunchtime soon after Tom's release, Deborah Kristal chanced to meet Charlie in a Fleet Street wine bar. The conversation soon got round to Middle Slaughter. 'I thought I might go down there again,' said Charlie. 'Care to join me, sweetie? Another cosy weekend in Wales?'

'Using my car, I suppose? No thank you, Charlie. Nothing personal, just the price of petrol these days. What do you want to go to Middle Slaughter for?'

'Tom Hunt's out. I thought of offering the poor devil a tenner for his story. It's worth another airing in the Sundays. It made a big enough impact when it happened.'

'I shouldn't if I were you,' said Miss Kristal.

'I'll be all right, my love. He had no grudge against me. I won't antagonise the fellow.'

'It's a waste of time going,' said Miss Kristal emphatically. 'He won't tell you a thing.'

But Charlie would not be dissuaded. He drove down to Middle Slaughter alone the following weekend.

'Sometimes I think you really are clairvoyant,' he told Deborah Kristal the next time they met. 'Ruddy fellow clammed up completely. Wouldn't say a word. And nor would anyone else in the village. His father still runs the pub, and he's no help. Nor are his customers. I spent a fortune at the bar trying to coax something out of 'em.'

'I did warn you.'

'But how did you know I was wasting my time?'

'Because they don't want the story opened up again. It was full of holes when he made the confession.'

Charlie's eyes narrowed. 'What do you mean?'

'Tom didn't kill Rufus Peel. A man as strong and as angry as he was didn't need to lie in wait with a tractor. He could have strangled Rufus with his bare hands.'

'But he confessed, for heaven's sake!'

Miss Kristal shook her head and gave a smile. 'For *Alison*'s sake, darling. She was the killer of Rufus Peel. Tom took the rap for her, and served eleven years. That's the measure of true love. Everyone in that village knows it, but no one will say a thing. And nor will you, if you've any romance left in you at all.'

Charlie, wide-eyed, said, 'Are you seriously telling me that an eighteen-year-old girl murdered a man by driving a tractor at him? A vicar's daughter? How do you know she could drive a tractor at all?'

'I went to see the school she attended. A boarding school for daughters of the clergy. They believe in self-sufficiency, a wonderful training for the good life. Every girl is taught to plough on the school farm.'

'You checked on this?' said Charlie. 'You're a dark horse, if ever I met one. But the story still takes some swallowing. Why would she have wanted to kill Rufus?'

'Really, Charlie, if you can't see that, you'll never understand the way a woman thinks. Alison was outraged by what Rufus insinuated in the Harrow. He slandered her reputation in front of her future husband, her prospective father-in-law and most of the village. Instead of going home, as Tom's confession suggested, she went to the farm and took out a tractor and took her revenge on Rufus when he came along the road. My guess is that Tom went the other way towards the vicarage and only met Alison later and heard what she had done. He must have helped her hide the body.'

'And when it was found, he made the false confession to save her,' said Charlie. 'It takes an awful lot of love to make a man accept eleven years in prison. If this is true, he's a very single-minded young man.'

'He would be,' said Miss Kristal. 'When I was casting their horoscopes that night in the Harrow, I said that one was governed by the sign of Virgo, and the other Taurus. Everyone jumped to the wrong conclusion. You see, he was the virgin and she was the bull.'

The Staring Man

When she returned from the honeymoon, Donna took two rolls of film to a shop in Kensington High Street that printed them the same day. She was dying to see herself in all the exquisite clothes Jamie had bought for her in Vienna. There were traditional Austrian dirndls and a dazzling selection of designer suits and dresses from the big-name couturiers in the Graben. Thoughtfully, she had travelled light. All she had taken on the honeymoon, apart from jeans, T-shirts and underclothes, was the Sonia Rykiel gown that she had been married in, a gorgeous cerise-coloured creation. It might have been made for her. Jamie would never know it was from the Nearly New shop in Fulham Palace Road.

She collected the photos and slid them from the package as soon as she was out of the shop. The first few were taken on the steps of Kensington Registry Office. Just a handful of friends. Donna would have liked the full works: a pony and trap to the parish church, bridesmaids, Mendelssohn, and Jamie in a grey top hat. But she could never have afforded it herself, and she refused to ask her appalling mother to foot the bill. Jamie, who was certainly capable of writing a cheque, had been through a church wedding once before, and had gently pressed for a civil ceremony this time. Donna had gracefully given way. She had not been prepared to make an issue of it. She had her priorities, and number one was to land her catch.

The first of the Vienna pictures. The Figaro House where Mozart had lived. Obviously they had not found the dress shops at that stage, because she was still in blue jeans. A pity. The narrow street with its sombre greys and greens would have been a perfect backdrop for the crimson dirndl and white blouse that Jamie had bought her later that afternoon.

Absorbed, she worked her way through the prints, assessing her outfits and finding them mostly as elegant as when she had tried them on. She was slightly disappointed that Jamie had taken so many pictures of buildings, but she hardly glanced at those, except one of the front of the hotel in which she was waving from their bedroom window. It had been lunchtime, she remembered, and she was still in the pale blue silk nightie he had draped across her pillow as a surprise the previous evening. She smiled at the recollection. He was captivated by her. He had woken her every morning with a kiss and a caress. They hadn't eaten a single breakfast in the two weeks.

She looked through the photos several times more that afternoon. It was partly self-congratulation, but there was something else. She was looking for reassurance. She had not been entirely honest with Jamie. The truth couldn't be hidden from him much longer.

She showed him the pictures after dinner that evening. They now lived in Jamie's beautiful Georgian riverside house at Strand-on-the-Green, near Kew Bridge. He had already asked his solicitor to make Donna the co-owner. Jamie believed marriage was a partnership in every respect. On Friday, they had an appointment with his bank manager to open a joint account.

He reached for her waist and pulled her on to his lap on the sofa in front of the real-flame gas fire. She picked the photos off the ceramic-tiled table nearby, and started going through them, holding them for Jamie to inspect. He was nibbling her ear lobe.

'Pay attention, lover boy,' she chided him lightly. 'I gave up my lunch to collect these for you today. I want to show them to you.'

He touched his lips to hers. 'Show me anything you like.'

'Jamie!'

He pretended to take an intelligent interest in the photos,

reaching to take one out of her hand. 'That's come out well.'

'My Italian suit?'

'The entire picture. The way the trees line up, giving that wedge of sky on the right. It makes an interesting composition. The park at Schönbrunn, isn't it?'

'I don't remember,' said Donna, and she might have added that she didn't care.

'Obviously you made a strong impression on someone.'

She perked up. 'The cameraman?'

'I meant the guy on the seat.'

She hadn't noticed anyone else in the picture. She took it back to look. To the right of the gravel path, partly in shadow, was a garden seat. On it, a youngish man in a tan-coloured bomber jacket had turned in an obvious way to look at Donna as she posed.

She commented modestly, 'He's probably looking at the palace.'

'I wouldn't bet on it.'

She turned to the next pictures, a series of shots that Jamie had taken on the Fiaker tour. They had sat side by side in the carriage, and he had snapped his camera at each old building the driver had pointed out. She didn't tell Jamie, but she thought he might just as well have bought a set of postcards.

There was one picture at the end, when she had posed with the driver in his brown bowler and grey velvet jacket that handsomely set off her peacock blue.

'There he is again – the same bloke!' said Jamie.

'The driver?'

'No, silly. The guy in the other picture. Look, he's there in the background, leaning against the scaffolding beside the Stephansdom.'

Donna studied the picture. 'It's just someone wearing a similar jacket.'

'No, look at his face. Where's the first picture?'

They compared them. Certainly the two jackets were identical and the faces looked similar, pale in colour with gaunt cheeks and deep-set, shadowy eyes. In each picture, they were fixed on Donna.

'Your secret admirer,' said Jamie.

'I hope not. He looks weird to me. Anyway, I've got an admirer.'

'And he doesn't make a secret of it,' murmured Jamie, sliding his hand over her left knee.

She let the photographs drop on the carpet.

After they had made love on the sofa, they drank iced Perrier water. Donna decided that if any moment was going to be right for a confession, this was it. 'Darling, I haven't been entirely honest with you. I feel very ashamed. I'd like to tell you about it.'

'Don't worry, angel,' he answered with consideration. 'If it's about the past, forget it. I'm a realist. I can't believe someone as pretty as you would have got to twenty-four without experience.'

'That isn't what I mean, Jamie.' She looked into his confident blue eyes and prepared to see them swivel with amazement. 'I married you under false pretences. All that stuff I told you about working as a company director in the family business wasn't true. I'm an out-of-work actress. When I go up to town, I don't really go to work in the City, I do the rounds of the theatrical agencies.'

Jamie smiled and squeezed her hand. 'Darling, that's nothing to be ashamed of! I'd much rather be married to an actress than a boring old company director.'

'My family isn't in business. We don't have a country house in Cheshire,' she went on, determined to clean the slate. 'Daddy wasn't a Master of Foxhounds, he was a tobacconist in Balham High Street. When I was twelve, he had an affair with one of the girls from the supermarket across the street. My mother divorced him and went to live in Scotland.'

'I married you, my sweet, not your parents,' Jamie pointed out with durable good humour.

'Yes, but you still don't know the truth about me. My cottage in Devon doesn't exist. I invented it to impress you. I don't have any furniture of my own. I've lived in furnished accommodation since I left school.'

'School? You mean Cambridge University?'

She sighed. 'Darling, that was another fabrication. I feel so terrible telling you all this. I didn't go to public school or university. I was at a tin-pot drama school that didn't even put us in for CSEs. All I got there was a plummy accent from the elocution lessons. It didn't even get me any parts worth having. It simply fitted me for what I am – a con-artist.' She lowered her eyes. The penitent look was something else she had learned in drama school.

Jamie had let go of her hand. He was sinking under the torrent of revelations, but slowly. He was still thinking about the cottage in Devon. 'You don't possess any property, then?' he said slowly. 'Nothing at all?'

'Not a brick. That's what I'm trying to tell you, Jamie. I'm a wicked liar. I wanted you so much that I lied through my teeth to get you.'

She watched him with wide, fearful eyes. In her mind, she had acted out this scene a dozen or more times and endured every kind of retribution from obloquy to a physical beating.

He said in a voice that was still struggling to come to terms with what he had been told, 'But we agreed to share everything, our property, our money, everything.'

'Yes. And I have nothing except the few things I moved in with.'

'But you have some money of your own. We agreed to open a joint account. Surely you have a bank account?'

'An overdraft,' admitted Donna, thankful that she had found the courage to tell him everything.

The colour had drained entirely from Jamie's face. He stared into the fire for a long time.

Donna moved closer to him and said, 'I love you. I lied because I love you. I could see you were unhappy living alone and I wanted you for myself.'

The last statement was true. She had met Jamie through an escort agency. It was a classy place that employed a lot of actresses between shows. They treated you like the Civil Service and sex was definitely not in the contract. The clients were mostly wealthy businessmen like Jamie who needed to socialise and paid everything with Diners' and American Express. When Donna had filled in her form with a couple of other girls she knew from drama school, it had all seemed a huge joke, and she had laughingly invented posh parents and a cottage in the country. But when she had met Jamie, the joke was over. He wasn't fat and middle-aged, like most of the clients. He was the most eligible guy she had ever met, tall, twenty-seven, good looking and, above all, rich, rich, rich. He was a widower, and it was practically written all over him that he was desperate to marry again.

She wondered whether this was the moment to sway towards him and solicit a forgiving kiss. His blitzed look was not encouraging.

He said in an expressionless voice, 'I think I'll go to bed.'

Donna decided that the appropriate action for a remorseful wife was to remain downstairs and spend the night on the sofa. A few hours' sleep would probably bring Jamie round.

She washed in the kitchen and fetched a car blanket from the Mercedes. She would sleep in her underclothes tonight.

While she was arranging the blanket, the bare sole of her foot touched something cold on the carpet: one of the honeymoon photographs. She picked it up. It was a flashlight shot taken in one of the wine gardens – what did the Viennese call them? – *Heurigen*. She was in the sweet little black number with the *diamanté* brooch and the reckless plunge. With her long, blonde hair, she always looked stunning in black. That evening, people had turned to stare as she had walked among the scrubbed pinewood tables. She hadn't imagined it; they were there in the photograph casting sideward glances at her. One, she now noticed, looked remarkably like the guy in the tan-coloured jacket in those other pictures. But this one was in a dark brown suit.

Well, Donna told herself, he wouldn't wear the same thing all the time, would he?

She had to be sure. She went to the sideboard drawer and took out the magnifying glass that Jamie kept there. She examined the photo minutely.

It was him. It was definitely him, that washed-out, cadaverous face, those hollow eyes, watching her. She shuddered. Even here in the security of her new home, she felt creepy. He must have been following her around Vienna. How else could he have appeared in three photographs taken in different places? A pulse was beating in her forehead.

Suddenly, irrationally, she felt afraid to spend the night downstairs alone. She pulled the blanket around her shoulders and hurried up to their bedroom without even turning out the light.

In bed, she pressed close to Jamie's broad back and the fears receded.

He said, 'Are you all right? You're shaking.'

She didn't tell him the reason. It would have seemed like a cheap bid for affection. Naturally, he was still brooding over her deceit. She murmured, 'It's a reaction, I expect. Darling, will you forgive me?'

He was silent for an agonising interval before he said, 'At least you had the decency to tell me the truth.'

'You were bound to find out soon,' admitted Donna. 'I should have told you before the wedding, but I was so afraid of losing you.'

'As it happens, I haven't been entirely frank myself,' Jamie unexpectedly volunteered. 'There's something I've been keeping from you. You've been honest with me, so I want to clear my own conscience. I didn't tell you the whole truth about Fiona.'

'Your wife?'

He turned on to his back. 'Yes. I told you she died. I didn't tell you the circumstances.'

'There's no need, my darling,' Donna assured him.

'Yes, you ought to know.' He hesitated. 'You see Fiona was murdered.'

She caught her breath. 'How?'

He answered in a voice that was low, but determined to recite the facts, 'Someone strangled her. It was while I was in Paris on a business trip. I think I told you that I have to go there periodically to visit our sales rep there. Someone broke into the house in the night and strangled my poor Fiona with a length of flex. I found her when I got back on Sunday night.'

'Oh, Jamie! Who?'

'They never found out. There was no reason why anyone should have wanted to kill Fiona. She wasn't the sort to make enemies. She was sweet-natured, loved by everyone who knew her.'

'Was she...?'

'Sexually assaulted? No. And the motive wasn't theft, because nothing was taken. We had some beautiful things around the house. Pictures, silver, antiques. Her family were very well off. I wouldn't be living in this style if it weren't for Fiona, poor darling. They questioned me, of course. I suppose if you think coldly in terms of motive, I had one. I certainly profited from her death. But I was in Paris from Friday night until Sunday. They checked with British Airways and the hotel and found it was true.'

'So who could have done it?'

'Nobody knows. They went through her diaries, questioned her friends, the neighbours, her family. It's a mystery. God knows, I've tried to think of an explanation. I think her family still feel it would never have happened if she hadn't married me.'

'Poor Jamie! That's unfair.'

'But understandable. There have been times when I've wondered whether the killer had some grudge against me.'

Donna frowned. 'He hated you so much that he strangled your wife? It doesn't sound very plausible.'

'Doesn't it? In business, you make enemies sometimes without knowing it, people whose ambitions you frustrate, people who regard you as a threat or a menace.'

'Is there anyone you suspect?'

'No one. That's just the point. It could be someone I didn't even know I had crossed. I try not to think about it now. I could easily get paranoid. Do you understand?'

'I understand, and I'm glad you told me, darling,' said Donna; she smiled in the darkness. Her own unscrupulous conduct seemed of less importance now.

No more was said that night. She drifted into sleep without giving another thought to the man in the photographs.

Next morning, they went to some trouble to behave considerately to each other. If the revelations on each side had tested the relationship, at least there were indications that they both wanted it to prosper. Jamie announced that he would clear Donna's overdraft and still open the joint account. Donna put up her hair in the style he liked best and promised him a candlelit dinner when he got home. He kissed her before he left for work.

The fears of the previous night seemed trivial as she went

about the house that morning. She picked the rest of the photographs off the living-room floor and put them in their wallet without looking at them again. She had more important things on her mind, such as which dress to wear that evening.

After lunch, she walked into Kew to the butcher who sold the best steaks and bought two large fillets. At the chemist's next door, she picked up a new lipstick and a musky perfume that she had not tried before. She had always envied the women with enough money to treat themselves to whichever luxuries they fancied.

She strolled back in the autumn sunshine, stopping for a moment by the bridge to watch an eight at practice on the Thames. The house overlooked the river, and all the activity on it was a happy discovery for Donna.

She was still watching the oarsmen as she approached the house. They appeared to be heading straight for a group of ducks, but she need not have worried. The ducks judged their escape to perfection, without even seeming to hurry. She was so wrapped up in this drama that she failed to notice the figure standing on the embankment opposite the house until she was within a few yards of him.

'Darling, I almost passed out on the spot,' she told Jamie that evening as soon as he came in. 'It was him – the man in the photographs. He stared at me just like he did in Vienna. He was standing outside the house as if he was waiting for me. It was horrible! My blood ran cold. I walked past him, past the house, trying to pretend I didn't live here.'

'And when you came back, he had gone?'

Donna's eyes filled with tears. 'You don't believe me, do you?'

'How could it be the same fellow? Why?'

'I don't know, but I'm not mistaken. I don't imagine things.'

'Of course you don't, but you must admit that you over-reacted a little when you looked at the photos. He made a strong impression on you. The image stays in the mind, and next time you see a thin-faced guy near the house...'

'It isn't like that, Jamie! It was him. I know it was him.'

Over dinner, Jamie tried a different tack. 'Okay, let's

accept for a moment that you're not mistaken. He was the same guy. There's no reason to feel afraid. He hasn't threatened you, has he?'

'I feel threatened.'

'Because it's all in your mind.'

'No!'

'After dinner, we'll take another look at the photos, and I think you'll find you've made a mistake.'

'I burned them in the grate this afternoon. I couldn't bear to have them in the house.'

'Our honeymoon pictures?'

As a romantic occasion, the meal was already a disaster. They drank the wine and Jamie ate his steak, but Donna pushed her plate aside. She couldn't stomach food in her present state of mind. She went off to make coffee.

'By the way,' Jamie said, when she returned, 'I think I told you that I have to make the occasional trip to Paris to confer with our rep over there. He's asked me over next weekend to meet some clients.'

'You're going to Paris?' she said in disbelief.

'Don't look so alarmed, darling. It's strictly business, I assure you. I'll be back on Sunday night.'

'Take me with you, Jamie.'

'That won't be possible. Company policy. Wives don't go on business trips.'

'To hell with the company! You can't leave me here alone after what has happened!'

'Nothing has happened.'

'I shall go out of my mind!'

'You're being melodramatic, Donna.'

'How can you contemplate a trip like this after what happened to your first wife?'

'Come now, that's unfair. What am I supposed to do: give up my job altogether?'

Donna said, 'They never found Fiona's killer. What if it were the man who watches me?'

'That's crazy! Why should it be him?'

'You said yourself that it was possible he killed her because he had a grudge against you. He might be planning to murder me.'

'Donna, you're overwrought. We've been through a heavy time together. Why don't you see the doctor in the morning and get some tranquillisers? In a couple of days you'll feel entirely different. By Friday, you won't care a damn about my Paris trip. Listen, I've had a good idea. You could go up to Harrod's on Saturday and buy yourself something exciting to wear when I come home. They stock some very exotic underwear.'

'I'd rather have it from Paris, thank you.'

'All right, I'll see what I can bring back for you.'

He was intractable. The next morning, he drove her to the doctor's. She was given some capsules and a lecture about the stress of the first few months of marriage. She had already decided not to take the tranquillisers. If she saw the staring man again, she didn't want Jamie telling her she was muzzy.

But she didn't see him, and by Friday she was more or less reconciled to spending the weekend alone in the house. She had told herself sternly that she would have to face it some time; when she was over the first weekend, she would feel less anxious about any others.

He was booked on the 5.15 p.m. Air France flight from Heathrow and Donna drove him there in the Mercedes after she had confessed to flushing all the tranquillisers down the toilet. He was amused, rather than angry. He seemed pleased that she had conquered the fears herself.

Before he left her at the gate for United Kingdom passport holders, he embraced her and told her where to locate the brandy in case she needed it for her nerves.

She answered that she wouldn't need it now. As he moved towards the ticket check, she called out, 'Jamie!'

He turned. 'Yes?'

'Don't get black, will you? White or pale yellow.'

'Oh!' He smiled, blushed, and went through the gate.

As Donna turned away, she looked into the eyes of the staring man. He had been standing within a yard of her. This time there could be no doubt. It was the skull-like face of the photographs, the cavernous eyes, the sallow colouring.

She blurted out, 'Who are you?'

Furrows of apparent surprise formed on the high forehead. 'I beg your pardon?'

'What do you want? Why have you been following me?'

He shook his head. 'I think you are mistaken.' He backed away and she quickly lost sight of him among the crowd around the departure gate.

For a moment she considered running after Jamie to tell him, but the security people on the gate would never have let her through. She might have asked to have his name called over the public address system, but what was the use? The man was gone now, and Jamie would say she had imagined it.

She had not imagined it. She was trembling and she had to find a place to sit down, but she was sane. She had to hold on to her sanity, her certainty that she was not mistaken.

After a while she had a coffee and then drove home. Along the motorway, she weighed the possibility of moving into a hotel for the weekend. Jamie would laugh when he got back, but he could well afford the cost. He would probably charge it to the company.

The other prospect was to sit at home in the terrifying knowledge that the staring man knew she was alone in the house.

She decided to go home, collect her night clothes and a couple of paperbacks and then drive back and check in at the Post House, the hotel near the airport. She would spend the next two nights there and meet Jamie when he flew in on Sunday evening.

Just before Junction 2, the Kew exit, she glanced in the rearview mirror and noticed a black Volvo trailing her quite closely. In the twilight, she couldn't see much of the driver. She took the right turn under the elevated section, down Lionel Road, past the station and briefly into Kew Bridge Road before turning into Strand-on-the-Green. The Volvo was still close behind.

Her garage entrance was electronically controlled. She turned on to the drive, pressed the remote control and drove swiftly inside. The door closed behind her. She had intended leaving the car outside while she fetched her things, but that would have meant entering the house by the front door and possibly being intercepted between the car and the house.

Once inside the garage, she used the interior door to enter the kitchen. She ran into the front room and watched the street from behind the curtain.

The Volvo was drawing up outside. She still couldn't see the driver properly. He was apparently content to sit at the wheel of his car. But only for a minute. The door swung open. Donna drew back nervously into the shadows, but the street lamp gave her a clear view of the man as he slammed his car door and turned towards the house.

It was him. He was even wearing the tan-coloured bomber jacket. And he was stepping up to the front door.

The sound of her own door chimes was petrifying to Donna. She stood with her back against the wall, praying that she was not visible from outside.

He pressed the bell push a second time. Donna held her breath.

She saw him crouch and peer through the letterbox. Was he going to force the door? She had mentioned only the previous week to Jamie that the catch on the fastening was not very strong. There was no bolt or chain to secure the house against an intruder.

He took a step away as if he might be about to try using his shoulder. First, he took a glance around him to see if he was being watched.

Donna shivered as those piercing eyes turned in her direction, peering through the window, apparently staring straight at her. Then, thank God, he turned and walked back to the car, opened the door, sat in the driver's seat and took out a cigarette.

There was no question now of escaping to the hotel for the weekend. She was trapped here. Thanks to the automatic door on the garage, she had driven in unobserved. Now her best chance was to stay out of sight and not use the lights. She felt sick with fear at the prospect of spending the evening in a darkened house, but it had to be so. There was no phone to use because Jamie had refused to have one installed, insisting that for peace of mind in his own home he preferred to be inaccessible.

As dusk deepened into darkness, and the car remained in the street, Donna summoned enough courage to lower herself to a crouching position and crawl out of the front room into the hall and out to the kitchen. By the light of the fridge kept marginally open, she managed to make some sandwiches and pour herself some red wine. It warmed her. She began to make plans. She would spend the night on the sofa in the front room, where she would be instantly alerted if the man broke into the house. She preferred that to lying upstairs in bed ignorant of what was happening downstairs.

Nine-thirty was not too early to make preparations. She improvised a bed with cushions and several coats. Outside, in the lamplight, the Volvo was still there. He was sitting inside, waiting. Donna could see the glowing tip of his cigarette as he inhaled. She had no intention of sleeping, but she stretched out on the sofa in a position from which she could see the window.

The strain of the past few hours must have taken a toll, because as she got warmer under the coats, it was increasingly difficult to keep her eyes open. But she was startled into wakefulness when she heard a sound outside. She turned her watch towards the lamplight. 4.20 a.m. She had slept for hours. Had she really heard a sound, or was it part of her dream?

There was definitely a sound. Footsteps on the gravel outside the window.

She propped herself up sufficiently to see the white, terrifying face of the staring man briefly illuminated by torchlight as he shone it around the window, searching for an opening.

Donna screamed.

She lost all control and dashed from the room and upstairs to the bedroom. She flung herself on the bed and moaned into the pillow for what seemed a long time.

Then a new sound entered her consciousness: footsteps on the stairs, moving upwards, towards her. Her flesh crawled.

The steps approached along the passage. The handle of the bedroom door made a slight scraping sound as it was turned. The door opened, the light came on, and there, unbelievably, was Jamie.

'Jamie! Oh, Jamie!' Donna sprang up and flung her arms around him. 'Jamie, my darling, how did you know?' She tried to kiss him, but something was preventing her.

It was pressing against her neck, holding her away from him, pressing her down towards the bed.

'Jamie, what is it?'

She lost her balance and fell backwards. In that split second she saw the ligature stretched between his hands, the piece of white plastic flex with which he was about to strangle her. She saw the look of hatred and contempt in his face and she understood that her husband Jamie was a killer, a ruthless murderer.

He said nothing, simply pressed the flex against her throat and began to draw one hand behind her neck to encircle it. She could do nothing to stop him. He was straddling her body, with his knees pinning down her arms. She was unable even to scream.

Then abruptly Jamie gave a grunt and the pressure on her neck slackened.

She was overwhelmed by a suffocating darkness, but she was not dead. Jamie had fallen on her. He was smothering her with his body. She struggled to get free, finding the strength to raise her knees and force him to one side. Amazingly, he did not resist. His body had gone limp.

Suddenly his weight was off her chest and she could breathe. She was looking up at a face, but it was not Jamie's. It was the face of the staring man.

Donna whispered, 'No!'

'All right. It's all right, my dear,' he told her. 'I won't hurt you. I'm a private detective. I just knocked your husband on the head. You're safe. He's out cold and handcuffed. He would have killed you like he killed his first wife. It was all set up.'

'What do you mean?'

'The trip to Paris. His alibi. He flew over, checked in at the hotel and went straight out and took a train to Calais. He was on the 10.45 night ferry back to England. Seventy-five minutes for the crossing, another train trip and he was able to get here quite anonymously to carry out the murder. Then he planned to take the same route back and be in Paris again for a business lunch. That was the method. The family of his first victim felt sure he was guilty, but they couldn't work out how he had done it. They hired me to investigate him. I had my doubts about his alibi, but I couldn't prove anything. So I had to be patient. The family backed me, paid my expenses, and I followed him, waiting for him to give something away. I was in Vienna, watching you.'

'I know.'

'It was only a theory, so I couldn't warn you until he actually showed signs of repeating the murder. I tried to speak to you earlier this evening, but you weren't answering the door. I simply had to sit out there and wait. I chose a window to force an entry, so when he turned up, I was right behind him.'

'You knew he planned to strangle me?'

'It was a carbon copy of the first killing. Why not? That appeared to succeed. I presume he fixed a joint account to grab your money? You're rich like the first one, I take it?'

Donna looked up at the detective and thought about what she would answer. Really, when he wasn't staring he was quite attractive. 'Quite rich,' she said with a beguiling smile. 'Yes, I suppose I have more money than sense.'

Woman And Home

Anita Sullivan adored Cornwall. One of her most vivid childhood memories was of sitting on a suitcase in the corridor of the Cornish Riviera Express waiting for the first glimpse of that level band of blue that would stretch across her vision through the blissful days of the family holiday. From Exeter onwards each sighting made her throat ache with anticipation until they approached Penzance, when St Michael's Mount, the fairy castle of her storybooks, suddenly appeared in the golden light of late afternoon. Cornwall was an enchanted place.

It was on the evening of their tenth wedding anniversary that Tom told her that he had been offered the position of manager of the Penzance branch of the bank.

'Darling, that's wonderful!' Anita cried out. She flung her arms around him and kissed him. Her eyes misted over with tears of joy.

'Hold on,' said Tom. 'I haven't accepted yet. It's a big decision to take.'

She drew back from him to see whether he was serious. 'Darling, it's the chance of a lifetime. There's nothing to decide – is there?'

Tom's face stiffened into an expression that Anita had noticed increasingly at moments of stress in recent years. It seemed to have started at about the time he had been appointed sub-manager at Croydon. His lips would tighten and the muscles would tense along his jawline. He would have appeared a picture of dogged resolution if it were not for his eyes, which registered something between hesitation and fear.

Anita asked, 'What is it, Tom?'

'I have a feeling I shouldn't take it. I know I shouldn't turn down a chance of promotion, but Penzance is a bit of an outpost, isn't it, right down there on the tip of the South-West?'

'It's a marvellous place,' said Anita. 'I was taken there year after year as a child. It's full of atmosphere and charm. I love it, Tom.'

'For a holiday, yes – but this is something else. Living and working in the place is another thing altogether.'

'We'll find a beautiful cottage. Property is sure to be less expensive down there than it is in the suburbs. We can look in the Sunday paper. I'm sure I've seen hundreds of lovely places advertised.'

'It's only a small branch,' Tom persisted. 'There are fewer staff there than I have in my charge at Croydon. The salary would be slightly better, but I'd lose my London allowance. I don't know whether it's worth it.'

Anita kissed him lightly and said, 'Tom Sullivan, you're beginning to talk like a banker now. Didn't we always say that money isn't everything? You still believe it, don't you?'

'It isn't just the money. It's my career prospects. If they shunt me down to Cornwall, they'll forget about me. I'll see out the rest of my service there.'

'What's wrong with that?' said Anita. 'You've done enough since you started in the bank to earn heaps of self-respect. You've worked your way up to sub-manager at thirty-three. You've passed all those exams. You've plenty to be proud about, Tom, and I'm proud, too. But let's not pretend that it's been easy. We've both felt the strain at times. Now that you've earned a very good position in the bank for a man of your age, why shouldn't you take the reward of a more relaxed job in a very congenial place?'

'I suppose there is a danger of getting caught in the rat race.'

'There are other dangers, worse than that. Remember that chief clerk at Epsom who had the breakdown? And Mr Beazley's ulcers? I don't want the man I love ending up like that. I've seen the danger signs already, Tom. You need this change. Of course it won't be a push-over, managing Penzance, but I'm sure it's less hectic than Croydon, or any of the London branches.'

Tom smiled. 'You mean that I ought to buy a set of golf clubs?'

Anita played her strongest card. 'I don't see you playing golf, darling, but I'll tell you one thing...' She picked up a prism of crystalline quartz from his collection of mineral stones on the shelf unit and stroked her fingertip along its highly polished surface. 'Cornwall has the most amazing rocks and minerals.'

Tom said, 'You're a devious, scheming woman and I love you.' He reached for the Sunday paper and turned to the property page.

They found a buyer for their house in Croydon within a few days of putting it on the market. It was all so quickly arranged that Anita was apprehensive of Tom taking fright and backing down, but he seemed genuinely delighted. Cornwall had really taken a grip on his imagination.

They travelled down the following weekend to begin their house hunt.

They spent two nights at the Esplanade Hotel, Penzance, and visited all the estate agents in the town. They looked at more than twenty cottages that weekend, but not one was suitable. As Anita tried to explain to each of the agents, she and Tom weren't interested in places with 'scope for modernisation'; they wanted to invest their money in a property already fitted with kitchen units, elegant bathrooms and gas-fired central heating. Tom was no handyman, and anyway they could afford to buy at the top end of the market. But they were disappointed. Although several of the cottages they were shown had been stylishly modernised, there was always some overriding disadvantage such as the pylon in the garden or the private airfield across the lane.

'We won't let it get us down,' said Tom on the drive home. 'We're learning a lot about the district. I have a suspicion that whenever new people arrive, those agents start by showing them all the rubbish they've had on their books for months. You have to sift through it before they come up with the good stuff. Let's see what they have to show us next weekend.'

Comforting as Tom's theory was after a disappointing weekend, it proved to be false. The properties they were shown on their next visit were for the most part bizarre or at least eccentric by their suburban standards: a water mill, the wing of a former monastery and a house built into the side of a cliff.

'Haven't you anything better than this in our price range?' Tom asked.

'I've shown you everything I can,' the agents replied with depressing regularity. 'It's not a good time to buy.'

'We've discovered that,' said Anita.

When they got back, they found a letter from their solicitor. There was a danger of losing the sale of their house in Croydon if contracts were not soon exchanged.

They were reading the Sunday papers in bed before turning out the light when Anita gave a cry of excitement.

'Darling, this is it! Listen: *Near Penzance. Immaculate granite-built cottage in idyllic setting, superbly restored and modernised. Inglenook with wood burner. Open beams. Luxury fitted kitchen. Two reception rooms. Cloak/shower. Spiral staircase to three good-sized bedrooms, one with bathroom en suite. Double garage. Landscaped garden. Offers invited in excess of £60,000.*'

Tom snatched the paper from her. 'Is there a number to call? Yes.' He reached for the phone.

'It's eleven at night,' said Anita. 'You can't call them now.'

'Try stopping me,' said Tom. He dialled the number.

Anita put her head close to the phone to try to catch the conversation.

The call was answered almost at once. Tom gave his name and apologised for calling so late.

'That's all right,' said the gentle-sounding voice. 'I expect it's about the cottage, is it?'

'Actually, yes. I would have rung before, but we've only just got back from Cornwall ourselves. We've been looking at cottages, and found nothing suitable. When my wife noticed your advertisement, I felt I just couldn't let this chance slip by.'

'I understand.'

'Could you tell me some more about the cottage, Mr, er...?'

'Glass. Wilfred Glass. Well, I could, Mr Sullivan, but it's only fair to warn you that I've been inundated by calls about the cottage. You must be at least the twentieth.'

'I see. But you haven't sold it?'

'Not yet. Several people are coming to see it tomorrow, however.'

'Tomorrow? I don't know if we could manage that.' Tom turned with eyebrows raised to Anita.

She nodded her head vigorously and mouthed the word 'yes'.

'Wait a minute,' said Tom. 'I think we could make a special effort to get there.'

'I'd hate you to come a long way and be disappointed,' said Mr Glass.

'I presume you won't make a decision before everyone's had a chance to see it tomorrow. I mean, if someone were to make an offer before we got there...'

'Rest assured that it won't be gone,' said Mr Glass. 'There are so many factors one has to take into consideration in selling a house.'

'Exactly,' said Tom. 'I think you could regard us as reliable purchasers. As a matter of fact, I'm about to take up an appointment as manager of a bank in Penzance. And we have already sold our own property.'

'Yes,' said Mr Glass. 'I also have in mind that I want the cottage to go to people who will treat it well. I'm very attached to the place. It's been an important part of my life. I wouldn't be leaving now if it were not that my mother is in her eighties and needs looking after. She lives in Plymouth and refuses to leave the house. But there – she looked after me as a child, and I'd hate to put her in some old people's home. What time can you get here tomorrow?'

Tom estimated two o'clock, and that was allowing for a very early start to beat the morning rush-hour around London. There was not even the chance to let them know at the bank that he would not be coming in. He was sure the manager would be sympathetic – he had more than once suggested Tom took a few days off for house-hunting – but it ought to have been arranged in advance. It wasn't the same thing at all to call the bank from one of the service points along the motorway. He didn't like doing it, but for once in his life the bank had to take second place.

They found Stennack Cottage on the St Just Road a few miles west of Penzance. The country here was more stark and dramatic than the outskirts of the town with its sub-tropical shrubs and palms. An ancient engine-house and chimney stack, relics of the great days of tin mining, stood on the skyline, covered in ivy. Below was the sea, more green than blue in the brilliant sunlight.

'It's wilder than I expected,' said Tom.

'I'm going to love it,' said Anita.

The cottage was set back from the road and surrounded by a low granite wall topped by blue hydrangeas and flame-coloured montbretia. It was a solid-looking whitewashed building with a grey slate roof. Wilfred Glass was standing in the porch dressed in faded blue jeans and navy fisherman's smock, a smiling neat-featured man in his forties with straight, light-coloured hair.

'The kettle's on the stove,' he told them as they introduced themselves. 'Come in and have some tea. What stamina you must have to make a journey like this twice in two days!'

'Needs must, when the devil drives,' said Tom.

'I hope the devil had nothing to do with your promotion, darling,' Anita said with a smile at their host. 'This is a beautiful room, Mr Glass. And the fire as well – so welcoming.'

'Not the real thing, I'm afraid,' said Mr Glass. 'It's one of those gas burners, but it is quite realistic.'

With the tea he offered them buttered buns, distinctly yellow in colour. 'Saffron,' he explained. 'They're very popular here, and they taste better than they look. As a bachelor, I'm very reliant on the cakeshop in St. Just. Do you enjoy cooking, Mrs Sullivan?'

'She's marvellous at it,' said Tom.

'I think you'll like the kitchen, then. I had it designed by some people in Penzance who specialise in kitchens.'

It was the first room they inspected when they got up to

start the tour of the cottage. Mr Glass was right: it was a dream of a kitchen, fitted with pine-clad units, a ceramic electric hob, eye-level grill, double-bowl sink with waste disposal unit, fridge-freezer and microwave oven. The view from the large double window was across open fields to the sea. It was the first time Anita had seen a kitchen she would not want to alter in the least.

'Everything's included,' Mr Glass told her, 'and that goes for the washing machine and drier and the washing-up machine in the utility room as well.'

The rest of the rooms were just as impressive, with coved ceilings and subtle lighting and stylish decoration. As they came down the white spiral staircase, Anita turned to Tom and whispered, 'This is the one.'

'I'll show you the garden,' said Mr Glass.

'I think we've decided already,' said Tom. 'I believe the asking price is sixty thousand – is that right?'

Mr Glass gave a small shrug. 'I think the phrase I used was "offers in excess of...".'

'Yes, of course,' said Tom. 'Tell me, did you have a particular figure in mind?'

Mr Glass put his hand to the side of his face in a gesture of meditation. 'Well, it's like this. Do sit down, won't you? I've owned Stennack Cottage for seven years now, and as you have seen I've spent a lot of money getting it to my liking. I'm very attached to the place.' As he was speaking, he put his hand on the chimney breast and moved it lightly across the surface, almost in a caress. 'It's probably ridiculous, but I would only agree to sell it to people who seem to be in harmony with the surroundings.'

'You can rest assured that we appreciate the place,' said Tom. 'We'd keep it up.'

'I'm sure you would, but it's more than that.' Mr Glass turned from the fireplace and asked, 'Would you think it frightfully impertinent if I asked you some personal questions?'

Tom glanced in Anita's direction. 'If you want to know a little more about us, we'll do our best to oblige you.'

'What would you like to know?' said Anita, more curious than apprehensive.

'First of all, how would you expect to spend your time here?'

'Well, I'm in the bank, as I explained,' answered Tom. 'That's five days a week accounted for, but Anita would be here. The cottage wouldn't be empty.'

Mr Glass turned to Anita. 'Then you're not a working wife?'

She smiled. 'I don't go *out* to work, if that's what you mean. There's plenty of work in running a house, even one so well equipped as this.'

'But you have no children?'

'No children,' said Anita evenly.

'There's nothing to prevent you from going out to work if you wished?'

'Nothing at all,' said Anita. 'But this is the style of life we both prefer. I'm not one of those women who feel deprived and demeaned by not going out to work. Our marriage is a partnership, and I do my share, and have my share of the rewards.'

'A partnership, yes,' said Mr Glass, and he seemed to approve of it. 'Does that mean that you would jointly own the cottage if I sold it to you?'

'Of course.'

'Look here,' said Tom. 'If you're worried about us not getting a mortgage, forget it. As a member of the bank, I can have as much as I like within reason, and on very good terms. Would you settle for sixty thousand?'

Anita put her hand on Tom's arm and said, 'Tom, dear, don't rush things. Mr Glass wants to know more about us.'

'You're both being very patient,' said Mr Glass. 'Now, Mr Sullivan, I like to have a picture of what will happen here in the evenings and at weekends, when you are both at home. Do you watch much television?'

'Very selectively,' said Tom. 'I spend a lot of time with my hobby of lapidary – stones, you know.'

'Really? Well, there's plenty of opportunity for that in Cornwall. I know of several local collectors. In fact, there's a shop in St Just.'

'I prefer to find my own specimens,' said Tom. 'I do a lot of walking at weekends.'

Mr Glass asked Anita, 'And does the partnership extend to joining your husband's expeditions?'

She shook her head. 'I'm not much of a walker. I think it's important to have your own thing to do. I'm the gardener.'

'I'm sure you'll do better than I have. You may even find some interesting minerals out there. *Stennack* is Cornish for tin-bearing ground. There are several mines hereabouts, some of them still being worked.'

Anita said with a smile, 'A pity it isn't a gold mine.'

He gave her an interested look, and said, 'It's not impossible.'

Before they left, Tom offered sixty-two thousand pounds.

Mr Glass agreed to consider it. 'I ought to tell you that I've had a considerably higher offer,' he told them, 'but as I explained, I want the cottage to go to the right people, and you may well be the ones. Can I phone you tomorrow?'

On the long drive back to Croydon, Anita tried hard to suppress her excitement. In her mind, she explored the cottage repeatedly for some flaw that she could seize on as a consolation in case Mr Glass decided not to sell to them. But secretly she believed he would. She knew from the way he had looked at her that she had made a favourable impression on him, and Tom had definitely scored a hit with his stone collecting.

'Offering silent prayers?' asked Tom.

'Something like that.'

'Odd sort of character, wasn't he? He seems so possessive about the cottage that I couldn't help wondering whether he really means to sell it at all.'

'Don't say that!' said Anita fearfully. 'Surely he wouldn't bring people all that way if he wasn't serious?'

'Well, you have to admit it was strange, asking those questions.'

'They didn't embarrass me.'

'That isn't the point. If you want my opinion,' said Tom in the voice he used in the bank, 'he's spent too much on the place. Overstretched himself. Can't keep up the payments. I don't believe the story about his old mother in Plymouth. If that were true, he could easily let it furnished for a year or two, until he's ready to go back.'

'I don't really care, as long as we get that cottage,' said Anita.

Next morning, Mr Glass phoned and said that he accepted the offer. Anita went out and bought a bottle of champagne.

There were no complications in the sale. At the end of July, six weeks after they had seen the advertisement, Anita and Tom became the joint owners of Stennack Cottage. They moved in a week later. Mr Glass had put flowers in the hall to welcome them.

They had purchased the curtains and carpets with the cottage, so once their furniture was arranged, it was easy to settle in. Anita rather wished Mr Glass would call on them and see how right everything looked. She was sure he would approve. She found that her thoughts often turned to him as she went about the house when Tom was at work. But he didn't come. He must have gone to Plymouth after all.

So she thought, until one Sunday evening Tom returned from one of his walks and said, 'I believe I saw that fellow Glass this afternoon. I was looking for specimens in that old mine near Sancreed and for some reason I turned round and saw someone higher up the hill near the prehistoric site. He was looking down at me through a pair of field glasses. As soon as I turned, he ducked out of sight. I can see a long way, as you know, and I'm certain it was Glass. That fairish hair and slim figure. Damned if I know why he was behaving like that. A very odd man.'

'I expect he was embarrassed,' suggested Anita. 'Perhaps he'd just got you in focus when you turned round. He didn't want you to think he was spying on you.'

'Perhaps you're right,' said Tom. 'It doesn't bother me. If he starts spying on *you* I'll have something to say about it. What do you think of this, then?' He took a large encrusted stone from his bag and held it to the light so that Anita could see its emerald green surface. 'Malachite. Isn't it beautiful? I dug it out of the tip beside the old pit-head up there. I think there must be more of it there.'

Later that week, he told Anita, 'I was right about Wilfred Glass. I had lunch today with the manager of the bank across the street. I happened to mention that I bought the house from Glass and he told me the fellow banks with them. It was just as I surmised – he overspent on the cottage and got himself in deep water. His old mother died eight years ago, so it was pure invention about Plymouth. He used her money to buy this place, with a hefty mortgage. He's living in a small terraced house in St Buryan now.'

'Poor man.'

'Yes, we all have our pride,' said Tom. 'I understand now why he didn't want to be seen the other day.'

But Tom's understanding of Wilfred Glass never went any further than that. The following weekend, he went off for one of his walks in search of rock specimens and did not return. When it got dark and he was still missing, Anita phoned the police. They promised to radio their patrols and they sent a young constable to take down the details, but little could be done in the way of a search before morning. Anita suggested that they should concentrate the search around the old mineworks near Sancreed.

Tom's body was found at the foot of the shaft. His neck was broken. His bag of rock specimens lay beside him. It contained two pieces of malachite.

The verdict at the inquest was misadventure. Everyone was very kind to Anita. Someone came from the bank to talk about the pension she would get. The cottage became hers on Tom's death. There was no more mortgage to pay, because it had been covered by an insurance policy. She decided she could afford to remain at the cottage.

Several weeks later she met Mr Glass in the cakeshop in St Just. She bought some bread and turned from the counter and there he was, facing her. He didn't seem at all surprised. He touched his hat and said, 'How are you now, Mrs Sullivan? What a terrible thing to have happened. I was so deeply shocked when I heard.'

'Yes,' said Anita, 'but I'm beginning to get over it now.'

'I know what it's like...' My mother... But of course she wasn't young like your husband. Are you still at the cottage?'

'Yes, in spite of everything, I think I shall stay.'

'I thought you would,' said Mr Glass, adding quickly, 'You were the one who fell in love with it. How are you managing there?'

'Quite well, thank you.'

'Everything in working order? No trouble with the electricity? It has been temperamental in the past.'

'None that I've noticed.'

'Oh.' Mr Glass looked thoughtful for a moment. 'I'm living in St Buryan now. Not the same at all. I passed the cottage on my way. I walked, actually.'

'Perhaps I can give you a lift,' said Anita because it seemed the decent thing to say.

'How kind! I'll tell you what: I'll buy some saffron buns. It will be such a treat to see what you've done with the cottage.'

She was really rather pleased. He was a sweet man. It was Tom who had kept saying he was strange.

On the drive back, she asked him whether he possessed a pair of field glasses. 'Tom thought he spotted you one afternoon at Sancreed, near the old tin-mine,' she explained.

'He must have been mistaken, my dear,' said Mr Glass. 'What would I be doing with a pair of field glasses?'

She heard him give a sigh of happiness as he stepped into the cottage. She went into the kitchen to make some coffee and put the buns on a plate. She called out, 'Black or white, Mr Glass?'

He answered, 'White, if you please, Mrs Sullivan.'

She said from the kitchen, 'You can call me Anita.'

Mr Glass smiled to himself. She was quite the prettiest of all the young wives who had come with their husbands to look at the cottage. In a month or two he would marry her and the place would be his again. He stood by the fireplace and passed his fingers fondly over the brickwork. Woman and home. It had all worked out according to plan, a plan as easy as falling off a log. Or pushing a man down a mineshaft.

The Locked Room

Sometimes when the shop was quiet Braid would look up at the ceiling and give a thought to the locked room overhead. He was mildly curious, no more. If the police had not taken an interest he would never have done anything about it.

The inspector appeared one Wednesday soon after eleven, stepping in from Leadenhall Street with enough confidence about him to show he was no tourist. Neither was he in business; it is one of the City's most solemn conventions that between ten and four nobody is seen on the streets in a coat. This was a brown imitation leather coat, categorically not City at any hour. Gaunt and pale, a band of black hair trained across his head to combat baldness, he stood back from the counter, not interested in buying cigarettes, waiting rather, one hand in a pocket of the coat, the other fingering his woollen tie, while the last genuine customer named his brand and took his change.

When the door was shut he came a step closer and told Braid, 'I won't take up much of your time. Detective Inspector Gent, CID.' The hand that had been in the pocket now exhibited a card. 'Routine enquiry. You are Frank Russell Braid, the proprietor of this shop?'

Braid nodded, and moistened his lips. He was perturbed at hearing his name articulated in full like that, as if he were in court. He had never been in trouble with the police. Never done a thing he was ashamed of. Twenty-seven years he had served the public loyally over this counter. He had not received a single complaint he could recollect, nor made one. From the small turnover he achieved he had always paid whatever taxes the government imposed. Some of his customers – bankers, brokers and accountants – made fortunes and talked openly of tax dodges. That was not Frank Braid's way. He believed in fate. If it was decreed that he should one day be rich, it would happen. Meanwhile he would continue to retail cigarettes and tobacco honestly and without regret.

'I believe you also own the rooms upstairs, sir?'

'Yes.'

'There is a tenant, I understand.'

So Messiter had been up to something. Braid clicked his tongue, thankful that the suspicion was not directed his way, yet irritated at being taken in. From the beginning, Messiter had made a good impression. The year of his tenancy had seemed to confirm it. An educated man, decently dressed, interesting to talk to and completely reliable with the rent. This was a kick in the teeth.

'His name, sir?'

'Messiter.' With deliberation Braid added, 'Norman Henry Messiter.'

'How long has Mr Messiter been a lodger here?'

'*Lodger* isn't the word. He uses the rooms as a business address. He lives in Putney. He started paying rent in September last year. That would be thirteen months, wouldn't it?'

It was obvious from the inspector's face that this was familiar information. 'Is he upstairs this morning, sir?'

'No. I don't see a lot of Mr Messiter. He calls on Tuesdays and Fridays to collect the mail.'

'Business correspondence?'

'I expect so. I don't examine it.'

'But you know what line Mr Messiter is in?'

It might have been drugs from the way the inspector put the question.

'He deals in postage stamps.'

'It's a stamp shop upstairs?'

'No. It's all done by correspondence. This is simply the address he uses when he writes to other dealers.'

'Odd,' the inspector commented. 'I mean, going to the expense of renting rooms when he could just as easily carry on the business from home.'

Braid would not be drawn. He would answer legitimate questions, but he was not going to volunteer opinions. He busied himself tearing open a carton of cigarettes.

'So it's purely for business?' the inspector resumed. 'Nothing happens up there?'

That started Braid's mind racing. Nothing *happens*...? What did they suspect? Orgies? Blue films?

'It's an unfurnished flat,' he said. 'Kitchen, bathroom and living room. It isn't used.'

At that the inspector rubbed his hands. 'Good. In that case you can show me over the place without intruding on anyone's privacy.'

It meant closing for a while, but most of his morning regulars had been in by then.

'Thirteen months ago you first met Mr Messiter,' the inspector remarked on the stairs.

Strictly it was untrue. As it was not put as a question, Braid made no response.

'Handsome set of banisters, these, Mr Braid. Individually carved, are they?'

'The building is at least two hundred years old,' Braid told him, grateful for the distraction. 'You wouldn't think so to look at it from Leadenhall Street. You see, the front has been modernised. I wouldn't mind an old-fashioned front if I were selling silk hats or umbrellas, but cigarettes—'

'Need a more contemporary display,' the inspector cut in as if he had heard enough. '*Was* it thirteen months ago you first met Mr Messiter?'

Clearly this had some bearing on the police enquiry. It was no use prevaricating. 'In point of fact, no. More like two years.' As the inspector's eyebrows peaked in interest, Braid launched into a rapid explanation. 'It was purely in connection with the flat. He came in here one day and asked if it was available. Just like that, without even seeing over the place. At the time, I had a young French couple as tenants. I liked them and I had no intention of asking them to leave. Besides, I know the law. You can't do that sort of thing. I told Mr

Messiter. He said he liked the situation so much that he would wait till they moved out, and to show good faith he was ready to pay the first month's rent as a deposit.'

'Without even seeing inside?'

'It must seem difficult to credit, but that was how it was,' said Braid. 'I didn't take the deposit, of course. Candidly, I didn't expect to see him again. In my line of business you sometimes get people coming in off the street simply to make mischief. Well, the upshot was that he *did* come back – repeatedly. I must have seen the fellow once a fortnight for the next eleven months. I won't say I understood him any better, but at least I knew he was serious. So when the French people eventually went back to Marseilles, Mr Messiter took over the flat.' By now they were standing on the bare boards of the landing. 'The accommodation is unfurnished,' he said in explanation. 'I don't know what you hope to find.'

If Inspector Gent knew, he was not saying. He glanced through the open door of the bathroom. The place had a smell of disuse.

He reverted to his theme. 'Strange behaviour, waiting all that time for a flat he doesn't use.' He stepped into the kitchen and tried a tap. Water the colour of weak tea spattered out. 'No furniture about,' he went on. 'You must have thought it was odd, not bringing furniture.'

Braid passed no comment. He was waiting by the door of the locked room. This, he knew, was where the interrogation would begin in earnest.

'What's this – the living room?' the inspector asked. He came to Braid's side and tried the door. 'Locked. May I have the key, Mr Braid?'

'That isn't possible, I'm afraid. Mr Messiter changed the lock. We – er – came to an agreement.'

The inspector seemed unsurprised. 'Paid some more on the rent, did he? I wonder why.' He knelt by the door. 'Strong lock. Chubb mortice. No good trying to open that with a piece of wire. How did he justify it, Mr Braid?'

'He said it was for security.'

'It's secure, all right.' Casually, the inspector asked, 'When did you last see Mr Messiter?'

'Tuesday.' Braid's stomach lurched. 'You don't suspect he is—'

'Dead in there? No, sir. Messiter is alive, no doubt of that. Active, I would say.' He grinned in a way Braid found disturbing. 'But I wouldn't care to force this without a warrant. I'll be arranging that. I'll be back.' He started downstairs.

'Wait,' said Braid, going after him. 'As the landlord, I think I have the right to know what you suspect is locked in that room.'

'Nothing dangerous or detrimental to health, sir,' the inspector told him without turning his head. 'That's all you need to know. You trusted Messiter enough to let him fit his own lock, so with respect you're in no position to complain about rights.'

After the inspector had left, Braid was glad he had not been stung into a response he regretted, but he was angry, and his anger refused to be subdued throughout the rest of the morning and afternoon. It veered between the inspector, Messiter and himself. He recognised now his mistake in agreeing to the fitting of the lock, but to be rebuked like a gullible idiot was unjust. Messiter's request had seemed innocent enough at the time. Well, it had crossed Braid's mind that what was planned could be the occasional afternoon up there with a girl, but he had no objection to that if it was discreet. He was not narrow-minded. In its two centuries of existence the room must have seen some passion. Crime was quite another thing, not to be countenanced.

He had trusted Messiter, been impressed by his sincerity. The man had seemed genuinely enthusiastic about the flat, its old-world charm, the high, corniced ceilings and the solid doors. To wait, as he had, over a year for the French people to leave had seemed a commitment, an assurance of good faith.

It was mean and despicable. Whatever was locked in that room had attracted the interest of the police. Messiter must have known this was a possibility when he took the rooms. He had cynically and deliberately put at risk the reputation of the shop. Customers were quick to pick up the taint of scandal. When this got into the papers years of goodwill and painstaking service would go for nothing.

That afternoon, when Braid's eyes turned to the ceiling, he was not merely curious about the locked room. He was asking questions. Angry, urgent questions.

By six, when he closed, the thing had taken a grip on his mind. He had persuaded himself he had a right to know the extent of Messiter's deceit. Dammit, the room belonged to him. He would not sleep without knowing what was behind that locked door.

And he had thought of a way of doing it.

In the back was a wooden ladder some nine feet long. Years before, when the shop was a glover's, it had been used to reach the high shelves behind the counter. Modern shop design kept everything in easy reach. Where gloves had once been stacked in white boxes were displays of Marlboro country and the pure gold of Benson and Hedges. One morning in the summer he had taken the ladder outside the shop to investigate the working of the sun blind, which was jammed. Standing several rungs from the top he had been able to touch the ledge below the window of the locked room.

The evening exodus was over, consigning Leadenhall Street to surrealistic silence, when Braid propped the ladder against the shop front. The black marble and dark-tinted glass of banks and insurance blocks glinted funereally in the street lights, only the brighter windows of the Bull's Head at the Aldgate end indicating that life was there, as he began to climb. If anyone chanced to pass that way and challenge him, he told himself, he would inform them with justification that the premises were his own and he was simply having trouble with a lock.

He stepped on to the ledge and drew himself level with the window, which was of the sash type. By using a screwdriver from his pocket, he succeeded in slipping aside the iron catch. The lower section was difficult to move, but once he had got it started, it slid easily upwards. He climbed inside and took out a torch.

The room was empty.

Literally empty. No furniture. Bare floorboards, ceiling and walls, with paper peeled away in several places.

Uncomprehending, he shone the torch over the floorboards. They had not been disturbed in months. He examined the skirting board, the plaster cornice and the window sill. He could not see how anything could be secreted there. The police were probably mistaken about Messiter. And so was he. With a sense of shame he climbed out of the window and drew it down.

On Friday, Messiter came in about eleven as usual, relaxed, indistinguishable in dress from the stockbrokers and bankers: dark suit, old boys' tie, shoes gleaming. With a smile he peeled a note from his wallet and bought his box of five Imperial Panatellas, a ritual that from the beginning had signalled goodwill towards his landlord. Braid sometimes wondered if he actually smoked them. He did not carry conviction as a smoker of cigars. He was a quiet man, functioning best in private conversations. Forty-seven by his own admission, he looked ten years younger, dark-haired with brown eyes that moistened when he spoke of things that moved him.

'Any letters for me, Mr Braid?'

'Five or six.' Braid took them from the shelf behind him. 'How is business?'

'No reason to complain,' Messiter said, smiling. 'My work is my hobby, and there aren't many lucky enough to say that. And how is the world of tobacco? Don't tell me. You'll always do a good trade here, Mr Braid. All the pressures – you can see it in their faces. They need the weed and always will.' Mildly he enquired, 'Nobody called this week asking for me, I suppose?'

Braid had not intended saying anything, but Messiter's manner disarmed him. That and the shame he felt at the suspicions he had harboured impelled him to say, 'Actually there *was* a caller. I had a detective in here – when was it? – Wednesday – asking about you. It was obviously a ridiculous mistake.' He described Inspector Gent's visit without mentioning his own investigation afterwards with the ladder. 'Makes you wonder what the police are up to these days,' he concluded. 'I believe we're all on the computer at Scotland Yard now. This sort of thing is bound to happen.'

'You trust me, Mr Braid, I appreciate that,' Messiter said,

his eyes starting to glisten. 'You took me on trust from the beginning.'

'I'm sure you aren't stacking stolen goods upstairs, if that's what you mean,' Braid told him in sincerity.

'But the inspector was not so sure?'

'He said something about a search warrant. Probably by now he has realised his mistake. I don't expect to see him again.'

'I wonder what brought him here,' Messiter said, almost to himself.

'I wouldn't bother about it. It's a computer error.'

'I don't believe so. What did he say about the lock I fitted on the door, Mr Braid?'

'Oh, at the time he seemed to think it was quite sinister.' He grinned. 'Don't worry – it doesn't bother me at all. You consulted me about the damned thing and you pay a pound extra a week for it, so who am I to complain? What you keep in there – if anything – is your business.' He chuckled in a way intended to reassure.

'That detective carried on as if you had a fortune hidden away in there.'

'Oh, but I have.'

Braid felt a pulse throb in his temple.

'It's high time I told you,' said Messiter serenely. 'I suppose I should apologise for not saying anything before. Not that there's anything criminal, believe me. Actually it's a rather remarkable story. I'm a philatelist, as you know. People smile at that and I don't blame them. Whatever name you give it, stamp collecting is a hobby for kids. In the business, we're a little sensitive on the matter. We dignify it with its own technology – dies and watermarks and so forth – but I've always suspected this is partly to convince ourselves that the whole thing is serious and important. Well, it occurred to me four or five years ago that there was a marvellous way of justifying stamp collecting to myself and that was by writing a book about stamps. You must have heard of Rowland Hill, the fellow who started the whole thing off?'

'The Penny Post?'

Messiter nodded. '1840 – the world's first postage stamps,

the Penny Black and the Twopence Blue. My idea was not to write a biography of Hill – that's been done several times over by cleverer writers than I – but to analyse the way his idea caught on. The response of the Victorian public was absolutely phenomenal, you know. It's all in the newspapers of the period. I went to the Newspaper Library at Colindale to do my research. I spent weeks over it.' His voice conveyed not fatigue at the memory, but excitement. 'There was so much to read. Reports of Parliament. Letters to the Editor. Special articles describing the collection and delivery of the mail.' He paused, pointing a finger at Braid. 'You're wondering what this has to do with the room upstairs. I'll tell you. Whether it was providence or pure good luck I wouldn't care to say, but one afternoon in that Newspaper Library I turned up *The Times* for a day in May, 1841, and my eye was caught – riveted, I should say – by an announcement in the Personal Column on the front page.' Messiter's hand went to his pocket and withdrew his wallet. From it he took a folded piece of paper. 'This is what I saw.'

Braid took it from him, a photocopy of what was unquestionably a column of old newspaper type. The significant words had been scored round in a ballpoint.

A Young Lady, being desirous of covering her dressing room with cancelled postage stamps, has been so far encouraged in her wish by private friends as to have succeeded in collecting 16,000. These, however, being insufficient, she will be greatly obliged if any good-natured person who may have these otherwise worthless little articles at their disposal, would assist her in her whimsical project. Address to Miss E.D., Mr Butt's, Glover, Leadenhall Street.

Braid made the connection instantly. His throat went dry. He read it again. And again.

'You understand?' said Messiter. 'It's a stamp man's dream – a room literally papered with Penny Blacks!'

'But this was—'

'1841. Right. More than a century ago. Have you ever looked through a really old newspaper? It's quite astonishing how easy it is to get caught up in the immediacy of the events. When I read that announcement, I could see that dressing room vividly in my imagination: chintz curtains, gas brackets, brass bedstead, washstand and mirror. I could see

Miss E.D. with her paste pot and brush assiduously covering the wall with stamps. It was such an exciting idea that it came as a jolt to realise that it all had happened so long ago that Miss E.D. must have died about the turn of the century. And what of her dressing room? That, surely, must have gone, if not in the Blitz, then in the wholesale rebuilding of the City. My impression of Leadenhall Street was that the banks and insurance companies had lined it from end to end with gleaming office buildings five storeys high. Even if by some miracle the shop that had been Butt's the Glover's *had* survived, and Miss E.D.'s room *had* been over the shop, common sense told me that those stamps must long since have been stripped from the walls.' He paused, smiled and lighted a cigar.

Braid waited, his heart pounding.

'Yet there was a possibility, remote, but tantalising and irresistible, that someone years ago redecorated the room by papering over the stamps. Any decorator will tell you they sometimes find layer upon layer of wallpaper. Imagine peeling back the layers to find thousands of Penny Blacks and Twopence Blues unknown to the world of philately! These days the commonest are catalogued at ten pounds or so, but find some rarities – inverted watermarks, special cancellations – and you could be up to five hundred a stamp. Maybe a thousand. Mr Braid, I don't exaggerate when I tell you the value of such a room could run to half a million pounds. Half a million for what that young lady in her innocence called worthless little articles!'

Braid had a momentary picture of her upstairs in her crinoline arranging the stamps on the wall. His wall!

As if he read the thought, Messiter said, 'It was my discovery. I went to a lot of trouble. Eventually I found the *Post Office Directory* for 1845 in the British Library. The list of residents in Leadenhall Street included a glover by the name of Butt.'

'So you got the number of this shop?'

Messiter nodded.

'And when you came to Leadenhall Street, here it was, practically the last pre-Victorian building this side of Lloyd's?'

Messiter drew on his cigar, scrutinising Braid.

'All those stamps,' Braid whispered. 'Twenty-seven years I've owned this shop and the flat without knowing that in the room upstairs was a fortune. It took you to tell me that.'

'Don't get the idea it was easy for me,' Messiter pointed out. 'Remember I waited practically a year for those French people to move out. That was a test of character, believe me, not knowing what I would find when I took possession.'

Strangely, Braid felt less resentment towards Messiter than the young Victorian woman who had lived in this building, *his* building, and devised a pastime so sensational in its consequence that his own walls mocked him.

Messiter leaned companionably across the counter. 'Don't look so shattered, chum. I'm not the rat you take me for. Why do you think I'm telling you this?'

Braid shrugged. 'I really couldn't say.'

'Think about it. As your tenant, I did nothing underhand. When I took the flat, didn't I raise the matter of redecoration? You said I was free to go ahead whenever I wished. I admit you didn't know then that the walls were covered in Penny Blacks, but I wasn't certain myself till I peeled back the old layers of paper. What a moment that was!' He paused, savouring the recollection. 'I've had a great year thanks to those stamps. In fact, I've set myself up for some time to come. Best of all, I had the unique experience of finding the room.' He flicked ash from the cigar. 'I estimate there are still upwards of twenty thousand stamps up there, Mr Braid. In all justice, they belong to you.'

Braid stared in amazement.

'I'm serious,' Messiter went on. 'I've made enough to buy a place in the country and write my book. The research is finished. That's been my plan for years, to earn some time, and I've done it. I want no more.'

Frowning, Braid said, 'I don't understand why you're doing this. Is it because of the police? You said there was nothing dishonest.'

'And I meant it, but you are right, Mr Braid. I am a little shaken to hear of your visit from the inspector.'

'What do you mean?'

Messiter asked obliquely, 'When you read your newspaper, do you ever bother with the financial pages?'

Braid gave him a long look. Messiter held his stare.

'If it really has any bearing on this, the answer is no. I don't have much interest in the stock market. Nor any capital to invest,' he added.

'Just as well in these uncertain times,' Messiter commented. 'Blue chip investments have been hard to find these last few years. That's why people have been putting their money into other things. Art, for instance. A fine work of art holds its value in real terms even in a fluctuating economy. So do jewellery and antiques. And stamps, Mr Braid. Lately a lot of money has been invested in stamps.'

'That I can understand.'

'Then you must also understand that information such as this' – he put his hand on the photostat between them – 'is capable of causing flutters of alarm. Over the last year or so I have sold to dealers a number of early English stamps unknown to the market. These people are not fools. Before they buy a valuable stamp, they like to know the history of its ownership. I have had to tell them my story and show them the announcement in *The Times*. That's all right. Generally they need no more convincing. But do you understand the difficulty? It's the prospect of twenty thousand Penny Blacks and Twopence Blues unknown to the stamp world shortly coming on to the market. Can you imagine the effect?'

'I suppose it will reduce the value of stamps people already own.'

'Precisely. The rarities may not be so rare. Rumours begin, and it isn't long before there is a panic and prices tumble.'

'Which is when the sharks move in,' said Braid. 'I see it now. The police probably suspect the whole thing is a fraud.'

Messiter gave a nod.

'But you and I know it isn't a fraud,' Braid went on. 'We can show them the room. I still don't understand why you are giving it up.'

'I told you the reason. I always planned to write my book. And there is something else. It's right to warn you that there is sure to be publicity over this. Newspapers, television – this is the kind of story they relish, the unknown Victorian girl, the stamps undiscovered for over a century. Mr Braid, I value my privacy. I don't care for my name being printed in the newspapers. It will happen, I'm sure, but I don't intend to be around when it does. That's why I am telling nobody where I am going. After the whole thing has blown over, I'll send you a forwarding address, if you would be so kind . . .'

'Of course, but—'

A customer came in, one of the regulars. Braid gave him a nod and wished he had gone to the kiosk up the street.

Messiter picked up the conversation. 'Was it a month's notice we agreed? I'll see that my bank settles the rent.' He took the keys of the flat from his pocket and put them on the counter with the photostat. 'For you. I shan't need these again.' Putting a hand on Braid's arm, he added, 'Some time we must meet and have a drink to Miss E.D.'s memory.'

He turned and left the shop and the customer asked for twenty Rothmans. Braid lifted his hand in a belated salute through the shop window and returned to his business. More customers came in. Fridays were always busy with people collecting their cigarettes for the weekend. He was thankful for the activity. It compelled him to adjust by degrees and accept that he was a rich man now. Unlike Messiter, he would not object to the story getting into the press. Some of these customers who had used the shop for years and scarcely acknowledged him as a human being would choke on their toast and marmalade when they saw his name one morning in *The Times*.

It satisfied him most to recover what he owned. When Messiter had disclosed the secret of the building, it was as if the twenty-seven years of Braid's tenure were obliterated. The place was full of Miss E.D. That young lady – she would always be young – had in effect asserted her prior claim. He had doubted if he would ever again believe it was truly his own. But now that her 'whimsical project' had been ceded to him, he was going to take pleasure in dismantling the design, stamp by stamp, steadily accumulating a fortune Miss E.D. had never supposed would accrue. Vengeful it might be, but it would exorcise her from the building that belonged to him.

Ten minutes before closing time, Inspector Gent entered the shop. As before, he waited for the last customer to leave.

'Sorry to disturb you again, sir. I have that warrant now.'

'You won't need it.' Braid cheerfully told him. 'I have the key. Mr Messiter was here this morning.' He started to recount the conversation.

'Then I suppose he took out his cutting from *The Times*?' put in the inspector.

'You *know* about that?'

'Do I?' he said caustically. 'The man has been round just about every stamp shop north of Birmingham telling the tale of that young woman and the Penny Blacks on her dressing-room wall.'

Braid frowned. 'There's nothing dishonest in that. The announcement really did appear in *The Times*, didn't it?'

'It did, sir. We checked. And this *is* the address mentioned.' The inspector eyed him expressionlessly. 'The trouble is that the Penny Blacks our friend Messiter has been selling in the north aren't off any dressing-room wall. He buys them from a dealer in London, common specimens, about ten pounds each one. Then he works on them.'

'Works on them? What do you mean?'

'Penny Blacks are valued according to the plates they were printed from, sir. There are distinctive markings on each of the plates, most particularly in the shape of the guide letters that appear in the corners. The stamps Messiter has been selling are doctored to make them appear rare. He buys a common Plate Six stamp in London, touches up the guide letters and sells it to a Manchester dealer as a Plate Eleven stamp for a hundred pounds. As it's catalogued at twice that, the dealer thinks he has a bargain. Messiter picks his victims carefully: generally they aren't specialists in early English stamps, but almost any dealer is ready to look at a Penny Black in case it's a rare one.'

Braid shook his head. 'I don't understand this at all. Why should Messiter have needed to resort to forgery? There are twenty thousand stamps upstairs.'

'Have you seen them?'

'No, but the newspaper announcement—'

'That fools everyone, sir.'

'You said it was genuine.'

'It is. And the idea of a roomful of Penny Blacks excites people's imagination. They *want* to believe it. That's the secret of all the best confidence tricks. Now why do you suppose Messiter had a mortice lock fitted on that room? You thought it was because the contents were worth a fortune? Has it occurred to you as a possibility that he didn't want anyone to know there was nothing there?'

Braid's dream disintegrated.

'It stands to reason, doesn't it,' the inspector went on, 'that the stamps were stripped off the wall generations ago? When Messiter found empty walls, he couldn't abandon the idea. It had taken a grip on him. That young woman who thought of papering her wall with stamps could never have supposed she would be responsible over a century later for turning a man to crime.' He held out his hand. 'If I could have that key, sir, I'd like to see the room for myself.'

Braid followed the inspector upstairs and watched him unlock the door. They entered the room.

'I don't mind admitting I have a sneaking respect for Messiter,' the inspector said. 'Imagine the poor beggar coming in here at last after going to all the trouble he did to find the place. Look, you can see where he peeled back the wallpaper layer by layer' – gripping a furl of paper, he drew it casually aside – 'to find absolutely—' He stopped. 'My God!'

The stamps were there, neatly pasted in rows.

Braid said nothing, but the blood slowly drained from his face.

Miss E.D.'s scheme of interior decoration had been more ambitious than anyone expected. She had diligently blocked out each stamp in ink – red, blue or green – to form an intricate mosaic. Penny Blacks or Twopence Blues, Plate Six or Plate Eleven, they were as she had described them in *The Times*, worthless little articles.